MA

ESCAPE FROM AZERBAIJAN

MARINE I: SBS

ESCAPE FROM AZERBAIJAN

David Monnery

First published in Great Britain 1996
22 Books, Invicta House, Sir Thomas Longley Road,
Rochester, Kent

Copyright © 1996 by 22 Books

The moral right of the author has been asserted

A CIP catalogue record for this book is available
from the British Library

ISBN 1 898125 83 X

10 9 8 7 6 5 4 3 2 1

Typeset by Hewer Text Composition Services, Edinburgh
Printed in Great Britain by Cox and Wyman Limited, Reading

1

'Let's go for a drink,' McClure said, surprising both himself and her.

He was in one of his stranger moods, Annie thought. She wasn't at all sure she wanted to spend time in a pub with him, but there was nothing on telly and it would be nice to get out for once. 'OK,' she said.

He swung himself off the bed, pulling the sheet with him. 'I need a shower first.'

'Help yourself,' she said, not bothering to pull the sheet back across her breasts. It would have been quicker to have a shower together, but she knew instinctively that he wouldn't like the idea.

Ten minutes later they were both dressed and ready to go. 'I left the money on the pillow,' he told her as they started up the street towards the pub on the corner. It wasn't one she would have chosen, but at least he wasn't wearing his uniform. These days that was like a red rag to a bull to some people.

As he got the drinks – a pint of bitter for him, a pint of Guinness for her – she sat and wondered what they would talk about after four years of nothing but fucking.

For the first half-hour they talked about her – mostly, she suspected, because he didn't want to talk about himself. 'My dad was killed in Korea,' she volunteered, 'before I was born. Mum brought me up on her own. She's still going – she lives in Southampton on her war pension, playing bingo and watching telly.'

'What do you do when you're not . . . ?'

'Working? I go places. Twice a year. Nowhere really exotic – just package tours. They're dead cheap if you take last-minute cancellations, and since I don't have many advanced bookings myself . . .' She grinned at him.

'Where'd you go this year?'

'Tunisia. And I got to ride a camel in the Sahara.'

For a while they talked about places they'd been, and it seemed to her that he might even be opening up a little.

'Where do you come from?' she risked asking after he'd bought another round.

'London,' he said, without too much reluctance.

'Whereabouts?'

'I grew up in Kilburn.'

'So why did you join the Marines – being a Londoner, I mean?'

He almost smiled. 'Swimming. I was a good swimmer.' He was being modest – he'd been the West London junior freestyle champion. 'And I wanted to be a soldier, so it had to be the Marines. They're the only soldiers that swim.' This time he did smile, and it transformed his face. Only the eyes resisted – the feeling from them was like a bruise.

Annie felt a rare sense of confusion. She wanted to reach out and comfort him, and knew that he'd be outraged at the thought. 'I have to go to the Ladies,' she said.

He sipped his pint, still thinking about the swimming.

2

He knew now that it had saved him from either an early death or a life in prison. Before he'd discovered, almost by accident on one of his European football trips, that he could swim better than the average fish, he'd been well into a downward spiral. 'Going bad' as they said in American films.

He'd been kicked out of three schools, had run with the Chelsea Shed lads and been arrested several times. He'd had no interest in football, but the violence had excited him, taken him out of himself. It was the only thing he'd ever been good at until he discovered how fast he could swim.

That had been the year it had happened. He had always been angry, but up until then he had just let it out – there had been no control, no using it. That year he had turned it inwards, learnt to use the anger like fuel. It had given him back his control, allowed him to make it as a Marine, all the way up to a sergeant's stripes in the SBS.

Annie was walking back across the room, hips slightly swinging, red hair dancing on her shoulders. She'd once admitted to being over thirty, and McClure would have added another ten years, but she was still a sexy woman.

A man at the bar said something to her and she stopped to say something back. One of her regulars, he supposed; it didn't upset him.

Then the man said something else, and she turned away from him, her face hardening.

'What was that about?' McClure asked when she got back to their table.

She could see the glint in his eyes. 'Nothing,' she said. A year or so ago the man had screwed her, short-changed her, and then hit her when she complained – all of which was par for the course. What had upset her just now was the realization that he didn't even remember doing it.

'What about your parents?' she asked McClure.

He took his eyes off the man at the bar and shook his head, as if he was trying to shake himself free from their memory. 'My dad was Irish. He left when I was three. My mum liked to think she was a hippie.' She did what you do, he thought, but she couldn't get it together to charge for it. 'She walked in front of a bus when I was thirteen,' he said.

By accident or on purpose? Annie wanted to ask, but she didn't suppose it mattered very much to him.

There was a silence. He was remembering visiting his mum's grave in Kensal Green Cemetery the year before. He'd stood there in the sunshine, wondering why the fuck he'd come. He had no good memories of her, just the smell of dope and knowing from an early age that he had only himself to rely on. And yet, for the first time he could remember, the tears poured down his face.

She'd had red hair too.

'I'd better be getting back,' Annie said. 'I may work on my back, but I never seem to get enough sleep.'

He gave her another half smile and drained his pint.

She was still fastening her coat on the pavement outside when the man she'd spoken to at the bar emerged behind them. He was probably still in his thirties, slightly balding, wearing jeans and a tan leather jacket. He looked like he fancied himself, McClure thought.

'Hey, hold on a minute,' the man said.

'What do you want?' Annie asked coldly.

He laughed. 'What do you think I want – a palm reading? I want what you sell – a quick fuck.'

4

'Not tonight,' she said, and turned away.

He laughed again. 'I thought whores were like taxis – not allowed to refuse a fare.'

'Get lost, mate,' McClure told him, resisting Annie's tug on his arm.

'Gary, come on,' she urged.

'Yeah, Gary, come on,' the man mimicked. 'She's old enough to be your fucking mother!'

The next thing McClure remembered Annie was pulling at his arm and shouting in his ear. The man was lying on the pavement in front of him, blood streaming from his nose and forehead, breath rasping from his throat. A small crowd of people had poured out of the pub and were now staring at him from a safe distance, a mixture of awe and hatred on their faces.

'Someone get an ambulance,' Annie snapped at them, pulling McClure away.

Seconds later she heard the first sirens. 'You'd better disappear,' she told him. 'I'll tell them I've never seen you before tonight. They won't waste much time looking.'

He looked at her, and she thought she could see gratitude and resentment warring in his eyes. 'Thanks,' he said curtly, and started running.

2

Uday al-Dulaini checked his appearance in the glass window of the door which led down to the basement, rearranged his tie a few millimetres to the left and descended the steps. Kusai Hussein was waiting for him, standing with his hips up against the rim of the large bath which had earned the whole building its nickname of the 'Sheep Dip'. On Uday's last visit to the basement some months before, the pitted vat had still been full of industrial acid and a dead Kurdish rebel had been hanging from the scaffolding above, his legs and lower torso half dissolved from their immersion in the bath.

This time Kusai was alone, and the various pieces of apparatus, which at first sight reminded visitors of a Western work-out gym, were not in use. Uday wondered once again why his superior had chosen this place for the meeting, and hoped once again that complete privacy was the only reason. He didn't like the idea that Kusai might be threatening him. The Mukhabarat boss was not invulnerable, but he was Saddam's brother, and Uday wanted to keep on his good side until such time as he could afford not to.

Kusai certainly wasted no time on civilities. 'So where is the little shit?' he asked coldly.

'He's in Istanbul,' Uday said. 'He's been there for two days. Staying in a small hotel.'

Kusai raised an eyebrow, and ran the fingers of his right hand along the rim of the bath. 'So how did he get away?'

Uday sighed. 'He just took a bus to Makhmur, walked across into the northern zone and got the Turks to let him across the border.'

'Why wasn't he under guard?'

'He was, but the two men concerned . . . I dealt with them personally.'

Kusai smiled to himself. 'So what does he know and who has he told?'

'He hasn't told anybody anything specific. At the moment he's still haggling with several English and German papers, trying to push up the bidding for his story. All he's told anyone so far is that he has sensational new facts about our nuclear programme.'

'Does he?'

Uday knew Kusai wanted a definite answer, but he shrugged anyway. 'It's hard to say. He was told he would be moving in order to work on the new programme, but not the location. He knows what the programme is, of course. And as to where, it's possible he picked up one of the rumours that have been flying around, and he may even have believed one of them . . .'

'The location is the only thing that matters,' Kusai said.

'Of course,' Uday said, allowing himself a trace of irritation. 'I don't think he knows, but if he does, he hasn't told anyone else. My . . . our people have the phones covered and he hasn't posted anything.'

My people, Kusai thought, noticing the slip with amusement. Uday had always been an arrogant little puppy, and here he was, all five foot six of him,

7

with his over-long hair and his immaculate suit, practically usurping Kusai's own position as head of the Mukhabarat. But Kusai had to admit that the little puppy was very efficient. 'I assume you'll also be dealing with this in person,' Kusai said.

'Of course.' Uday looked at his Rolex. 'I have a plane in just over an hour.'

Kusai massaged his moustache. 'You must walk a fine line on this one. I want him thoroughly discredited as far as the rest of the world is concerned, but our scientists have to find out what the penalty for treason is. You understand?'

Uday resented the tone, but knew it would not be prudent to let the feeling show. 'I already have a team working through the man's records, and by the time they've finished editing his life story no one will believe he was interested in anything other than money and vices.' He allowed himself a thin smile. 'By the way, the woman he took wasn't his wife but his mistress. And the wife's angry and frightened. She'll say whatever we need her to.'

Kusai straightened his back, causing the bath to rumble on its foundations. 'OK,' he said. 'Call me from Istanbul.'

They went up the steps together and parted in the lobby, Kusai heading up to his office on the second floor, Uday walking straight out to the waiting limousine. His driver scuttled forward to open the rear door.

'The airport,' Uday told him, and pushed a button on the CD player, flooding the air-conditioned car with En Vogue. He wasn't that crazy about the music, but the videos of the group which he had seen on MTV had fuelled his fantasies for several weeks.

At the Tigris the Mercedes took the bridge lane reserved for government vehicles, surging past the grid-locked traffic in the other lanes. Further downstream the reconstruction of the bridges destroyed by American bombs seemed to be making no appreciable headway.

Uday thought about snorting a line of coke, but decided against it. At the other end of the bridge a crowd of people was trying to cross the road, and the driver slowed slightly, allowing a flashing glimpse of the faces. Some were staring angrily at the car, some almost flinched, but most managed to hold their expressions in neutral. Uday was enjoying the variety when a particularly beautiful girl – a Kurd, probably – caught his eye. He glanced at the Rolex and sighed. There was no time to stop and invite her into the back seat – not today.

A little over four hours later, Barzan al-Hassan watched as the Turkish Hava Yollari airbus from Baghdad came in to land at Ataturk International, and lit a cigarette as it began taxiing towards the terminal. He felt nervous, though there was no real reason why he should. He had followed his instructions to the letter, and nothing had gone wrong. The traitor scientist was living on borrowed time.

But Colonel al-Dulaini always made Barzan nervous. Uday, the colonel insisted on being called, as if they were young men out on the town together, rather than boss and subordinate in an organization not noted for its tolerance of anything other than unthinking obedience.

He had been in awe of Uday at the beginning, in awe of his good looks, his self-assurance, his lack of scruples, his certainty. And he supposed he still was, but after two years of working with the man, there was also something else, some other feeling for which Barzan had yet to find a name . . .

There was no point in thinking about it. He ground the cigarette under his heel, thinking that it would probably be his last for several hours, and popped a mint into his mouth before making his way downstairs to the arrivals gate.

The young colonel emerged with his usual alacrity – despite their country's current pariah status he never seemed to have any problems at airports. Officials melted away before Uday, happy to give him whatever he asked for. Women fell at his feet, or would have done if Uday had ever bothered to ask. Where women were concerned he simply took.

Barzan walked forward, trying to rid himself of negative emotions. 'A good flight?' he asked, taking his superior's suitcase.

Uday grunted. He was glad to be off the wretched plane. Flying bored him, and lately . . . It didn't frighten him of course, but there was a feeling of being caged, of powerlessness, which he found thoroughly distasteful.

The two men walked out to the car, a Mercedes identical in all but colour to the one Uday had left behind in Baghdad. In the spacious rear they sat facing each other, and Barzan found himself wishing that the drinks cabinet by his side was primed with more than fruit juice and mineral water. But alcohol, like tobacco, was forbidden in Uday's presence, allegedly on religious grounds.

'Any new developments?' Uday asked, as the car gathered speed on the highway into the city. To their right the Sea of Marmara stretched away like a lake of oil, with only a few pinpricks of light visible on the distant Asian shore.

'One,' Barzan told him. 'About three hours ago he phoned the *Sunday Times* in London, and agreed to send them the first two pages of a document he says he has. The document itself is fifty pages long. The newspaper will examine the two pages and then agree a price for the whole document.'

'Has he sent them?'

'No. If he had tried then I would have prevented it. He told the English paper he would send them tomorrow morning by express post.'

'Excellent,' Uday said. 'Now tell me about the hotel they are staying in.'

'It is in Binbibdirek, in a quiet street only a few hundred metres from the Blue Mosque. It is small – three storeys, four rooms on each, and Abas Naji has taken one of the front rooms on the top floor, the one on the left as you look from the street.'

'We'll go straight there,' Uday said, and Barzan instructed the driver accordingly.

The lights on the Asian shore drew steadily closer as the Sea of Marmara narrowed towards the Bosphorus, and within half an hour the car was pulling up a street away from the defecting scientist's hotel. 'I rented a room across the street,' Barzan explained. 'It was expensive, but I didn't want to risk scaring him off.'

'You acted correctly,' Uday said, as Barzan had known he would. His boss had never shown any inclination to worry about expenditure. If the Mukhabarat had accountants, they were doubtless of the creative variety.

The back way to the rented room led through a dark

and muddy alley, which did nothing for the shine on Uday's Gucci loafers, and up a flight of outside steps. A Turkish woman was sitting smoking at the top of the latter; she looked at them with interest but said nothing. The rest of the Mukhabarat team were in the room, one with his binoculars trained on the street and opposite hotel, the other lounging in a chair.

Uday examined the view through the window. The Feneri Hotel looked like a haunt of travelling salesmen or an urban port of call for visitors up from the country. It would not be on any tourist list.

The curtains of the relevant room were pulled shut, but moving shapes could be seen through the thin material.

'What's the woman like?' Uday murmured.

'She must be over forty,' Barzan said disparagingly, 'but she's good-looking just the same.'

'Have you fixed me up for tonight?' Uday asked.

'The embassy arranged it. She'll come to your room at ten.'

Uday spent another thirty seconds watching the opposite room, then abruptly turned away. 'Let's go.'

Fifteen minutes later he was checking into the Sophia Hotel, where Barzan had booked him a luxurious three-room suite overlooking the Golden Horn. After dismissing his subordinate – who retired to the bar for a much-needed cigarette and whisky sour – Uday stripped off his clothes and stood under the shower for several minutes, thinking about the task which Kusai had set him. Nothing had occurred to him when there was a knock on the suite's outer door.

He wrapped a towel round his waist, removed the Mauser from the diplomatic bag, and took a look through the peep-hole. A blue-eyed blonde in a red dress stood there, looking like she hadn't a care in the world. He let her in.

She studied the room appreciatively, then walked across and laid an index finger on the top of the towel. 'Shall we begin?' she asked in English.

'Why not?' he replied in the same language.

She carefully unwrapped the towel, let it fall, and sank down to her knees in front of him. With a few strokes of her tongue he began to harden, and once he had attained what seemed the maximum elevation, she stood up again and began to undo the buttons on the front of the red dress.

He reached forward and tore at the fabric, scattering the buttons everywhere. She started to protest, but he slapped her across the face, drawing blood at the corner of her mouth, and pushed her back down on to the floor. He ripped off her knickers, plunged himself violently into her and began pumping, his eyes fixed on her face.

'Open your eyes,' he ordered, and she stared up at him with that mixture of fear and loathing which he loved.

He had almost come when the idea struck him, and he laughed out loud, filling her eyes with fear. Slowing his pace, he went into spasm, finally collapsing on top of her like a dead weight. Then abruptly he clambered off her and got to his feet.

She lay there, getting her breath back.

'Get lost,' he said, throwing the torn dress at her.

'Who'll pay for this?' she asked.

'See the man in 474,' he told her, giving her Barzan's room number.

She put the dress on and, holding it across her body,

walked to the door. 'You bastard,' she shouted over her shoulder.

He grinned and reached for the phone as the door slammed behind her. 'I want a number in Baghdad,' he told the hotel switchboard.

Ten minutes later, having passed on the relevant instructions to the Mukhabarat office in the Iraqi capital, he called Barzan on the cellular phone and explained just what he intended doing with Abas Naji.

Looking out of his hotel window on the following morning, the Iraqi scientist found Istanbul enveloped in grey cloud. The last few days had been sunny, hinting at an early spring, but this seemed more like the weather he would need to grow used to in an English or American exile.

At least it would not be as lonely as he had once expected. Taliha was walking towards the hotel, bringing back their breakfast from the café she had found in a nearby street. He watched her graceful stride, remembering the day, less than a month before, when he had risked everything by asking her to accompany him. They had not even been lovers then, but they had been in love, and she had agreed to give up her home, her family, everything she knew, for him.

His eyes caught sight of the sealed envelope waiting on the table. If it hadn't been for her, he would simply have sent everything he had to as many Western newspapers as he could afford. But in return for her loyalty he had felt honour-bound to use his information to buy them a new start in the West. She might have given up everything for him, but there was no reason she should get nothing back.

She knocked three times on the door, and he let her in. She rubbed her hands to warm them up, pulled the flask of fresh coffee from her bag and collected the two cups she had bought the previous day in the souk. He took the custard pastries out of their wrapping, waited till she had finished pouring the coffee, and handed her one.

For the next five minutes they abandoned themselves to the joys of breakfast.

'I must go to the post office,' he told her, once he had finished licking his fingers.

She looked up. 'I'll come with you.'

'No,' he snapped. He didn't see how they could have been traced, or at least not yet, but there was always a chance. And he knew he would feel more vulnerable if she was with him. Both of them would have a better chance of escape if he went alone.

She didn't argue, and a couple of minutes later he was venturing out on to the street, wishing that he had the cash to pay for a decent coat. He looked both ways, failed to see anyone loitering suspiciously, and started up the street, clutching the large manila envelope to his chest with both arms. The street was busy with both cars and pedestrians, which bolstered his confidence.

At the first corner he was turning right when he heard a car stop behind him, and footsteps hurrying in his direction. He turned to see two men almost on top of him, and before he could even think of running they each had one of his arms in a vice-like grip. One of the free hands reached down to recover the fallen envelope, and then he was being half dragged, half carried towards an anonymous-looking black saloon. He squirmed in his captors' grasp and shouted for help, first in Iraqi and then in English. As he was bundled into the car he had one fleeting glimpse of faces staring his way – curious faces, anxious faces, even sympathetic faces – but no one raised a voice in protest at his abduction, far less came to his defence. And as the car moved away he felt a knot of fear tighten in his stomach.

In the front seat Uday carefully opened the envelope, took out the two sheets of paper and read through what they contained. There was nothing of great importance, though perhaps the reference to a 'new and highly secret location' would energize the Western intelligence services for a week or two.

He looked up to see they were crossing the Galata Bridge over the Golden Horn, and turned to take a look at Abas Naji. The scientist seemed to be in shock – either that or he had acquired a stoicism beyond the reach of most men. Uday's money was on shock.

They were driving along beside the Bosphorus now, following the European shore north toward the Black Sea. Earlier that morning Barzan had rented a *yali* – a house by the water – in Tarabya, some fifteen kilometres outside the city, and he was waiting for them there. But first they had another port of call. Five kilometres short of Tarabya the driver turned the car inland, and ten minutes later they were deep in the Belgrad Forest.

They drove slowly down several deserted tracks before Uday decided to call a halt, and then he strode off into the trees, leaving the other two Mukhabarat men to drag Abas Naji along in his wake. The scientist was recovering from the shock of capture, but it was like a dentist's anaesthetic wearing off – pain replacing numbness. He knew he would tell his captors everything, but there was no knowing whether they would believe him. Maybe, he thought, if he was strong enough, he could use what they needed to know to buy Taliha's freedom.

Uday was also thinking about interrogation, though from rather a different standpoint. He had brought the traitor here to question him, but now that the moment had arrived he realized there was nothing he needed to know. It was unfortunate but true. Lighting a slow fire between the man's legs – a Red Indian trick he had picked up from a Western and honed on several Shiite rebels – might offer a satisfying revenge for the man's treason, but would otherwise be futile.

And there was always the woman for entertainment.

Uday walked forward and pushed the barrel of the Mauser into Abas Naji's mouth, angled it upwards, took a lingering look at the man's terrified eyes, and pulled the trigger.

Birds fluttered out of the surrounding trees, screeching violently.

'Take him back to the car and put him in the boot,' he told his men. 'And put a plastic bag over his head – we don't want all those high-powered scientific brains dribbling out.'

They drove back to the coast road and on up to the *yali*.

Shortly before dawn the following day Uday's local helpers took the villa's boat out into the middle of the moonlit Bosphorus and dumped the weighted corpses of both Abas Naji and Taliha over the side. Their boss had joked that it wasn't every couple who got the chance to decompose in both Europe and Asia.

3

Woken by the telephone, Martin Sommersby groaned, rolled over on to his back and waited for someone to leave a message. 'It's Jen,' the familiar voice said. 'That package you asked me to look out for . . .'

He picked up the phone. 'Hi, Jen. Has it arrived?'

'That's why I'm ringing. Shall I send it over?'

Sommersby rubbed his eyes. 'Er . . .' Through the open bedroom door he could see empty heat-and-serve cartons precariously balanced on each arm of the sofa and two empty wine bottles standing sentry on the TV set. Why did he let things get like this when she was away on tour?

On the other side of the curtains the sun seemed to be shining. 'I'm coming in,' he decided.

'See you soon,' she said cheerfully, and hung up.

He dressed, cursed the lack of milk, and walked out into the cold air. Across the street the night's frost was still glimmering on the grass of Victoria Park, but his ten-year-old Volvo proved its usual reliable self. Sommersby drove south towards Wapping with feelings of expectation, for once hardly noticing Canary Wharf's beacon of ugliness looming through the skyline, and picked up the envelope from a smiling Jen in reception. Upstairs, in the small space left by the computer monitor which had colonized his desk, he eagerly opened the envelope and read through the two typed pages which it contained.

It was not what he had expected. In their last conversation the Iraqi had talked about a new location, but the information here concerned the reopening of an old installation in the desert about a hundred miles west of Baghdad.

Perhaps he had misunderstood Abas Naji, Sommersby thought. Perhaps the Iraqi's English had let him down, and he had mixed up new with renew, or something like that.

It didn't really matter. This was still a good story, and the first solid evidence for some time that Saddam hadn't given up the idea of providing himself with a nuclear arsenal. So much for the pious hopes of the UN inspection team, who kept reiterating their belief that Iraqi's nuclear programme had been comprehensively halted in its tracks.

He got himself a cup of coffee and read through the material again. It all seemed straightforward enough, but, just in case, he called up the paper's regular consultant on nuclear issues, explained the situation and faxed him copies of Abas Naji's two pages. Ten minutes later the man called back to say everything was as it seemed.

The managing editor hadn't yet arrived, so a decision on the Iraqi's fee would have to wait. Sommersby sat down at his monitor and began sketching out the structure of a possible piece for the next day. His preferred course of action would have been to wait for the bulk of the Iraqi's manuscript and carry the whole story the following week, but there was always the chance the paper's legal experts would insist on the government's immediate right to know, and once the information was loose in Whitehall any chance of a real exclusive would vanish out of the Wapping windows.

He was still on the first paragraph when his phone rang.

'A call from Istanbul,' the switchboard operator told him. 'A woman who says she will only talk to you.'

'Put her through,' Sommersby said, turning on the attached recording device.

'Mr Sommersby?' the woman asked in a Middle Eastern accent.

'I am Martin Sommersby. Who are you?'

'I am Shura, the wife of Abas Naji. You are the man my husband send papers?'

'Yes, that's me. The woman sounded very upset.

'My husband disappear. I think he is kidnapped by Saddam Hussein.'

There was a moment's silence while Sommersby waited in vain for her to say more. 'When did this happen?' he asked. 'How did it happen?'

'It happen yesterday, in the afternoon. I go out to buy food for our dinner, yes, and when I come back he is gone. And the papers are gone. I am frightened.'

'Have you been to the police?' Sommersby asked.

'They say my husband just leave me, but I know he will not do this. I am frightened,' she repeated.

Sommersby thought for a moment. 'If you will go to the British Embassy,' he told her, 'I will telephone someone there and get them to help you.'

There was a pause. 'Where is your British Embassy?' she asked.

'Hold on, I'll find out for you.' He accessed the appropriate programme, and pulled the address on to the screen. 'Hello?' he said, but there was no reply. The line was dead.

In the villa by the Bosphorus the English-speaking secretary from the local Iraqi Embassy was looking nervously at Uday al-Dulaini.

'You did well,' he said matter-of-factly. 'Now Barzan will drive you back to the city. And do not speak of this to anyone,' he added, realizing as he did so that there was no need. The girl had played her part well enough, but she had no idea what it was all about.

He watched her walk to the car, regretting once more that she was a distant cousin of Saddam's and therefore off limits. Such timidity was a real turn-on . . .

'Start packing,' he told his men. Their work in Istanbul was done.

Ten days later David Constantine boarded the 8.30 train for King's Cross at Cambridge, managed to find a window seat in the first-class section, and started work on *The Times* crossword. By Royston he was only two words short, but these kept him busy until Stevenage, when the final inspiration struck.

Having done his duty, Constantine glanced through the rest of the paper. The royal family, the Conservative Party and English cricket were still in decline, but there appeared to be no new developments in the Iraqi story. He supposed he would find out that morning whether that was really the case, or whether the security lid had been lowered.

He had read Martin Sommersby's 'exclusives' on the previous two Sundays, and had to admit that he felt intrigued by the mystery of the two disappearances. He supposed that knowing Abas Naji helped, though their acquaintance had been both brief and almost twenty years in the past. But he could remember liking the man, and in his mind's eye he could still see the Iraqi sitting on the edge of his barstool during the conference lunch breaks, earnestly discussing whatever it was that had fired his imagination that morning. And though they had never discussed politics as such, Constantine could well believe that Abas Naji had not relished the role of a missile scientist in the service of Saddam Hussein.

After all, he thought, as the train surged into the first Hadley Wood tunnel, who in their right mind would?

From King's Cross he took a taxi to Whitehall, but the traffic was worse than ever, and after passing through the usual security checks, he arrived at Conference Room B to find only one empty chair at the large, polished table. Martin Clarke, a Junior Minister at the Foreign Office with whom he had not had any previous dealings, immediately did the round of introductions. The gaunt-faced man with the crew cut sitting opposite Constantine was Manny Salewicz from the American Embassy, the balding man with the thin moustache beside him Derek Lindquist, an MoD official whom he vaguely remembered from a meeting several years before. The young man beside him, whose name he missed, was from the Foreign Office Gulf Desk. More significantly, the grey-haired man at the end of the table was Sir Christopher Hanson, who was introduced as Chair of the Joint Intelligence Staff, but was better known to Constantine as the Director of MI6.

It was Hanson who opened the proceedings, with some news.

'It now seems unlikely that the missing woman was

Abas Naji's wife,' he said. 'The Iraqis have produced a woman whom they claim is the real wife, and she swears that Abas Naji had an affair with his secretary and then ran off with her. As far as our people can tell, she's speaking the truth.' He paused. 'However, the man has disappeared, and his choice of companion – who has also vanished – doesn't tell us anything about the reliability of the information he gave the *Sunday Times*. There was a nuclear research installation at Falluja, and it may have been reopened . . .'

'And as of this morning the Iraqis are still refusing access,' Salewicz interjected.

'David,' Clarke said, turning to Constantine, 'perhaps you could put the whole business into some sort of context for us laymen. How far have the Iraqis come? Should we be worrying about a single research centre in the desert?'

'Yes and no,' Constantine said wryly. Already he could tell that Clarke wanted grounds to dismiss, and Salewicz more evidence for the prosecution. 'At the simplest level,' he began, 'there are three components of a nuclear military capability. You need the material, you need a detonation assembly and you need a delivery system. None of which are easy for a country like Iraq to obtain.

'Having said that, we now know that on the eve of the Gulf War Saddam was not that far away from having all three. Since the Israelis destroyed their reactor at Osirak in 1977, the Iraqis had managed to buy both a significant amount of unenriched uranium ore – yellowcake, it's called – and the centrifuges necessary for turning it into fissionable material. Their scientists were apparently twelve to eighteen months away from a crude detonation device, and two to three years from working out how to mount a warhead on one of their Scud missiles.

'Of course, once the war was over every effort was made on our part to put a stop to this programme, and every effort was made on the Iraqi side to conceal and continue it. And it's my belief that only Saddam,' he said, looking round the table, 'knows how successful we and they have been.'

He looked at his notes for the first time. 'In September 1992 the UN Weapons Inspection team announced that Iraq's nuclear programme was, quote, "harmless". In November 1993 the International Atomic Energy Agency told the UN that the programme was, quote, "either destroyed or neutralized", though they did have the sense to admit that their knowledge was incomplete.

'But the Iraqis have hardly behaved like innocents. In '92, when the UN demanded the demolition of the Al-Athier facility, Saddam procrastinated for months and then suddenly backed down, which led quite a few people to suggest that the interval had been used to transfer the industrial plant. And then there were the centrifuges they bought from Germany for the enrichment process – several thousand of them. First the Iraqis denied their existence, then said they had been destroyed. The inspection team has never found any trace of them.'

Constantine looked at Hanson. 'And then last year there was the business of the plutonium the Iraqis tried to buy from a Soviet military establishment. The Germans foiled that particular deal, but who knows how many have gone through, both before and since.

Add to that the assassination of one defecting nuclear scientist in 1992 and the disappearance of another this month, and . . . well, there's no doubt in my mind that the Iraqi nuclear programme is still underway, that the necessary raw materials are being either stolen or secretly purchased, and that a weapons design group is hard at work. How advanced they are is impossible to say. Though of course Abas Naji might have been able to tell us.'

'Thank you, David,' Clarke said. 'As you say, the possibilities are horrendous, but I don't think we should trap ourselves in worst-case scenarios – this problem has already been with us for several years. The question is, how do we proceed from here? The Iraqis are pushing hard for an end to sanctions, and I think I can safely say that the government is leaning in that direction – there's a lot of pressure from industry, a lot of reconstruction contracts which the UK could fill. And if we can pull Saddam back into the international community – give him something to lose, so to speak – then he is less likely to think about using weapons of any sort.' He looked round the table, as if defying anyone to disagree with him.

'Without disputing a word of that,' Hanson said, 'I think we must make every effort to give Abas Naji what amounts to a posthumous vetting, and exert as much pressure as is necessary to persuade the Iraqis to open the Falluja site for inspection.'

'Seconded,' the American said. 'The thought of that bastard with even one bomb gives me the shivers.'

'That goes without saying,' Clark agreed. 'But for the moment can we assume that the disappearance of this man and the information he sent to the *Sunday Times* are insufficient reason for rethinking our current policy? If a UN team discovers a crate full of nuclear Exocets at this place, then of course we shall have to reconsider . . .'

There were murmurs of agreement, some more reluctant than others.

In other words, Constantine thought as he emerged into the thin sunshine, it would be business as usual, right up to the moment they found Saddam knee-deep in nuclear weapons. And of course the point of his own little speech had been that the Iraqis would not be caught so easily. When the site at Falluja was eventually inspected it would prove as innocent as a new-born babe, because by that time the lost centrifuges would be happily spinning in a new location.

Over the next few days Constantine followed the unfolding story courtesy of *The Times*, *The World at One* and *Newsnight*. Against all his expectations the Iraqis wasted little more time in allowing access to the Falluja facility, and the resulting photographs and video footage of the wind-blown shell offered convincing proof that Abas Naji's document was a forgery. Those in favour of dropping sanctions against Iraq were given fresh heart, and those who continued to advise caution were given less credence. Abas Naji, it seemed, had not only run out on his wife; he had also fabricated evidence to finance a playboy lifestyle in the West. The same tabloid editorial wondered out loud whether he and his mistress, realizing the game was up, had simply gone into hiding until the hue and cry died down.

The one problem Constantine had with this version of events was that he had actually known the Iraqi. He simply couldn't bring together this conniving schemer with the young scientist he had met at the conference twenty years before. And it irked him.

All his life he had been a man who loved puzzles. He had originally gone in for science because the universe seemed to offer the greatest mystery of all, and it was only in middle age that he had come to suspect human behaviour had the better claim. Now, as the February days dragged slowly by, he sat in his cottage outside Cambridge, listening to the big-band jazz he loved and wondering about the behaviour of Abas Naji.

A week to the day after the Whitehall meeting he telephoned the *Sunday Times* journalist who had been the Iraqi's contact, explained who he was, and asked for an off-the-record conversation. Sommersby, suitably intrigued, immediately invited him round to the flat in Hackney. Armed with glasses of Sémillon Blanc, the two men listened to the tape of his telephone conversation with the woman who had claimed to be Abas Naji's wife.

One question immediately came to Constantine: hadn't Sommersby been at all surprised that an Iraqi secretary should speak such good English?

Sommersby hadn't been at the time, but now that Constantine mentioned it . . . He poured another glass of wine and told the other man about the discrepancy between Abas Naji's mention of a new location and the reference in the posted pages to the reopening of an old facility. They both listened to the tapes Sommersby had made of his two conversations with the scientist, and Constantine thought he recognized more than just the man's voice. There was certainly nothing to suggest that his personality had been transformed over the previous twenty years.

But without such a change, it just didn't make sense.

On the train back to Cambridge Constantine tried fitting together the pieces of an alternative explanation. If the woman on the phone had been neither his wife nor his mistress, then what had been the purpose of her call? The answer was simple – to establish false times for both Abas Naji's disappearance and his posting of the papers. Why? That was simple too. If she was lying about the times it could only be because the enemy had got to Abas Naji before he posted the papers. In which case the papers were indeed forgeries, but not forgeries of Abas Naji's making.

There was a new facility somewhere, and the whole Falluja business was just a smokescreen.

The Iraqis would be cock-a-hoop, he thought – except for one thing. They had lost a valuable scientist – probably the best they had in that field. As he stared out through the window at the rapidly darkening countryside it occurred to him that they would be needing a replacement.

4

Raisa Karayeva wound down the Lada's window and let the evening breeze tug at her hair. On the shoreline below the picnic area the heads of the donkey derricks were nodding like the delegates at a Party conference; out to sea a distant tanker's horn softly boomed. High clouds were hurrying out across the sea.

She looked at her watch again, and found she had been waiting for more than a hour. He had never been this late before. In fact it seemed highly probable that he was standing her up for the first time.

The sensible thing would be to go home, to leave the picnic area before another vehicle, official or otherwise, drove in and parked beside her. But she stayed, watching night fall across the Caspian, remembering all the other secret assignations they had shared over the previous two years.

In the first few months they had rarely met twice in the same place. In summer they would leave their cars in the trees by the side of a mountain road and walk until they found a suitable trysting place; in the winter they would snuggle in the back seat of his Volga. But over the past year it had become increasingly unsafe to travel more than about fifteen kilometres from the city, for there seemed to be checkpoints everywhere, some of them manned by the army or police, others simply set up on

29

a freelance basis by criminals or refugees from one of the local wars. The latter posed a greater threat to life, limb and honour, but a run-in with the former was always a risky business these days, and carried the additional risk of publicizing their relationship. Over the past few months they had met regularly at this spot, which was as little frequented in winter as it was crowded in the summer.

The horn boomed again in the distance, a mournful sound. The ship was invisible now, cloaked by the darkness. She spent her days alone with this sea, working at the Caspian Research Institute, which was attached to Baku University, pondering the thousand-year-old riddle of the sea's changing size. It was shrinking now, and there were obvious explanations for that, but it had also shrunk before, and then expanded once again, for reasons that remained unknown. And until they were known, all the various polluters and water thieves in the five states which now bordered that sea could claim that since no one really understood the processes at work they might as well carry on with business as usual.

She spent her days alone with the sea, and now, it seemed, her evenings as well. He wasn't coming.

She smiled ruefully in the dark. His non-appearance was ironic, in that she had planned to end the affair that evening. It was going nowhere, and it never would. She liked him, liked his body with hers, enjoyed his mind. She could even have let herself love him if there was any chance of reciprocation, regardless of the thirty-year difference in their ages.

She smiled again. She did love him, but not enough to put her life on permanent hold.

And yet there was someone inside her who was glad

he hadn't come. That someone was frightened of casting herself adrift, of being as alone in reality as almost everyone assumed she already was. 'Be strong,' Aida had told her; and she would be, but it wasn't going to be easy. Tamarlan had given her emotions a focus, her life a centre. She had no family to fall back on – only one good friend. And if there was ever a good time and place to be alone, this wasn't it.

The darkness was almost complete now, and on the maze of wooden piers which stretched out to sea the drill-head flames looked like lighted candles on a giant birthday cake. Raisa turned on the car light and examined her face, her half-Armenian face.

On their visits to Yerevan in years gone by, her father's family had always insisted that she had inherited her Armenian grandmother's looks, but Raisa herself had never been able to see the resemblance. Perhaps there was a hint of mountain pallor in her skin colour, but the tumbling black hair could have come from either side of her family, and the deep-brown eyes were her Azeri father's. During the last seven years most of the Armenians in Baku had been forced out – some had been lynched by their former neighbours – but she had never been challenged, either by friend or foe. She didn't look Armenian *enough*, and she moved in the kind of circles, both social and geographical, which were generally considered safe. If she were to wander through one of the industrial suburbs or one of the shanty towns full of Azeri refugees from Nagorno-Karabakh, it might well be a different matter, but then such areas had always been dangerous for single women. Even seventy years into the Soviet era wife-stealing had been far from a lost art in the Socialist State Republic of Azerbaijan. And now that the nation was busy rediscovering its Islamic roots such practices seemed bathed in a nostalgic glow.

She had been there long enough, she decided, and reached for the ignition key. The Lada which her father had treated so lovingly until his death three years before still responded in kind. She turned it away from the dark sea and on to the road which wound round the Aspheron Peninsula.

Ten minutes later she was driving down the long slope into Baku. It wasn't yet warm enough for people to spend the evenings outside, and the streets seemed mostly deserted, with only the occasional tavern door offering a glimpse of light, sound and smoke. She parked the Lada in its garage and walked up the cobbled street to the flat which had once housed her family, and where she now lived alone. The smell of fresh bread still hung in the air beside the baker's on the corner, despite the fresh breeze which was ruffling the acacias.

She let herself in, turned on the light and stood for a moment with her back to the door. Then she shook her head impatiently and went to find something to eat. As a can of soup warmed up on the stove she watered the plants which framed the arched window and wondered if he would phone.

She ate the soup in front of the TV – one of the American shows which seemed to be on more and more often. The dubbing was so bad it was almost comic, but she doubted there was much in the way of depth to be lost. She poured herself a glass of vodka and wondered why he hadn't turned up.

Perhaps his son was visiting, and he hadn't been able to get hold of her in time. But he could still have called – *he* had no idea she was calling the whole thing off.

She thought about ringing him. She could always hang up if his son answered, or his wife. Even if he answered she could just put the phone down. At least she would know he was OK. Not that there was any reason why he shouldn't be – it just wasn't like him to stand her up like that.

She took another jolt of the vodka, reached for the phone and dialled the number she had never used, yet knew by heart. It rang once, twice, three times . . . She realized she was holding her breath, and let it out. Four times, five. It kept ringing and ringing. After twenty, she put down the phone.

The following morning she drove to work by a round-about route. She had been to see the Shadmanov house once before, near the beginning of the affair, but had never admitted as much to Tamarlan. She hadn't been able to explain to herself why she wanted to see the house, let alone explain it to him. And as luck would have it she had driven past just as Tamarlan's wife was climbing out of a taxi with a bag of shopping, looking a lot younger than her forty-five years and a lot more beautiful than Raisa had expected. The whole business – her own curiosity, the reality of his actual home, Farida Shadmanova's corporeal existence – had left her depressed for days.

This time, though, there was no one emerging from a taxi, and no sign of Tamarlan's Volga. She thought the house itself had an unoccupied look, but that might be just her imagination. Still, she didn't dare stop to take a closer look.

At the Research Institute she spent the morning on the annual hydrographical estimates. It had been a dry winter in the Urals and the Volga's rate of flow was down, which didn't augur well for the Caspian. Moscow's old plans to divert Arctic-bound water south were still on the drawing-board, but now that the Soviet Union was rather less than a fond memory the Russians were unlikely to make a present of their surplus water to Azerbaijan and the other Caspian states. The government in Baku would be needing all the money it could squeeze out of the Western oil company reps who were installed in the city's best hotels.

But what did they care if the sea died? In fact they would welcome such a development – it would make for easier drilling.

Raisa shut down the computer, walked across to the university's faculty canteen, and unenthusiastically devoured a cheese roll and an apple while she waited for Aida's class to finish. There was no sign of Tamarlan, but then he rarely used the canteen.

Aida Usubova arrived about fifteen minutes later, waved to Raisa and joined the queue. They had been friends for several years now, though Raisa sometimes wondered why Aida bothered with her. The younger woman, with her short, dark hair and mischievous face, was much more of an extrovert than Raisa, and much more inclined to take risks, both socially and politically. If Azerbaijan was headed for an Islamic state, then it wouldn't be because of any failure to express opposition on Aida's part.

She put down her tray and grabbed a seat. 'Well, did you tell him?' she asked. Aida was the only one of her friends who knew about Raisa's affair with Tamarlan.

'He didn't turn up.'

'What? Why not?'

'I don't know. He's . . .'

'Have you called him this morning?'

'No . . .'

Aida noticed the look in Raisa's eyes. 'What is it?'

Raisa told her about the empty-looking house.

Aida was not impressed. 'There could be any number of explanations for that. Look, if you don't want to call him, I will. Or I'll call his secretary anyway. I can say I'm collecting signatures for some campaign or other. If he's there, fine. If he isn't, I'll ask when he's coming in. OK?'

Raisa smiled. 'Thanks,' she said.

She had been back in her office only a few minutes when Aida called, and the change in her friend's tone was immediately noticeable. 'I got his secretary, and she told me he's on sabbatical, as of yesterday. She sounded as surprised as I felt. I mean, no one starts a sabbatical in the middle of the year, do they?'

'Did she say where?' Raisa asked.

'That was the other thing – she didn't know for certain. She said Moscow, but when I asked for the address she said she didn't have one. And when I pushed a bit, she clammed up completely.'

'Oh,' Raisa said. She felt more surprised than anything, but there was a sense of emptiness too.

'Still, I suppose the fates are trying to tell you something,' Aida went on, her spirits obviously recovering.

'What . . . ?'

'You were going to give him up, remember?'

'Yes, I know, but . . . Yes, you're right.'

After putting the phone down Raisa sat staring out of the window at the familiar view: the city on its hills, the curved bay, the artificial islands with their oil rigs.

35

It didn't feel right that it should end like this. In fact, it didn't feel right, full stop. She supposed it was absurd, her worrying about someone whom she'd been about to see for the last time. But she was.

She got up and started pacing. There didn't seem to be anything she could do without revealing their affair, and even if she did reveal it she wasn't family, so no one would have to answer her questions.

She had to talk to someone, and there was only one real possibility. Like Tamarlan, Arif Akhundov was a professor at the university, and the two men spent most of their summer weekends hiking together in the mountains. As far as she had been able to tell, he was Tamarlan's only real friend. She didn't know if he knew about her.

After three days of internal debate she finally phoned him on the Sunday evening. She had no rational grounds for concern, she told herself as the ringing tone started – just an underlying sense of 'wrongness' which she couldn't quite shake.

'Hello?' a male voice said, as if its owner was surprised to be receiving a call.

She took a deep breath. 'My name is Raisa Karayeva,' she began. It obviously rang no bells. 'I am a friend of Tamarlan Shadmanov,' she went on. 'A close friend,' she added, wincing at the cliché.

'Ah,' he said, as if something had just slotted into place.

'I am trying to get in touch with him,' she said. 'He often talks about you, and I thought perhaps you might know where he is.'

There was a brief silence. 'No, I don't, but I have had a letter from him . . .'

'A letter,' she echoed.

'A strange letter,' he added. 'He says that he will be away for several months working on a government project, but he doesn't say where or what the project is.'

'What sort of government project would need a physics professor?' she wondered out loud.

A long silence ensued, and for a moment she thought they had been cut off.

'He has only been an academic for a few years,' Akhundov said eventually. 'Before the break-up he worked for the Soviet Rocket Forces research division.'

Tamarlan had never told her that. 'Doing what?' she asked.

'I'm not sure – he doesn't like to talk about it much. Something to do with missile engineering, I think.'

She let that sink in. 'What was the postmark on the letter?' she asked.

'Baku,' he said promptly.

She had the feeling that both of them were now treating Tamarlan's disappearance as suspicious, without actually saying so.

'There was something else in the letter, something which I didn't understand until now. I still don't, but . . . wait a second and I'll read it to you.'

She listened to him walk across his room and back again.

'He says, "If Raisa calls tell her it's time to start her life and to stop chasing rainbows – there's no pot of gold at the end of mine." Does that mean anything to you?'

'No,' she said, but promised to think about it.

An hour and two glasses of vodka later she was no nearer to inspiration. There didn't seem much doubt that he was trying to tell her something, but she was damned if she could work out what.

She went back over the two years of their affair, trying to remember each meeting, each conversation. She relived their first meeting, at a scientific conference, the first time they had made love in his Volga, the first time they had done it in the forest. She found herself thinking how much fun it had all been, and then realized how selective her memory was proving. All the evenings and nights she had spent waiting for the phone to ring had been conveniently erased.

This was getting her nowhere. She poured another slug of vodka, curled up on the sofa once more and let her mind go blank. A pot of gold . . .

And then it came to her. It had been almost two years ago, a showery autumn day, and they had met in the same picnic area above the city, maybe even for the first time. She could see the arc of oil-drilling piers stretching out into the choppy water, and the rainbow which suddenly appeared in gloriously bright colours, one end caught in the clouds, the other seemingly rooted in the farthest tip of the man-made isthmus.

He was out there in the Caspian.

But doing what? Her department should have received notification of any new government project in the area, but there had been none. For a few moments her anger at this betrayal thrust Tamarlan to the back of her mind. What the hell were they doing in the middle of her sea?

Still, at least she knew where he was, and presumably his wife was with him. She reached for the phone to call Akhundov, then took her hand away. It was almost midnight – much too late to call. And now that she

38

had solved at least part of the riddle there seemed no reason for urgency.

Next morning she arrived at work to find the university buzzing with the news that a professor had been run down and killed by a car just outside the gates. It had been an accident, of course, but the car had not stopped.

5

Uday al-Dulaini padded down the richly carpeted underground corridor and rapped softly on the door of Kusai Hussein's Mukhabarat office.

'Come,' Kusai said, his voice only just audible above the whirr of the basement's air-conditioning.

Inside, Uday found his boss idly snacking, dipping Jacob's Cream Crackers into twin bowls of red and black caviar. There was something irredeemably provincial about the man, Uday thought. Like his brother, he was a peasant in urban dress. A peasant with the power of life and death over twenty million people.

Kusai poured them both a glass of bourbon and sat down on the white leather couch which lined one wall. 'So your sleight of hand with the scientist was a success,' he said encouragingly.

'It worked like a dream,' Uday agreed, lowering himself into Kusai's massage chair. 'We videoed the UN people as they arrived at Falluja. Their eyes nearly fell out of their sockets when they realized there was nothing there. For the next few months they'll think twice before voicing their suspicions, and in the meantime our people in Washington and Brussels will be using the proof of our innocence' – he allowed himself a smile – 'to strengthen the case for lifting sanctions. Abas Naji may not have intended it, but he served his country better in death than he ever did in life.' He took a sip of the bourbon.

'There are lingering suspicions,' Kusai argued, as much to put the arrogant puppy in his place as because he thought they mattered. 'There was an article in the London press a few days ago.'

Uday dismissed the matter with a wave of the hand. 'They are afraid of us,' he said, 'and frightened people are always suspicious. But I think we have given our friends enough ammunition already, and soon they will have more.'

'The Russian operation is underway?'

Uday looked at his watch. 'The call was made about two hours ago.'

Kusai shook his head and smiled. 'What makes you think they will take the bait?'

'How could they not?'

Kusai laughed at the sheer hubris of the younger man. 'I hope you're right.' He took a gold cigarette case from his pocket and extracted a cigarette, noting Uday's slight frown of disapproval. 'Do we have a new delivery date?' he asked, the Zippo lighter poised beside the cigarette.

'No. It's still eighteen months, assuming nothing goes wrong . . .'

'What could go wrong?' Kusai asked, realizing as he did so that seeing Uday fall flat on his face would offer at least some consolation for any future failure.

'Who knows?' Uday was saying philosophically.

'The Azeri scientist is not making difficulties?'

'It doesn't look like it.'

Kusai blew smoke in Uday's direction. 'So all we have to do is wait.'

*   *   *

The cast of characters in Conference Room B was much the same as it had been three weeks before, with a Lieutenant Colonel Colhoun in the seat previously occupied by the anonymous young man from the Foreign Office Gulf Desk. The presence of this newcomer, introduced by Martin Clarke as 'the Officer Commanding the Special Boat Squadron', had given David Constantine cause to hope that this particular meeting would generate more than words.

Neil Colhoun, who had been invited up from Poole at short notice, was hoping much the same thing.

'I'm afraid it's Saddam's bomb again,' Clarke began, with what he probably thought was a winning smile. 'The subject is becoming something of an old chestnut, but . . .' He raised his hands in mock helplessness.

'But we all know what happened to the boy who cried wolf,' Manny Salewicz interjected somewhat inappropriately.

'Quite,' Clarke agreed. 'Sir Christopher?'

The head of MI6 looked like he'd been up all night. 'We have received some information from St Petersburg,' he began. 'According to a man who telephoned our consulate there, a ship left port at dawn yesterday – that's about thirty-two hours ago – bound for the Syrian port of Latakia. The manifest claims the ship is carrying agricultural machinery, but our man on the phone says there's also sixty pounds of weapons-grade Uranium 235 on board. He even had the number of the hold and the markings on the crates. The shipment has been purchased by the Iraqis through a Russian syndicate of ex-military and neo-Mafia people.'

Clarke turned his gaze on Constantine. 'Enough for

two Hiroshima-power bombs or warheads,' the weapons science adviser said. 'Maybe three.'

'Shit,' Salewicz murmured.

Colhoun now knew the reason for his own presence, and his enthusiasm dimmed slightly. In the past the SBS had often been asked to act in circumstances which bent the rules of international law, but high-seas piracy would be something new. There was even an added element of irony – that very week an SBS team had just wrapped up an operation against organized piracy in the South China Sea.

'What are the chances of putting some real pressure on Syria?' the man from the MoD was asking. 'They would be guilty of sanctions-breaking, and they've never been that fond of the Iraqis.'

'Do they even know what's headed their way?' Salewicz asked.

'We don't know,' Hanson answered the American. 'But my feeling is, we can't afford to trust the Syrians to sort this out. Even if they're willing, they're unlikely to be competent.'

'Her Majesty's Government,' Clarke said ponderously, 'is of the opinion that this ship is already guilty of sanctions-breaking, and can be considered a rogue vessel according to international law. Lieutenant Colonel, do you think your men could board and search this vessel as it proceeds through the English Channel?'

'And remove the relevant contraband?'

'Exactly.'

Colhoun shrugged. 'I can see no *practical* difficulties. But if my men meet opposition they will obviously have to defend themselves, perhaps before they can verify the existence of the nuclear material. If people are killed and there turns out to be no contraband then there will be a major international incident. Is Her Majesty's Government prepared for such an eventuality? And can I have your assurance, Minister, that my men will not be left holding the baby if something like that happens?'

Clarke looked almost hurt, as if such a possibility had never occurred to him. 'We stand by our people,' he said shortly.

'Remember Gibraltar,' Salewicz said sardonically.

Colhoun realized that was all the assurance he was likely to get. 'Are we certain the ship is taking the Channel route?' he asked Hanson.

'According to the course they filed with Lloyd's. Our rough estimate, based on an average speed of fourteen to sixteen knots, puts the ship in mid-Channel sometime between sunset on Monday and dawn on Tuesday. But of course we'll be getting more precise updates from air reconnaissance once she enters the North Sea.'

Which gave him almost four days to prepare his team, Colhoun thought. He hoped the ship would oblige them by moving through the Channel at night. In such matters darkness might provide no more than a fig leaf, but a fig leaf was always better than nothing.

Once ensconced in his first-class compartment for the return journey to Poole, the SBS boss turned his mind to choosing a team for the job. The four-man team led by Callum Marker had the most active-service experience – the real thing was distinctly hard to come by in this day and age – but it was still in Hong Kong, and in any case lacked the specialist knowledge needed for this assignment. Gary McClure and Paul Noonan, on the other hand, had finished a course in nuclear-related issues only a few weeks earlier, and presumably now knew one end of a Geiger counter from the other.

'McClure,' Colhoun murmured out loud, causing the woman sitting across the aisle to stare in his direction. To his certain knowledge, Gary McClure had a perfect service record. He had graduated from the Marines to the SBS with flying colours, and in hardly any time at all had passed through the SC3, SC2 and SC1 courses, passed the Senior Command Course, and been promoted to sergeant. He was probably the best swimmer in the Squadron, a veritable wizard when it came to explosives, and his leadership of a behind-the-lines team in the Gulf War had won him a Military Medal. He seemed to live for the SBS.

And yet there was something about the twenty-eight-year-old Londoner which made Colhoun less than a total fan. Something which he had never been able to put his finger on. He could point to certain things – McClure was too dedicated, too willing to put aside ordinary physical and mental needs, too good at turning off his own humanity the way a soldier sometimes has to do. These sounded like positive attributes, and of course in certain situations they were, but . . .

Colhoun sighed, and watched the outskirts of Guildford slide by. Over the last few years he supposed he had come to see McClure as someone who existed at the very edge of what was acceptable in a soldier. He remembered Raymond Chandler's description of the perfect private eye – a man who was able to walk the mean streets without becoming mean – and thought that a perfect soldier could be described in much the same way. McClure's record made him look like one, but Colhoun sometimes had the sense that he had chosen to walk the mean streets – or in SBS terms, swim the mean waters – because he felt most at home with meanness.

He sighed again. You were supposed to get more resigned with age, not more moralistic. If McClure got the job done, what did it matter if he had a heart of stone?

It mattered, Colhoun told himself, if McClure was so tightly wrapped that one day he simply lost control of himself. And it was with such a possibility in mind that he had asked for a psychiatric profile the previous year. The psychiatrist had reported back that McClure was a very angry man and a very controlled man, and that it was hard to imagine a career in which he could make more productive use of his anger than the one he was currently in.

There had been no indications, either then or since, that an explosion was imminent. There was only a hunch in Colhoun's gut which he couldn't substantiate, and which might well be playing him false.

Besides, McClure had just acquired the extracurricular knowledge he would need for an otherwise straightforward mission. There was really no choice, no matter how much the man in the back of Colhoun's mind wanted there to be one.

Paul Noonan took a sip of bitter without taking his eyes off the door of the Ladies. She emerged, and he found that the sight of her walking towards him was as bad for his blood pressure as the sight of her walking away had been. It wasn't just the shape – it was the motion.

The jewelled stud in her nose glinted in the lights as she sat down. A few days ago he would have imagined something like that putting him off, but now it just seemed an extra come-on. He was glad she didn't have a ring through her lip or tongue though – no matter what people said, things like that had to get in the way of all-out kissing.

And he did hope to be kissing her before the evening was over, on the mouth at least. And then, either tonight or sometime in the very near future, he wanted to lick his way down her lovely throat towards the nipples that were pushing against the tight sweater.

But first, he thought with a sigh, they had to get to know each other.

Julie seemed to have the same idea. 'So how long are you in for then?' she asked, making life in the Marines sound like a stretch in prison.

'Until I feel like quitting,' he told her, with scant attention to the truth.

'But you like it?' she asked, licking the Guinness foam from her upper lip with a perfect pink tongue.

'Oh yeah.'

'It doesn't just feel like you're playing soldiers?' she asked mischievously.

'No,' he said indignantly.

'I told my dad what you did, and he just said it must be better than working for a living.'

Noonan made a face. I can't wait to meet her father, he thought.

'Well, there's no wars, is there?' she persisted. 'And the Cold War's finished. It's just terrorists these days, right?'

'You never know,' Noonan said. 'We have to be ready for anything. We have to be the best.' And the SBS was the best, but he couldn't tell her he was a member of that. 'It's not just combat skills,' he said seriously. 'You have to be a mechanic, a parachutist, a sailor, a radio operator, a bomb disposal expert . . . You can tell your dad it's bloody hard work.'

Julie grinned at him. 'You'll probably get to tell him yourself one of these days.'

'I can't wait,' he said sarcastically, though the implication behind her remark made him feel good.

'He's OK really. Are your parents still in Liverpool?'

'Yeah. My dad's like one of those mobile phones you can't take too far from its base, only in his case it's his football team. If he moves more than a mile away from Anfield his circuits start shorting. My mum's a councillor – spends her life trying to stir up the neighbours.'

'What's your dad do?'

'Building, when there's any work. He was a merchant seaman for twenty years, but the unionized jobs just disappeared – it's all Filipinos these days.'

'My dad lost his job about four years ago. He can get seasonal work in the summer but there's nothing else around here. I think they'd have trouble making ends meet if I wasn't bringing in any money.'

He took another sip of beer, and wondered if it was too cold to suggest a walk on the beach. 'You like being a nurse though, don't you?' he said.

'Most of the time. It's really depressing sometimes. People die.' She looked at him with a rueful smile. 'And I never get enough sleep.' She arched her back and yawned, tightening the sweater in the process.

Noonan was about to suggest the walk when a uniformed Marine loomed over her lovely head. For reasons that he couldn't begin to guess at, much less excuse, he was needed back on base.

*   *   *

48

The surprises continued. For one thing, it was the CO himself who required Noonan's presence; for another, as he walked in through the great man's door the first person he set eyes on was his monosyllabic partner from the recent nuclear course. Exchanging Julie's company for Gary McClure's was like trading in Meg Ryan for a depressed Arnold Schwarzenegger.

'Sit down, Corporal,' Colhoun said, gesturing Noonan towards the one empty seat in the ring of four facing his desk. Sitting beside McClure were two SC3s whom Noonan knew by little more than name. Davies was a curly-headed giant from East Anglia who looked like he could lock horns with a combine harvester and win. Appleton was a slightly smaller, straight-haired Geordie who seemed about as verbose as McClure.

Their Scottish CO was sitting in his famous tattered leather chair, notes and charts spread liberally across the desk in front of him. 'We've been given a job to do,' Colhoun told the four men. 'And I've provisionally selected you four to do it. It may be that once you've considered all the possibilities and done some draft planning you'll come to the conclusion that more bodies are needed. If so, we'll bring more in.'

He looked round the semicircle of faces in front of him, noting the nervous excitement of three, the hungry look in the eyes of the fourth.

'The job,' he went on, disentangling a map of Europe from the other papers and turning it round for his audience. 'Two days ago a Russian ship, the *Red Voyager*, sailed from St Petersburg here' – he pointed it out, knowing from long experience how many of his men were geographically illiterate. 'By now it should be somewhere around here, about ten miles south of Copenhagen. The ship is headed for Latakia in Syria with a cargo of agricultural machinery. It's also, according to information received, carrying about sixty pounds of enriched uranium for Saddam Hussein.'

'Christ,' Noonan said out loud.

Colhoun smiled at him. 'And according to the latest estimate it should be forty miles away from here at around 01.30 hours on Tuesday. Which is when you will board her, locate the uranium and bring it away with you.'

A slight smile was creasing McClure's lips. 'Do we have any other information about the ship?' he asked in his soft voice.

'The normal crew complement is twenty-six – six officers, five deck crew, ten in the engine room, five in the galley. As far as we know they're all Russian. We have no idea how many of them are armed, or how many of them know about the uranium. We do know which hold the stuff's in, and what the markings on the crate are.'

McClure raised an eyebrow. 'How come?' he asked.

Colhoun explained about the tip-off. 'There a possibility that it's just a hoax, but I'm afraid there's only one way of finding out for certain.'

To Noonan's astonishment, McClure actually grinned.

'The ship will be passing through the Oresund in a couple of hours,' Colhoun went on, 'and the Danes have promised to take some pictures for us.'

'Should give us an idea of the lighting,' McClure murmured, as if he was talking to himself.

'You have three days to plan and prepare. First thing in the morning, I want the four of you to start considering your options. I'm probably teaching my grandmother to suck eggs, but it seemed to me there are three separate questions to answer: how you're going to get on to the ship, how you plan to spend your time on board, and how you intend to get home with the booty. I should add at this point that our political masters would prefer that you manage all this without alerting the Russian crew, but I doubt if that will be possible, and I told them as much. However, it's important you don't leave any evidence behind – it won't be hard for them to work out who their visitors were, but we want proving it to be another matter.'

'Understood,' McClure said.

'The RAF will keep track of the ship for us once it's in the North Sea. OK, I think that's all for now. Any questions?'

The two SC3s looked at each other; McClure shook his head. The four men filed out. 'Canteen at eight,' McClure told the others with what might even have been a smile, and strode off without waiting for a reply.

Noonan asked the other two if they fancied a drink.

'Does a fox shit in the woods?' Davies asked him.

It was only ten o'clock. McClure left the base and headed for the centre of town on foot, his mind mulling over this sudden change in his circumstances. The fucking nuclear course had been worth it after all. He would be seeing some real action, going up against real enemies.

He found he was heading for Annie's flat without having really intended to. Since that night in the pub he'd stayed away – he felt too ashamed of the way he'd lost control. And he hadn't really wanted to be reminded of it either, though lately just about anything seemed to get him going. Sometimes he felt like he had been born with this vast pool of anger somewhere in his brain, and all anyone had to do was tap into it.

But he had a job now, and it was always better on a job. The rage seemed to evaporate somehow, and he felt completely in control of himself, the job in hand, everything.

Annie's light was still on. He rang the bell and listened to her descend the stairs. When she saw it was him her face darkened for an instant, but then she must have seen something in his eyes because she smiled. 'Come in, lover,' she said.

6

Looking back on the days which followed Arif Akhundov's fatal encounter with the unidentified car, Raisa Karayeva found it easy to retrace her path through a series of emotional reactions. The first of these, which grasped at her heart and then sat like lead in her stomach, had been simple fear.

The police, the newspapers, all those around her – everyone thought it had been an accident. Witnesses had seen the professor step out in front of the speeding car; the driver's failure to stop had certainly been callous, but the collision itself had not been his fault. Even Aida accepted this version of events, preferring to see Tamarlan's vanishing trick and Akhundov's accident as coincidental, though she did concede that his friend's disappearance might have upset the professor enough to make him careless. According to his colleagues and secretary he had been absent-minded at the best of times.

Raisa had been planning to tell her friend about the conversation with Akhundov and the deductions she had herself made, but after his death the sudden rush of fear – for herself, for Aida too – compelled her silence. One whole day went by, and then another. She tried to work at the office, tried to relax at home, but the terrifying expectation of a knock on either door only gradually faded.

By the evening of the third day she was at least ready to hope again. Perhaps they had not found the letter, or perhaps there were too many Raisas in Baku to make an investigation worthwhile. On reflection, she found it hard to believe that the letter had not been vetted before it was sent, but then who was she to second-guess the KGB, or whatever it was they called themselves these days?

Whoever they were, they had apparently not discovered that Tamarlan was having an extramarital affair before they took him away. It was ironic, she thought, that the secrecy which she had so resented seemed to have been her salvation.

As the fear receded, curiosity filled the emotional space it left behind. Where exactly had they taken him? What were they doing out there? Finding an answer to the first question was not so difficult – at the institute she had access to all the available information concerning activities taking place around, on or under the surface of the Caspian Sea. After two days of intermittent research she had ruled out all the facilities at the end of the artificial isthmus, and thus narrowed the search to the huge twin rig – Aliyev A and Aliyev B – which lay just beyond it. The two interconnected structures, built in the last years of the Soviet Union, had been intended as a test-site for deep-drilling equipment, but there was no record of their being used as such during the past few years.

The twin rig was certainly large enough to house a scientific project, and seclusion could be almost guaranteed. It would be hard to escape from.

On the Friday after Akhundov's death she manufactured an excuse to join one of the Institute's regular water-sampling trips, and went to see for herself. The twin rig was still there. In daylight, several kilometres away, it was impossible to detect movement or light, but she felt sure enough of her conclusions.

Having satisfied herself on that score, the second question took precedence. What were they doing out there? A small part of Raisa was still hoping that Tamarlan had been taken for his non-military skills, but with such levels of security it was hard to escape the conclusion that the military were involved, and that her lover's old work had come back to claim him.

But what could they be doing? She found it hard to believe that the Azeri government would allow the Russians to develop new nuclear weapons in Azeri waters, and even harder to imagine the same government starting its own nuclear weapons programme. She supposed the raw materials could be had for a price – maybe from the Ukraine or Kazakhstan – but what would be the point? What possible use could Azerbaijan have for nuclear weapons?

Fate conspired to tell her that very day. Shopping for vegetables in the Sharg Bazary market, she witnessed an argument and near brawl between two women. One, a refugee from Nagorno-Karabakh, had been trying to jump the queue, and when challenged launched a string of abuse at her accusers. Had they no generosity towards their fellow-countrymen? When their turn came to be raped and their husbands killed and their homes burnt maybe they would learn. If they couldn't treat their own people better than this then they deserved the coming Armenian invasion.

Raisa expected her fellow-shoppers to treat this out-burst with the laughter it deserved, but they didn't. In fact they seemed shamed, and the woman was almost hustled to the front of the queue.

Back at the flat she turned on the TV to the same subject – someone was obviously trying to tell her something. There was footage from the front – a burnt-out Armenian tank, a shot-down Armenian plane, both surrounded by smiling Azeri soldiers – and interviews with the survivors of another Armenian massacre in occupied Azerbaijan.

She turned off the TV and poured herself a drink. She knew all this, so why did it come as a surprise? When it came down to it, she realized, she had assumed that none of it really mattered. It was hard on those involved, but all this crazy flag-waving was just an aberration, a sort of school's-out hysteria to follow the Soviet break-up. It would all blow over.

But it hadn't. Armenians had been fighting Azeris for seven years now, and there was no prospect of a lasting peace. It was she who was the aberration, not the flag-wavers. She was a child of mixed parentage, someone who had always felt that the official Soviet distaste for nationalism made perfect sense. Her work as an environmentalist had only strengthened this feeling – nature, and the need to protect it, certainly knew no boundaries. She had kept her eyes firmly on the east, on the multinational problems of the Caspian, while the rest of her countrymen and women had their gaze locked on the West, and the potentially genocidal feud with Armenia.

They would understand the need for an Azeri bomb. Parts of their country were already occupied, and what was there to stop a continuing Armenian advance? The Azeris were a peaceful race, a race of farmers, not infidel mountain warriors. The more sophisticated could even argue that Azerbaijan's maintenance of the economic blockade would eventually give the Armenians no choice but to attack.

She felt a shiver race up her spine, and took a gulp from her glass.

Tamarlan would feel no better about this than she did, and he – she was now sure – had been dragooned into helping. There was no way he would have volunteered for such work, for he was as little moved by nationalism and power politics as she was. Working for the Soviet Union was one thing, but building nuclear weapons for use in a war over who owned a few desolate mountains . . . What would there be left but desolation?

And now that she knew of his past work, she thought she could understand the inner sadness which had occasionally seeped to the surface, the rueful asides which had previously seemed inexplicable. Knowing that he had been dragged back into it made her sad, and angry too. How dare they steal people! It was no less than a modern form of slavery. And how dare they put her sea at risk by placing a nuclear facility at its heart!

She had to do something, tell someone.

But whom? And how? There was no point in raising the matter here in Azerbaijan, and an international phone call would probably seal her fate. If she was serious about this, she would have to get out of the country.

The rigid inflatable Fast Patrol Craft bobbed in the Channel swell, its twin 700hp outboard motors idling in neutral. Over the past few months considerable ingenuity had been applied by the technical branch to muffling the sound of these motors, and though the work had been done principally with 3rd Raiding Division's Hong Kong anti-smuggling duties in mind, McClure's team was now sharing the benefits. The FPC's approach was unlikely to be heard above the engines and passage of the target ship, and on this particular night it was no more likely to be seen. Mist had been cloaking the Channel since shortly after nightfall, and the succeeding hours of darkness had been filled with the doleful horns of passing ships. These were visible, if at all, as nothing more than moving constellations of fuzzy lights.

Fate had apparently decided to favour the SBS team, but the four men in the FPC were taking nothing for granted. The radar operators on the frigate HMS *Gloucester* were tracking the target ship's approach, and as the fixes grew steadily nearer, the three subordinate members of McClure's team could each feel the butterflies dancing in their stomachs and the adrenalin coursing through their veins.

McClure himself felt perfectly calm. He always did at such times, when action was imminent. He thought of it as the stillness before the storm, and relished the moment – it was really the only time in his life when he felt able to simply *be*. For those few hours, or even minutes, the world seemed a different place. The colours were brighter, sounds sharper. It seemed ridiculous on such a misty night, but everything was so clear.

Sitting beside McClure, Paul Noonan was more conscious of his own nerves than the team leader's lack of them. The minutes seemed to be dragging by, and yet he knew that when the moment came, and the freighter loomed through the fog, everything would happen at breakneck speed. He could feel the excitement of the two men in front of him, and could vividly remember his own baptism of fire three years before. For what seemed like hours of waiting the thought 'please don't make a complete fool of yourself' had carved a rut in his brain.

He hadn't, and he doubted whether Appleton or Davies would either, but he could almost hear them praying.

McClure was receiving on the radio. 'Over and out,' he said softly. 'She should be on top of us any minute now,' he told the others.

Appleton's hand tightened on the FPC's wheel and eight eyes strained to pierce the darkness and the mist.

A minute went by, and another, but no engine noise carried across the rolling water, no dark shape swam into view. 'Where the fuck is she?' McClure muttered, and at that moment Noonan heard the distant hum of a ship in motion.

'I can hear her,' he said.

They all could, but a visual sighting was something else, and already the sound seemed to be fading.

'Take us south-south-east,' McClure told Appleton, 'at twenty knots.'

Appleton obliged, and the sound of the FPC's engines, even with their new muffling, immediately drowned out the noise of the other ship's passage. Noonan was just beginning to fear that the mist had proved more of a foe than a friend when a dim light appeared almost dead ahead. For a moment it seemed to be floating wraith-like in mid-air, and then a ship's bow materialized out of the mist, shadowy at first but then increasingly substantial, the prow sharpening as they drew closer.

In his mind's eye each of the four men could visualize

the rest of the ship. They had carefully studied the photographs flown in from Copenhagen two days before, and made a trip to Southampton to look over an almost identical ship. About a hundred and fifty of these SD14 cargo vessels had been built since the mid-1960s; they were about 140 metres in length, with the superstructure set three-quarters aft and the two large twin derricks occupying the foredeck. Their top speed was fourteen knots. The one now looming above them had been built at the Sunderland yards of Austin & Pickersgill in 1969, and picked up cheap by the Soviets when the original buyer failed to make the initial payment.

They could see the ship's name now, stencilled in a lighter colour on the black hull, but the superstructure a hundred metres further back was only a dim shape in the mist. There was no way that anyone on the bridge could see them, and there was no sign of life on the foredeck.

Appleton angled the FPC in slowly towards the starboard bow, adjusting his speed to keep pace with the other ship, and Noonan had a mental picture of a cowboy positioning his speeding horse to leap aboard a runaway stagecoach. The Russian ship was actually moving slower than they had expected – it couldn't be doing much more than eight knots at this moment, which should make boarding it that much easier.

The wall of the hull now rose above them, and McClure was standing up, the rope curled in his hand like a lasso. He wheeled his arm twice and sent the grappling-hook soaring up and over the starboard rail. There was a muffled clang as it caught. McClure tugged to make sure and then started up the rope hand over hand, his Heckler & Koch MP5SD sub-machine-gun hanging loosely across his shoulder and back. The other three watched his indistinct figure scramble across the rail, and then a few seconds later a tug on the rope announced the all-clear.

Noonan followed him up, thinking as he did so that he didn't envy Appleton's job of keeping the FPC in position for however long it took to find and move the crate containing the uranium. Not that Noonan himself fancied having anything much to do with the crate, since the course he had just finished in the nuclear aspects of possible terrorist situations had hardly been comforting. As far as he could tell the availability of the deadly stuff in the old Soviet states was only matched by the carelessness with which they seemed to treat it. Noonan was half expecting to find the whole ship already irradiated by a wodge of plutonium that someone had casually stuffed in a plastic bag.

Once over the rail he tugged on the rope for Davies, knelt down on the deck and checked the liquid crystal display on the Geiger counter. The background radiation was negligible. Either the sanctions-breakers had been suitably careful with their illicit cargo or the SBS team was on a wild-goose chase.

McClure, meanwhile, was still staring down the length of the ship, searching for any sign that their arrival uninvited had been noticed. The distant superstructure grew alternately fainter and more substantial as the mist swirled around it, and the strip of yellow light which marked the bridge seemed to be flickering on and off like a faulty fluorescent strip-light. Besides that intermittent glow there were only the fuzzy red, green and white navigation lights to tell the SBS man that he had not boarded a ghost ship.

The entrance hatch to No. 2 Tween-decks, where the crate was supposedly stored, was about thirty metres away. McClure waited while Noonan and Davies hauled up the rope cradle which had been chosen to carry the crate, and then hand-signalled them to follow him. The three men advanced down the slippery deck, the lighted window of the bridge growing clearer as they did so, but even when the mist was at its lightest no human figures could be seen inside. Visibility to either side was no more than fifty metres, and above them it was even less, so that the tops of the derricks were hidden in the clouds.

They reached the entrance hatch. Davies swung it open and the three men dropped through on to the ladder which led down on to the tween-decks. McClure closed the hatch behind him, plunging them into total darkness, and then for several moments the three men waited in silence.

'OK,' McClure said at last, switching on his torch. The others followed suit.

The tween-decks was arranged like a wide, four-sided balcony overlooking the inner courtyard of the main No. 2 hold below. McClure gestured Noonan and Davies to go one way while he went the other, their torch beams dancing on the walls and piles of crates on pallets. Noonan had another mental picture – this time of the space travellers searching the nesting place at the beginning of *Alien* – and decided it was time he stopped going to movies. Or at least the scary ones.

'Over here,' McClure called softly. He had found the crate with the marking.

This was becoming too easy, Noonan thought, as he hurried across with the Geiger counter.

The LCD didn't go mad – in fact it hardly moved at all. If there was Uranium-235 in the crate it was better shielded than anyone could have hoped.

'Nothing,' he told McClure.

'We'd better open it up.'

'I was afraid you'd suggest that.'

It wasn't difficult, as the crate was no better clamped shut than the average tea chest of crockery in transit. And no lead or similar containment vessel appeared in the light of their torches – just four heavy-looking cylindrical canisters packed in straw.

McClure tried to lift out one of the canisters and found they were lighter than they looked. The writing on the side contained several figures and two tell-tale words in English – 'Red Mercury'.

Noonan searched his memory for what the course instructor had told them about it. It had been confusing enough at the time – according to some people the stuff could be used to make nuclear weapons; it was the poor man's plutonium – but other, equally reputable scientists dismissed it as a hoax.

'This must be it,' McClure announced.

'There's no indication of anything radioactive down here,' Noonan confirmed.

McClure banged the lid back down on the crate with the butt of the MP5. 'Let's get it out of here,' he said.

Noonan and Davies carried the crate to the bottom of the ladder, and once there lowered it into the rope cradle. McClure went up the ladder, pushed the hatch ajar and examined the visible deck. If anything the mist was a little thicker, the bridge light faint enough to be a figment of the imagination. He climbed up on to the deck, gestured Noonan up with the rope, and together they hauled the crate up through the hole and on to the deck.

Davies was just emerging through the hatch when the Russian materialized out of the mist. He was wearing a dark parka, which he hadn't bothered to close at the front. The hood was also down, exposing a bearded face and longish hair slicked flat by the moisture in the air. He was swaying as he walked, and not merely with the motion of the ship.

He shouted at them in Russian, seeming to find something funny, and reached inside his parka.

He could have been going for a gun, but Noonan instinctively knew that he wasn't.

McClure's silenced MP5 triple-coughed, the Russian's knees buckled, and he fell forward on to the deck like a bull which had been given the *coup de grâce*.

McClure strode forward and checked inside the man's clothes for identification, his senses alert for any further interruption. There was nothing to say who the man was, nothing to connect him to this ship; it should be safe to throw the body overboard, bullet wounds and all. It would be better to weigh it down, but there was nothing suitable to hand.

He beckoned the others to help him get the body across the rail. Noonan snapped out of his trance and hurried across. As they lifted the corpse the parka fell open, revealing the corked vodka bottle resting in the large inside pocket. There was no sign of a gun.

After making sure that the FPC was not directly below, they let the body drop into the dark swell. Their boat was only ten metres or so away, and even in the darkness Noonan could see the expression of shock on Appleton's face echo that which his own had worn.

He and Davies turned their attention to the cradled crate, lowering it carefully into the other boat as Appleton kept the FPC in position and McClure kept watch. Then, with the rope reattached, they took their leave of the *Red Voyager*. A flick of McClure's wrist disengaged the grappling-hook, and Appleton turned the FPC slowly and almost silently away from the freighter. Within seconds it had been swallowed by the mist.

Noonan found he was expecting McClure to say something about the killing, but the team leader apparently felt no such compulsion. 'No witnesses,' they had been told, and McClure had obviously taken the order literally.

Noonan looked across the crate at the other man, who was now reporting in on the radio. He had an almost dreamy smile on his face, like a cat which has just tasted cream.

On the bridge of the *Red Voyager* Captain Vlasov was sharing a drink with First Mate Denikin. They had observed deck-hand Samsonov's ridiculous encounter with the British commandos through nightscopes, and the experience had cast a slight pall over an otherwise successful operation.

'What was the idiot doing out there?' Vlasov wanted to know.

'God only knows. It looked like he was going to offer them a drink.'

'Did he have any family?'

Denikin expressed his ignorance with a shrug. 'Maybe we can get compensation from the Iraqis,' he suggested.

Vlasov grunted. 'And maybe Yeltsin is a teetotaller,' he said, then drained his glass. 'Oh well,' he added, 'at least we can stop crawling along at this ludicrous pace now that our visitors are gone.'

Eight hours later Noonan was in the CO's office, feeling Colhoun's penetrating gaze boring into him. The team had been officially debriefed on their return, but something had obviously stuck in the Old Man's craw, and Noonan had a shrewd idea what it was. He felt like a schoolboy who had been called back in by the headmaster to rat on his fellows.

'This is off the record,' Colhoun said. He felt awkward himself, but there didn't seem any other way of getting to the bottom of this business.

'Yes, boss,' Noonan said noncommittally.

Colhoun leaned back in his chair. 'Take me through the shooting incident again.'

'It was like Sergeant McClure said. The man came out of nowhere, shouted something, then reached inside his jacket. He could easily have been reaching for a gun.'

'Did you raise your own weapon?' Colhoun asked.

'There wasn't time. The sergeant had already dealt with it.'

Colhoun sighed. 'According to our records, Corporal, you have consistently scored higher in instinctive response tests on the firing range than Sergeant McClure.'

Noonan looked at the floor. 'I didn't think the man was a threat,' he said, 'but I could have been wrong. And if I had been, then McClure's action would have saved the operation.' He looked up at Colhoun, and the distress in his eyes would have been hard to miss. 'It happened so fast, boss.'

7

Thirty-six hours after the boarding of the *Red Voyager* the SBS CO was back in the increasingly familiar environs of Conference Room B. As he waited for the meeting to begin, Colhoun stared idly at the landscape painting on the wall with its doomy skies and deep shadows. It suited the room, he thought. It suited Whitehall.

The roster for these meetings seemed to be shrinking. This time there were only five men gathered around the table: Colhoun himself, Junior Minister Clarke, scientific adviser Constantine, Salewicz from the American Embassy, and MI6 chief Sir Christopher Hanson.

Martin Clarke asked for Constantine's report.

'Well, it follows the prescription for red mercury,' Constantine confirmed.

'And what is red mercury?' Clarke asked, looking round. 'Or am I the only one here who doesn't know?'

'No one seems very sure,' Constantine said drily. 'The name has no scientific basis, but the stuff which usually goes with the name is a compound of mercury and antimony oxides. It's normally transported in powder form, as in this case, but it can be converted into a liquid with the application of pressure and radiation. In liquid form – so the manufacturers allege – it acquires explosive properties.'

He paused, wondering how to present his information in the simplest possible manner. 'Two things happen in a nuclear warhead or bomb,' he said. 'A conventional explosive is used to implode the plutonium core, crushing and destabilizing it. Then an electronic gun fires a stream of high-energy neutrons into the destabilized plutonium, starting the fission chain reaction – the nuclear explosion. What its proponents claim for red mercury is that it does both jobs – it provides both the conventional explosion and the burst of high-energy neutrons. And in doing both jobs it makes bomb or warhead design much simpler.

'That's the claim, and if it was true then red mercury would be a very significant discovery. The obvious hunger for the stuff – as evidenced by the number of seizures made by various police forces and customs officials over the last few years – suggests there might be something in it, but there's not a shred of scientific evidence to back up such a belief. Seized material has been analysed in a dozen countries, and no one has discovered any explosive properties in the stuff. The International Atomic Energy Authority doesn't believe in it. The Los Alamos National Laboratory says it doesn't exist. And the obvious conclusion is that a few Russian laboratories have thought up a product, given it an enigmatic name and an astronomic price tag, and counted – rather successfully – on the gullibility and deep pockets of the Saddams and Gaddafis of this world.

'Against that, the black-market trade in the stuff has been going on for twenty years now, which is a long time to run a bluff. It's possible that Russian scientists have made some sort of breakthrough which we either can't or won't recognize. There are British scientists – respected

British scientists – who believe there's something worth investigating here.'

'Is there any actual evidence that the Iraqis take it seriously?' Hanson asked.

'Yes. The UN inspectors found boxes of paperwork on the stuff when they raided a building in Baghdad a few years ago. Nothing conclusive there either,' he added, leaning back in his chair and looking at Clarke.

'That was a very judicious presentation,' the minister said. 'The only thing you neglected to give us was your own opinion of this stuff. Is it real or isn't it?'

Constantine smiled at him. 'I'm afraid I can't give a definite answer. I'm not sure. My experience suggests that when scientific opinions diverge this much about something, the truth is usually somewhere in between, but in this case it's hard to imagine a middle ground. Either red mercury simplifies the manufacture of nuclear weapons or it doesn't. And though the amount of energy which seems to be going into its procurement suggests that a lot of people think it can, the plain fact is that we have no evidence to suggest that it does. And twenty years down the line I find that significant.'

'You think it's a hoax?'

Constantine shook his head. 'I'm keeping an open mind. But if I was a betting man, I wouldn't be putting my money on its being a panacea for states in search of a quick nuclear fix.'

'None of our scientists believe in the stuff,' the American offered.

'The Iraqis seem to,' Hanson said, without a great deal of conviction. The intelligence chief was simply playing devil's advocate, Colhoun decided.

'They may do,' Constantine said carefully. He had his

suspicions about the whole business, but had decided that for the moment he would keep them to himself.

'So at least your boys weren't wasting their time the other night,' Salewicz told Colhoun. 'Whether the stuff works or not, Saddam's going to have to put in another order.'

'The SBS team performed in exemplary fashion,' Clarke added. Unlike the SAS, with whom the minister had also had dealings in recent months, Colhoun's men seemed capable of performing those tasks – and only those tasks – which had been set them.

Colhoun bowed his head slightly in recognition of Clark's praise. He didn't like the man, but in these days of sweeping military cut-backs any political endorsement of the Squadron's continuing viability was worth its weight in gold.

'Well, that seems to be that then,' Clarke said. 'I have to get across to the House,' he added, getting up. A nodded goodbye and he was headed for the door.

Colhoun, after making a more leisurely departure, found the scientific adviser waiting for him at the bottom of the stairs. 'I have a question,' Constantine said, falling in beside the SBS man.

'Yes?' Colhoun asked, surprised.

'In your report the speed of the Russian ship is estimated at eight knots. I know there was a heavy mist but that seems unnecessarily slow – I mean, these days ships aren't blind in those sorts of conditions, are they?'

'No, they're not. The *Red Voyager* had radar, of course.'

'So why such a slow speed?'

Colhoun shrugged. 'You'd have to ask the captain.'

'But there's no obvious reason you can think of?'

'No,' Colhoun said, wondering what the other man was getting at.

'And why didn't their radar pick up your men's boat?' Constantine asked, as if the question had just occurred to him.

'Too small, too low in the water,' Colhoun told him.

'Ah. Thanks. No doubt we'll meet again in similar circumstances.'

'No doubt,' Colhoun agreed with a grin. He watched the scientist thread his way through the Whitehall traffic, thinking that this was probably a man he'd like to know.

For his part Constantine spent the journey home to Cambridgeshire shuffling his suspicions about the whole business. A single telephone call to the British Embassy in St Petersburg had revealed that a ship carrying nuclear material would soon be passing through the English Channel. Despite the fact that this material was expensive, illegal and vital to the buyer's interests, the ship had obligingly slowed to a virtual crawl and left its decks unlit and unpatrolled. The only confrontation which had taken place had obviously been an accident. And no report of a missing seaman had been filed by the ship's captain.

It had to be a set-up.

Back at his cottage, Constantine phoned an acquaintance in the university's Russian department and passed on what Noonan had remembered of the unfortunate sailor's last words.

'What was the context?' the linguist asked.

'The person who said it was greeting some other people.'

'Then he was simply saying, "You're late".'

*　　*　　*

71

Noonan slowed to let the idiot with undipped lights sweep past, and then put his foot back on the accelerator. Next to him, Julie seemed to be lost in her thoughts, which wasn't very surprising – the evening had not been a great success. He knew now that he would have been better off taking her to a film than to his favourite country pub, but their first date had felt such a success that he'd been tempted to repeat it.

Trouble was, he couldn't seem to get the dead Russian out of his head, and it hadn't made him very exciting company.

'What's the matter?' she asked suddenly, as if she'd read his mind.

'Nothing really,' he said, giving her an awkward grin. 'I'm sorry . . .'

'You've been looking like your cat just died all evening. Is it me? Because . . .'

'Christ, no.' He exhaled noisily. 'Look, I shouldn't tell you this, right, but I was on duty the other night and someone got killed. It's just kind of shaken me up, know what I mean?' He glanced across at her, knowing that now she'd ask him what had happened and where and he'd have to say he couldn't tell her.

But she didn't.

'I know how a death can . . . well, it can take over, almost. It's happened to me at work. Sometimes you can't help letting yourself care – more than you should as a professional, I mean . . .'

'But I'm a Marine,' he interrupted. 'I'm not supposed to let caring get in my way.'

'Neither am I.'

He grunted. 'I suppose not.'

72

'Did you?' she asked. 'Let it get in the way.'

'No.'

'Well then, that's OK, isn't it? You did your job. If you didn't care *afterwards* then you wouldn't be someone I'd want to go out with.'

He smiled. 'No?'

'Pull the car over.'

'Now?'

'Now.'

He did as she asked and turned to face her.

'I've just thought of a way to cheer you up,' she said, uncoupling her seat-belt.

'Yeah?'

'Yeah.' She took his left hand, cupped it around her right breast, and leant her face towards his to be kissed. He couldn't remember ever seeing anything lovelier.

'I feel better,' he told her a few minutes later, as another car flashed past them. 'It's not very private, is it?' he added. 'And I'm afraid the back seat's not very comfortable.'

'In your dreams,' she said with a mischievous smile. 'When we eventually get to do what you want to do right now, I want a big bed, soft sheets and candlelight.'

He laughed. 'You'll have 'em.'

McClure knew it was crazy, but he felt let down. It had been too easy, too quick, like taking candy from a baby. He felt like a man who'd been offered one glass of water after days in a desert. Christ it tasted sweet, but when it was gone he felt thirstier than ever.

And instead of more action he'd spent nearly a whole day in a classroom instructing potential SC3s in UHF Morse transmitting and receiving.

A car pulled out of a side road unexpectedly, and as he braked McClure could feel the rage stirring inside him. 'Fucking cunt,' he muttered viciously. He thought about giving chase, and then found he was laughing at himself. Why was he feeling so angry? He'd just pulled off another successful mission, won a few more laurels for the SBS. He should be celebrating.

He was close to Annie's place now. He'd been seeing her a lot in the last few days, but why shouldn't he? He didn't spend his money on anything else, and going without sex wasn't good for anyone.

He parked the car and walked up her street. There was a light on in the bedroom, which might mean she had company. He rang the bell and waited, ready to leave if she didn't answer.

'Who is it?' her voice crackled through the tiny speaker.

'It's me.'

There was only a slight hesitation before she buzzed him in. He walked up the familiar staircase, and found her waiting at the top, wearing her dressing-gown.

She smiled at him, and, as she had learned to do over the years, searched his eyes for the tell-tale signs. His last visit had been one of the good ones, and on those occasions she knew he was the only one of her clients who gave her as much as she gave him. Times like that she would have happily not taken his money, but she knew that he would be horrified by the implications of such generosity.

That wouldn't be an issue tonight, she thought. There was no trace in the blue-grey eyes of that indefinable something which occasionally allowed him to share his feelings like a normal fucked-up human being. And sure enough, they had no sooner undressed than he was desperately pumping inside her, his body stiff as a board.

Afterwards he lay beside for the time it took to smoke a cigarette. It had taken her most of their five-year acquaintance to get him to stay that long, she thought, stealing a glance at his face. He had never talked about his past, and she had always assumed it would be futile to ask, but one thing had seemed abundantly clear to her from the very beginning: as a child, no one had ever given him the love he needed.

Colonel Azad Vezirov stood at the wide window and stared out across the blue-green sea at the distant hump of land. Baku was there, with its bars and its women, with his friends and his grown-up children. And on the other side of the Aspheron peninsula, some eighty kilometres north of the city, his beach-side dacha was lying empty. If the President had let him retire instead of insisting that he take charge of this project, Vezirov could have started enjoying the well-earned perks of his forty years in the KGB.

At least he could see land today; for most of the last fortnight the winds had been kicking up the water and hurling spray at his window.

There was a knock on the door. 'Come in,' Vezirov said, hoping that Shadmanov was going to be reasonable.

The scientist came in, took the offered chair, and wondered where to begin. He didn't expect anything to come of this meeting, but he felt he owed it to himself to have a try. At the very least he might get a fuller understanding of what his own government thought it was playing at.

'Professor Shadmanov,' Vezirov said curtly. 'You wanted to see me?'

'I have wanted to see you for two weeks.'

'Well, here you are.'

'Yes. Well, first, and even though I realize it is utterly useless, I would like to formally protest at the kidnapping of myself and my wife by the state organs which you represent here.'

'Noted,' Vezirov said. He could empathize with anyone who wanted away from the island, but there was no point in pretending that such dreams could come true. They were all there for the duration, however long that might be.

Shadmanov's mind was moving in the same direction. 'Are we to be kept here like prisoners, with no opportunity to visit our children or friends, for a period of years?' he asked.

'Every opportunity will be taken to make the prison a comfortable one – even a luxurious one – but yes, I'm afraid so. Azerbaijan is at war, Professor, and when the nation is at risk people have to make sacrifices. Particularly those people who have been best rewarded for their labours during the years of peace, I might add.'

Shadmanov wondered whether Vezirov actually believed what he was saying, and supposed it didn't really matter. 'Are you telling me that the weapons I am designing are for Azerbaijan, and only Azerbaijan?' he asked.

'Of course not. This is a joint project, undertaken by two states for reasons of mutual benefit. The Iraqis, as you are well aware by now, have contributed the lion's share of both the material and the research expertise.'

'That is obvious. The point I was trying to make was

that I have been dragooned by you and your bosses into working for a foreign regime, and one with which I have no sympathy whatsoever.'

Vezirov shrugged. 'Perhaps you would feel happier if you thought of your assistance to Iraq as a necessary but unfortunate by-product of your work for Azerbaijan. We need these weapons, Professor.'

'What for?' Shadmanov half shouted. 'You could never use them against Armenia without risking the destruction of our own country. Have you lived here all your life without noticing which way the prevailing winds blow?'

Vezirov seemed stung by that. 'We have no more intention of using these weapons than the Kremlin intended using the ones you designed in the past. They will deter an Armenian invasion, that is all. They will save lives.'

Shadmanov smiled coldly. 'And the Iraqis? Is that what Saddam Hussein wants them for? I seem to remember that a few years ago he threatened to irradiate the entire Gulf oilfield.'

'That's their business.'

'It's mine if they need my skills to do it!'

Vezirov decided he had let the scientist vent his frustrations for long enough. 'I will pass on your protest,' he said.

Shadmanov got slowly to his feet. Half of him recoiled from the idea of extracting a threat, but the other half was determined to know exactly where he stood. 'And what if I refuse to work?' he asked simply.

Vezirov chose his words carefully. 'I can make no specific predictions,' he said, 'but you will suffer for such a refusal. As will your wife, your son, your friends.'

Shadmanov felt a hollowness in his stomach, and a nervous desire to belch which he managed to repress. 'I understand,' he said, and turned for the door.

Concocting a reason to visit Moscow was not hard – much of the historical data relating to the Caspian and its water catchment area was still on paper in the old Soviet capital, and in happier financial times Institute workers had often journeyed to examine them. Once Raisa had told her superior that she had a friend to stay with, and would not be charging exorbitant Moscow hotel expenses to her employers, he was happy to OK the funds for the relatively cheap air fare.

Leaving, it seemed, was going to offer more in the way of emotional problems than practical ones. As the day for departure grew nearer the enormity of what she was about to do -- sacrificing career, country, the only life she knew – almost overwhelmed her. There was no one to argue her out of it – she had not told Aida anything of her plans, partly for that very reason, and partly because she feared to risk involving her friend. There was even the slight fear that Aida would not prove so immune to patriotic impulses as she herself seemed to be.

On the morning of her flight she took one last sad tour of her flat, gave her plants enough water to last them a few days, and took a taxi to the airport through the city which had been her only home. The wind was blowing as strongly as ever off the Caspian, grabbing at the flags on the old Muslim citadel, pulling at the long, black dresses of the old women perched like crows on the wooden benches.

At the airport the checking-in process had apparently been abandoned in favour of mob rule, but those in charge of passport control were made of sterner stuff. The official went through Raisa's passport twice, while his partner simply stared at her. 'This is not you,' the man eventually decided, tapping the picture for emphasis.

'Yes it is,' she said, with more authority than she felt.

'This woman has short hair.'

'It has grown since then.'

The man changed tack. 'Why are you going to Moscow?' he asked.

'On business. For the Caspian Research Institute.'

'You are travelling alone?'

'Yes.'

He gave her a disapproving look, which she ignored. It wasn't illegal for a woman to travel alone – not yet anyway. He went through the passport a third time, looking for something that was, but came up empty. He handed it back and gestured her through with a contemptuous flick of the head.

The delay had cost Raisa any chance of a seat on the plane, but she managed to get one of the better standing places, close to an emergency exit. An hour of waiting ensued before the Tupolev took off, climbing up over the Caspian and providing her with an unexpected bird's-eye view of the rigs which she believed were home to the Azeri nuclear programme.

A comic interlude was then set in motion by one of the standing passengers, who commandeered the seat of a toilet visitor and then refused to give it back. A loud shouting match ensued, and violence was only avoided by the aggrieved party's obvious inferiority in physique. A precedent having thus been set, the seated passengers were left to choose between their seats and relief, and by the time the plane was approaching Moscow it seemed to Raisa as if the strain was beginning to show on more than a few faces.

Domodedovo Airport was much as she remembered it – a concrete monstrosity built on the edge of the city, with an interminable bus ride to the centre. The latter at least gave her time to think through what she intended to do and say, and as the drab apartment blocks rolled by she checked through her reasoning for one last time. Everything seemed to make sense.

It was almost dark when she finally arrived, with suitcase, at the gates of the British Embassy. They were locked for the night, but she rang the bell anyway, and eventually a woman's voice sounded on the intercom.

'My name is Raisa Karayeva,' she responded in Russian. 'I am from Azerbaijan, and I have information for your government. It concerns a secret nuclear weapons programme in my country.

The woman told her to wait, and shortly thereafter a man appeared to open the gate for her. He introduced himself as Brian Cunningham, ushered her in and left her alone for a few minutes in a high-ceilinged reception room hung with English pastoral scenes, before taking her through to what was obviously his office.

He laboriously wrote down her name, and asked her to repeat what she had told the woman on the intercom. Raisa was ready to explain in English, but since Cunningham's Russian was grammatically as good as hers – though his accent left something to be desired – they agreed to speak in that language.

She did as he asked.

'OK,' he said, allowing scepticism to colour his tone. 'Now tell me about this secret programme.'

'I will only tell you this,' she said. 'My government is developing nuclear weapons to use against Armenia. I know where they are doing this, and I know at least one of the scientists involved – he is my friend, and he was abducted by the government two weeks ago to work on this project. But I will not divulge the exact location until I get a promise from your Prime Minister that no military action will be taken against this facility.' She looked across at her questioner, whose face had been through a rapid series of expressions, culminating in disbelief.

'I can give you references,' she said. This indeed was why she had come to the British, rather than the Americans. 'I work for the Caspian Research Institute in Baku – we monitor the state of the Sea – and I have been to several international conferences on hydrography, some here in Moscow, one in Athens and one in Vienna. I know several British scientists from these meetings, and I can give you their names. They will vouch for the fact that I am not a crazy person.'

He smiled at her for the first time, and picked up his pen. 'OK,' he said.

It was almost midnight, and David Constantine was in the middle of brushing his teeth, when the phone rang in his cottage. He hurried into the bedroom, almost tripping over one of his cats, and picked up the receiver. It was Glyn Sanford, his usual connection at the MoD.

'David? Sorry to call you so late, but we need your expertise in town tomorrow.'

Constantine groaned inwardly – he had already ear-marked the day for gardening and reading.

'. . . something that should interest you,' Sanford was saying. 'And nothing to do with the wretched Iraqis for a change. Some woman scientist has walked into our embassy in Moscow and claimed she has proof that Azerbaijan is developing its own nuclear arsenal. She wouldn't go into details, but she gave a list of British scientists she's had dealings with over the years, and they've all given her a clean bill of mental health. Of course, she could have fallen off her trolley in the last few weeks. We'll soon know – she's on her way to London now. We'll put her in a hotel overnight, and then start the debriefing around ten in the morning. I assume you can get here by then?'

'Of course. Did the woman say anything else?

'Not really. She dropped one name – Tamarlan Shadmanov. Mean anything to you?'

'Yes. He was one of the Soviets' top missile engineers in the 70s and 80s.' And he had specialized, Constantine remembered, in exactly the same field as Abas Naji.

'She sounds more kosher by the minute. I'll see you in the morning, then.'

'OK,' Constantine said absent-mindedly, and put the phone down. Azerbaijan, he thought. A country at the secular end of the Islamic spectrum, with a sophisti-cated technological base. A government involved in an unwinnable war.

Put like that, Azerbaijan sounded like an apt nest for a nuclear cuckoo.

In fact, it sounded very like the 'new location' which Abas Naji had been unable to divulge.

8

The Prime Minister put his palms together in front of his mouth, then abruptly lowered his hands into firing position, thumbs cocked. 'All the evidence seems to be circumstantial,' he said. 'But I take it that both of you are convinced?'

Sir Christopher Hanson and Martin Clarke both nodded, the latter with a sigh of reluctance.

'Right,' the PM went on, shifting in his armchair. 'So the next question is, how seriously do we take this? How much does it matter to us if Saddam Hussein gets hold of a few atom bombs?'

'We did go to war with him to prevent that from happening,' Hanson said mildly. 'With just a few missiles he could render the Gulf oilfields unusable for thousands of years. Or simply threaten to do so.'

'The Japanese and the Germans would be very unhappy,' Clarke added with a smile. 'And our North Sea oil revenues would probably rise tenfold.'

The Prime Minister smiled wryly. 'We might be the winners in the short run, but somehow I don't see our economy prospering in the aftermath of German and Japanese ruin, no matter how emotionally satisfying the latter might be. I think we have to assume this is our problem as much as anyone else's.' He looked at the other two. 'So the question then becomes, what can we do? Hand it over to the UN? Or to the Americans?'

'If the Iraqis have managed to fool the UN to this extent already, there's every reason to believe they'll be able to do the same in the future,' Hanson offered. 'As for the Americans . . .'

'They'll either make a huge production job of it and end up bungling things,' Clarke interjected, 'or they'll worry themselves to death over who they might be offending – the Turks, the Russians, their own Congress, anyone.'

'If you want something done properly, do it yourself,' the PM murmured. 'And this will require a little subtlety. If we just wanted to blow this research facility out of the water then no doubt someone would be happy to oblige – the Israelis would probably leap at the chance – but before we think about subcontracting, I think we have to be certain of exactly what is going on out there. We may be convinced, but I think the rest of the world will need rather more in the way of evidence than David Constantine's theories and a half-Armenian woman's suspicions. Someone will have to go in and check this place out,' he concluded, with a meaningful glance at Hanson.

The MI6 chief shook his head. 'We have no one suitable. We may not know the exact location of this facility, but we do know it's out at sea in a restricted military area, and that makes civilian infiltration almost impossible, even if we had any Azeri Turkish speakers, which we do not. If we want to check out this place I'm afraid there's no alternative to a covert military operation. This could be restricted to pure reconnaissance, or it could be stretched to include other objectives, like rescuing Tamarlan Shadmanov.'

'That's upping the stakes,' Clarke observed.

'Such a mission certainly decreases our chances of deniability,' the PM observed. 'In which case we have to consider the diplomatic implications. Who's going to get upset if British soldiers are caught paddling in Caspian waters?'

'The Azeris for one,' Clarke said, 'and they could try to take it out on BP. But basically they need the Western companies more than the companies need them, and if the worst comes to the worst we can probably use that fact to get a new government in Baku. The same goes for the Turks – as long as we can hold out the promise of EC membership they won't kick up too much of a fuss. The Russians will probably fume, but they're in too much of a mess to do anything, and nobody gives a damn what the ayatollahs think any more. I don't think we have to worry too much about diplomatic repercussions.'

'That makes a change,' Hanson said. 'And talking of Caspian waters – the SBS not only did a fine job in the Channel the other day, but they're also responsible for the security of our own rigs in the North Sea. It seems like they're tailor-made for this particular job.'

'How would they get there?' Clarke wondered out loud.

'If memory serves, at least some of them have parachute training,' Hanson told him.

The PM nodded. 'What exactly does this woman require from me before she'll divulge the location?' he asked.

'She wants your word that no military action will be

taken against this base,' Hanson said. 'She claims that she's concerned about the possibility of nuclear pollution in the Caspian – she is an ecologist – but I assume she's also worried about her boyfriend.'

The PM smiled. 'So she should be happy at the prospect of his being rescued,' he said. 'And of course I'll see her and make any promises she wants. Where is she, by the way?'

'In a hotel, under guard. Though as far as we can tell, no one knows she's in London, or indeed that she knows anything.'

'Send someone to talk to her,' the PM told Hanson. 'David Constantine would seem a good bet – she obviously likes scientific father-figures. And Martin,' he went on, turning to Clarke, 'get the SBS to work on a contingency plan.'

The following morning Constantine found Raisa sitting at the window of her hotel room gazing out at the budding trees in Hyde Park. The TV was on with the sound turned down, which somehow accentuated the loneliness of the scene.

She brightened visibly when she saw it was him, and he returned the smile. He had liked her from their first meeting four days before, but on asking himself why, Constantine had found it hard to come up with an answer. There was just something about her which was ... 'unspoilt' was the word that came to mind, but it didn't seem particularly adequate. There was an innocence and a stubbornness about her, qualities which Constantine associated with his own daughters in their mid-teens.

She liked him too. He was English in the way that she

had imagined Englishness – courteous, kindly, apparently honourable. His obvious tendency to introspection lent him a superficial resemblance to Shadmanov, but there was none of the latter's underlying sadness. This man, she thought, has led an easy English life, with not much more to worry about than the health of his children and the condition of his roses.

'Would you like to go for a walk in the park?' he asked in English, and her eyes seemed to light up at the prospect.

The two MI6 men trailed a few yards behind them as they walked slowly towards the Serpentine. 'The Prime Minister would like to meet you,' he told her, 'and give you in person the assurance you asked for. But they need to know the exact location of the production facility.'

'What they plan to do?' she asked.

Constantine assumed he was allowed to tell her. 'They plan to send a team of soldiers to investigate, to find out exactly what is happening.'

'They do not believe what I say?'

'They believe it. And they believe that Iraq is involved. We have new proof of that, by the way – certain high-ranking Iraqis have been seen in Baku. But for the international community to act, we need to know exactly what is happening on that rig.' He allowed a few seconds for that to sink in before adding, 'And if it is possible this team will attempt to bring back your . . . Professor Shadmanov.'

They walked along in silence as she thought this over. Think logically, she told herself – this man you are talking to may be a kind and honourable man, but that could be the very reason why he was chosen. If she were the leader of the British how would she see this? It would be best to bring Shadmanov out, certainly, since then he could tell the world what was happening. But if they could not do this – if Shadmanov refused to go with them, then it would be better for the British if he was dead than left to continue his work for the Iraqis . . .

She suddenly remembered something else, that same something she had spent so much of the past two years trying to forget – his wife. He might choose to stay on her account, and then . . .

And he spoke hardly any English at all, though there might be British soldiers who spoke Russian.

'I will go with them,' she said suddenly. It was the only way of continuing to exert any influence that she could think of, and she couldn't simply hand over the responsibility for him, for the Caspian, for the future of her two peoples, to the British. No matter how honourable they might be, they couldn't be expected to care for such things in the way that she did.

'I don't think that will be possible,' Constantine was telling her.

'Why not?' she asked.

He looked uncomfortable. 'This will be a military operation. You have no military training . . .'

'I know the place. I know the Caspian. I know the language. And you say yourself that it is only a reconnaissance. I will be help, not problem.'

He smiled in spite of himself. 'I don't know for certain,' he said, 'but I imagine these men will go in by parachute – you understand? – jumping from a plane into the sea.'

She shrugged. 'I know many Soviet boys who learn how to jump from plane – it cannot be so difficult.'

He laughed, but she knew that he wasn't laughing at her.

'You will tell your Prime Minister that I go?' she asked.

'I'll tell him. But he may not think it's such a good idea.'

'Then I don't tell the place.'

'OK,' he said equably. 'Now let's enjoy the rest of our walk.'

They circumnavigated the Serpentine, stopped for a coffee and pastry at an outdoor café, and walked back to the Park Lane Hotel. He told her about his grown-up daughters and she told him about her work in Baku. When he was gone she felt even further from home than before.

She sat by the window again, wondering at what had possessed her to demand a place in the British spy team. Her reasons had all seemed good ones, but jumping out of a plane . . .

The hotel, as far as she was able to judge, was a luxurious one, but for her it was still essentially a prison. She didn't know if anyone would physically prevent her from leaving, but her lack of money was just as effective a deterrent, and heaven only knew what the future held. Going with the soldiers would at least get her out of here, give her a chance to do something, to win some friends. She was going to need the latter, because at the moment she found it really hard to imagine a future for herself in any country but her own. All she knew was the Caspian, and such knowledge had no value elsewhere in the world.

But she knew she couldn't count on ever going home again. For the moment any interested party might assume she had simply stayed in Moscow, but, if they were not already, sooner or later the authorities would become suspicious, and would trace her movements, put two and two together. If it wasn't already too late to go home it soon would be. And if she was seen in the company of foreign soldiers then the door would be shut for ever. And if she was caught, she realized with a shudder, the chances were that she would be executed.

It seemed unreal, with the sun peeking through the English clouds. She left the window and turned on the TV to find horses racing each other beside a long white fence. Great clouds of breath were pouring from their mouths, and behind them the wet green grass faded into a misty distance.

She could no more live here than in the Russian far north, she realized. One way or another, she had to go home.

In his office in Poole, Neil Colhoun was cradling the phone in his right shoulder and using both hands to unwrap his afternoon Kit-Kat. 'There's no hope of changing her mind then?'

'According to Constantine she's adamant,' Martin Clarke told him.

'What's she like?' Colhoun asked. He had a mental picture of a frumpy Russian girl with a headscarf which probably bore no relation to the reality.

'What do you mean?'

'For a start, how old is she?'

'Thirty-four. She's about five foot six, not exactly thin but not plump either. She looks fit, but . . .'

'Is she excitable? Emotional?' Colhoun could imagine

the look on his wife's face if she'd heard him asking such questions.

'I wouldn't say so. I've only seen the video of her first interview but she seemed quite self-contained to me. But you'd probably be better off asking Constantine about her' – Clarke grunted with what sounded like amusement – 'though he may have become too besotted to give you an objective answer.'

'She's pretty, is she?'

'In a dark sort of way,' Clarke admitted grudgingly.

Colhoun did as the minister had suggested, and found Constantine quite willing to discuss Raisa Karayeva's character, personality and general suitability for such a mission. In general he agreed with Clarke, believing the woman unlikely to either give up or panic in adverse circumstances.

'So why not?' Colhoun asked himself once he'd hung up. If she wouldn't be a liability she probably would be a help, above and beyond her ability to pinpoint the facility's location. But whichever men he picked for this mission would need some convincing.

He had already decided that Major Derek Galloway would be the guiding hand, the producer, so to speak, of this particular epic. He would deal with the chosen team on a day-to-day basis, get them ready, find them everything they thought they needed. But who would lead the team?

Colhoun snapped the last Kit-Kat finger, popped half in his mouth and leant back in his chair. Who was he kidding? McClure had to be the leader. He'd conducted the Channel business with exemplary efficiency, even if, as now seemed certain, the enemy had been doing their best to make it easy for him and his men. The only question mark over the exercise had been McClure's ruthless dispatch of the Russian, but military behaviour which seemed dangerously close to the limits of acceptability in home waters might well offer a team operating beyond the reach of outside assistance its best hope of collective survival.

If he was the woman, Colhoun realized, he would be glad to have someone like McClure in charge. The only way anyone would get to her would be over his dead body.

And if McClure went, Noonan should go. Then, if either of them was captured or killed, there would still be someone with enough knowledge of nuclear matters to evaluate the facility.

The woman made a third, leaving one place to be filled. Marker's team had arrived back from Hong Kong a few days before, and for a few moments Colhoun considered sending McClure and Noonan under Marker's command! But he dismissed the idea – he had talked with Callum Marker only the previous day, and the man was obviously in the throes of a new love.

Colhoun smiled to himself as he imagined the tabloid headlines – 'SBS HERO RULED OUT BY ROMANCE' – but the plain fact of the matter was, and experience had proved it a thousand times, men in Marker's condition were permanently off balance. It affected different men different ways – some couldn't keep their minds on the business at hand, some became too cautious, some acted as if they'd acquired immortality – but it affected all of them. The disease only lasted a few weeks, and its symptoms were often hard to spot, but when it came to performing the sort of jobs the SBS performed, anything less than one hundred per cent proficiency might well prove fatal, not only for the man himself but for his comrades too. Marker was out.

Stuart Finn, on the other hand, seemed an ideal candidate. Marker had been full of praise for the way the young Londoner had handled himself in the South China Sea, and Colhoun could imagine that Finn and Noonan would get on well together. And between them they might well be strong enough to bring out the best in McClure.

It seemed like a nice blend, Colhoun thought. He wrote down the names on a virgin sheet of paper, asked his adjutant to find and summon Derek Galloway, and rewarded himself with the last piece of Kit-Kat.

Stuart Finn examined himself in the mirror, took out his comb and slicked his gelled hair even flatter, trying to see the resemblance to Ian Walker which the girl had noticed. Problem was, he could only remember seeing the Tottenham goalkeeper once or twice – he liked football but he wasn't nuts about it – and there hadn't been any reason to notice the lad's face.

He went back to the table his team was sharing, arriving just in time to add another pint to the order. He knew only two of the six – since his departure for the Far East a month earlier one couple had moved to London and two of the other women were off on a weekend break somewhere sunny. Their replacements included two *Sun* readers who knew everything there was to know about sport and royal gossip but nothing else, and the girl who thought he looked like Ian Walker. She had answered only two of the first fifteen questions, but in both cases she had been the only person at the table to know the answer. It was from such building blocks, Finn thought, that great pub-quiz teams were built.

He was enjoying the evening, but there was also an air of unreality about it all. It was hard to believe that less than ten days had passed since he and the others had sailed the hijacked freighter out of Communist China with its cargo of political prisoners and smuggled babies. He could still smell the warm wind blowing across the Pearl estuary, even after eating two bags of spring-onion crisps.

There was an ear-splitting screech from the microphone. 'Youse ready?' the familiar voice asked, eliciting the usual chorus of groans. 'Well, ready or not. Question sixteen: who was Patricia Holm? That's H-O-L-M. Patricia Holm.'

His team-mates stared blankly at each other, and looking round Finn could see the same reaction at the other tables. Yes, he told himself, but he waited for the hubbub of discussion to slowly rise before leaning forward and telling the others the answer.

'The Saint's girlfriend.'

'What?'

'You know – the Saint books. Roger Moore played him on TV, even worse than he played James Bond. She was his girlfriend in at least half the books.'

The team scribe dutifully wrote it down.

'The interesting thing,' Finn carried on, talking only to the girl, 'is whether they ever had sex. It's never mentioned, but she didn't seem to live anywhere else, and they were always sitting round in their dressing-gowns together.'

'That sounds conclusive,' she agreed, grinning at him. She had a nice mouth full of small, even teeth, with an ever-so-slightly upturned upper lip. Very kissable. Finn had been introduced to her at the beginning of the evening, but realized he'd forgotten her name.

He decided to wait; with any luck one of the others would use it.

'Question seventeen,' the voice boomed. 'How many official Rolling Stones have there been since the release of their first record?'

Finn and the girl counted them off on their fingers, and agreed on seven. 'Always assuming the new bass player isn't official,' Finn added as a caveat. She turned to argue the point with another team member, offering Finn a brief view of a neck every bit as kissable as the mouth.

'You're in the Marines, aren't you?' she asked him.

'Yep.'

'So's my dad.'

'Really?' Finn murmured, his heart sinking. 'What was your surname again – I missed it the first time.'

'Colhoun,' she told him.

Finn took a large gulp of his beer.

9

Colhoun slept on a final decision, but over breakfast the next morning he could think of no compelling reason to go back on his original resolve. Restraining the impulse to question his eighteen-year-old daughter about her hung-over expression – he could already see the look of exasperation, the eyes rolled towards the ceiling, if he tried – the SBS CO drove into Poole and summoned both Derek Galloway and Gary McClure to his office.

McClure, midway through administering a Morse test to his SC3 class, half reluctantly passed the teacher's baton to his best student, and made his way slowly towards the CO's office. He was glad to be out of the wretched classroom, but was not looking forward to another bout of questioning from Colhoun concerning his actions aboard the *Red Voyager*.

The CO welcomed him with a smile and an offer of tea, which was much more than he had expected, and the presence of Major Galloway offered further hopes that something new was brewing.

'We've been given another job to do,' Colhoun told him, and McClure had difficulty concealing the extent of his enthusiasm. 'Another ship?' he asked.

'You should be so lucky,' Colhoun said drily. He reached for the atlas beside him, opened it at the marked place, and placed it right way up in front of McClure.

'The Caspian Sea,' he said, tapping the appropriate spot with the teaspoon.

'Christ,' McClure murmured. The Caspian was a long way from anywhere he'd ever been. 'What's there?' he asked.

'An Iraqi nuclear production facility – or at least we think so.' Colhoun filled in those parts of the background with which the other man was not already familiar, most notably the story which the woman had brought out of Azerbaijan.

McClure listened patiently, hardly daring to believe his luck. This was going to be the biggest challenge of his life. 'And the job we've been given?' he prompted, once the CO had stopped talking.

'Someone has to take a look, confirm or rebut our suspicions. If the answer's yes, some proof would seem to be in order. If we can bring Shadmanov out that would fit the bill nicely – he has an international reputation and his testimony would be believed.'

Colhoun paused to take a sip of tea, and to watch the size of the task percolate into McClure's consciousness. 'Major Galloway here will be in overall command of the operation, and you'll lead the insertion team. But before you get too excited,' he added, seeing the excitement in McClure's eyes, 'I should tell you that the woman is going in as part of the team.'

McClure was surprised, and looked it. But contrary to Colhoun's expectations he didn't kick up a fuss. He didn't even protest.

'Is she physically capable?' he asked. The idea of taking her with them actually appealed to him, although he wasn't sure why. Maybe just because it increased the challenge.

'I'm told she is.'

'Why does she have to go?' McClure asked, more because he thought the question was expected than because he really cared.

Colhoun smiled. 'First off, because she's refused to give us the exact location until we promise to take her along. And second, because I think she'll probably be more of a plus than a minus – she knows the local geography, she's an expert on the Caspian Sea – it was her job – and as well as fair English she speaks Azeri Turkish, which I assume you don't.'

'No,' McClure said, as if it was a straight question. 'But why does she want to go? What's in it for her?'

'She was Shadmanov's mistress before the Iraqis snatched him and his wife. And I think she feels we may just destroy the place without caring too much about who gets hurt in the process.'

'Doesn't sound like too bad an idea,' McClure commented.

'It may come to that. First, we have to be sure what's going on there.'

'Makes sense. So do I get any say in who else goes along?'

'I'm afraid not – CO's privilege. You'll take Noonan, whom you already know, and Stuart Finn. Do you know him?'

'Only by sight.'

'He's young but he's got experience, including combat. He was in the team that was sent to Singapore to help with the anti-piracy campaign.'

'I thought they were still out there.'

'They got back a few days ago.'

'He sounds fine,' McClure said, wondering why

Colhoun hadn't asked Callum Marker to lead this mission. Someone up there was obviously smiling down at him.

Darkness had fallen over the Caspian, leaving the distant lights of Baku to shine like a forest of enchantment on the horizon. 'I'm sick of this place,' Farida Shadmanova said, turning away from the window and pacing across the large room she shared with her husband. 'There's nothing to do, and no chance of getting any exercise – I've put on two kilos in less than a month.'

Shadmanov looked up from his book, but didn't think it was worth reminding her that there was a well-stocked library or that she had never taken any exercise in her life. 'I thought you were pleased that I was working for the military again,' he said.

'I am. Though of course if you had agreed to stay on in Moscow where we had a good life . . . But no, you had to come back to Baku, which we outgrew twenty years ago.'

'We are Azeris, not Russians.'

'I know.' She stopped pacing for a moment. 'I was talking to someone in the recreation room. He said that once we have nuclear weapons and the Armenians are forced back, the West will help us develop the oilfields and Azerbaijan will become rich, like one of the Arab oil states. Do you think that's true?'

'Maybe.'

'And if you are the nation's top nuclear scientist . . .' She let the thought fade, but her husband knew where it was headed. The two of them would be back among the privileged élite again – not the second-class intellectual élite of university life, but the real thing, like in the old

Soviet days when he was one of the highest-ranking military scientists and she had rubbed shoulders with the wives of astronauts and politburo members.

She had started nervously pacing again. He could remember how exciting her overflowing energy had once seemed to him – that and her body had been attraction enough nearly thirty years ago – but nowadays it just made him feel tired. He supposed being locked up here was harder for her than him – he at least had work to occupy his time – but with any luck she would find someone to have an affair with. Pulling it off with discretion in such a small space and community should keep her busy for at least some of the time.

He sighed and went back to his book, thinking how unimportant such things were in the grand scheme of a nuclear universe.

The first team conference took place in the SBS briefing room on the day after Colhoun's initial meeting with McClure. Noonan and Finn had been given the time and place the previous evening, but neither had any idea what it was about. Raisa Karayeva had been brought down on the train by her MI6 minders, and eyed with a mixture of interest and concern the four men whom fate had thrown across her path.

All but the major were younger than her, and he didn't seem much older. None of them was particularly big, but they all looked tough and fit, and somewhat to her surprise there also seemed to be a watchful intelligence in each man's eyes.

The major cheerfully introduced them in turn. The team leader – the one who would actually be in charge where it mattered – acknowledged her with a diffidence which could have been shyness, could have been simple indifference. No doubt she would soon find out which. He told her to simply call him 'McClure', and seemed amused by her difficulty with the unfamiliar double consonant. As a colleague of male scientists she was used to men who were experts at shutting down their emotions, but within minutes of meeting McClure she knew she was in the presence of a master.

The other two were a different matter. The curly-haired one – 'call me Paul' – seemed the most uncertain of the three, but he had a friendly smile, and she felt right away that she could count on him to do the right thing in any given situation. The one with the slicked-back hair – 'just Finn' – was obviously a bit of a flirt, and it was hard to tell what the man inside was like.

The three SBS men were also taking her measure, almost literally in Finn's case. He and Noonan didn't yet know who she was; McClure, by contrast, was pleasantly surprised by what he saw. She looked fit enough, and she didn't look stupid.

Galloway began by outlining the background to the intended operation, casting occasional glances at Raisa to see if she wanted to correct anything, and then bluntly stated the bare bones of what was expected of them. Noonan seemed a bit taken aback, but Finn seemed almost amused by it all. McClure just sat there, only his eyes betraying his obvious excitement. 'This is just a preliminary briefing,' the major told them. 'We're not in any rush – this is one of those times when doing it properly is more important than doing it fast. What we have to work out today is a rough plan of action. Once we have that we'll have a better idea of what we still need to know.'

He reached behind him for a map, and spread it out on the table. It was an old Soviet map, Raisa immediately realized, covering the central third of the Caspian, with English translations neatly added in pencil alongside the Cyrillic Russian annotations.

'So where exactly are we going?' Galloway asked her.

She hesitated for only a second – Constantine and Clarke had both given their word, and if they betrayed her now it was just too bad. 'Here,' she said, pointing it out with her right index finger. 'There are two rigs, joined by a bridge. Aliyev A and Aliyev B.'

They asked her questions about the rigs themselves, the other man-made structures nearby, the local weather conditions, the Caspian itself. She answered them all without hesitation, and could see that they were impressed.

'So how do we get in, boss?' Finn asked Galloway.

'My preference is a HAHO drop. That means high altitude, high opening,' he explained to Raisa. 'We leave the plane at about 30,000 feet, open the parachutes immediately, and glide for about an hour before touching down. The advantages of this method are that the chances of the plane being seen are negligible, because it's so high up and because it doesn't have to come closer than forty kilometres to the target area.'

'The disadvantages are that your balls both freeze,' Noonan murmured. 'But that won't affect you . . .'

'I see from your records that you two both took refresher courses last year,' Galloway said to McClure and Noonan. 'But Finn here . . .'

'I haven't jumped out of a plane since initial training,' the man in question admitted.

'Well, assuming we take this route, you and Raisa

can go up to Brize Norton together. Either way, I don't think we'll have any problems getting in. The difficult part would seem to be getting out again.'

'I don't suppose we could just row to the nearest friendly port?' Noonan wondered.

Raisa suppressed a giggle, but Galloway didn't seem to see the funny side. 'The countries bordering the Caspian,' he said, 'are Azerbaijan, Russia, Kazakhstan, Turkmenistan and Iran. None of them are what you'd call friendly. The nearest friendly country is Turkey.'

'And that's stretching the definition of friendly,' Finn observed. 'How far away is it?'

Galloway produced another map, one that took in the wider region. 'About seven hundred kilometres,' he said. 'A Sea King could probably be fitted up to make the distance. But it would have to fly over either Armenia or Iran. Probably Armenia.'

'And it would have to fly damn low,' Finn added. 'Over this lot,' he added, running a finger down the spine of the mountains which lay across the potential route.

'Across Nagorno-Karabakh,' Raisa pointed out.

'Oh-oh,' Finn muttered. 'Is that war still going on?'

'It is peaceful now,' she said, 'but the war cannot end.'

'They've just stopped for a breather,' Finn suggested.

'We'd better find out what sort of anti-aircraft weaponry they've been using down there,' McClure suggested softly.

'Right. This is obviously not going to be a cakewalk, but let's just assume for the moment we can get ourselves in and out. The next question is, how long do we need on the ground? We might be able to manage a HAHO drop, check out the place, grab the professor, get to a pick-up point and fly back to Turkey, all in the one night, but a schedule like that sounds too tight for comfort. So . . . maybe we should think about spending one whole day on one of the rigs. Set up a concealed OP, get an idea of the routines and then do the business as early as we can on the second night.' He turned to Raisa. 'I'm assuming these rigs are big enough to hide out on?'

'They are big, like a house with ten floors, yes?' She shrugged. 'I think there are many places for hiding.'

'Some satellite photographs should be coming through tomorrow,' Galloway added. 'They should give us a better idea.' He looked at a map for a moment. 'OK. It seems to me that the professor and his wife could turn into another problem. They've no idea we're coming, and there's no way of letting them know. It's going to be a shock for both of them. How are they going to react?'

He was looking at her again.

'It is difficult to say,' she said. 'Tamarlan . . . I think . . . I am not certain of this, but I think he will be unhappy to work in this place making the nuclear bombs. He will be pleased to escape this.'

'And his wife?' Galloway asked. How would she react to the sudden arrival of her husband's mistress with a bunch of foreign soldiers. Did she even know a mistress existed?'

'I don't know,' Raisa admitted. 'I never met her.'

There was a silence while everyone tried to imagine themselves in Farida Shadmanova's shoes at the crucial moment. But there was simply no way of knowing.

'We shall need a plan which covers every possibility,' Galloway said eventually. 'Including knocking her cold and leaving her behind, or, if her husband objects to that, bringing her with us whether she's willing or not.'

He turned to Raisa. 'Will he want her to come, do you think?'

She shook her head. 'I do not know.' She *should* know, she thought.

'OK. Third problem. We need a location for the pick-up. Not too far from the rig, but not too close either. Say, between twenty and thirty kilometres away.'

'Narghin,' she said without hesitation. 'It is here,' she added, pointing it out on the map. 'It was Soviet prison island, but now no one is there.'

It was twenty-four kilometres from the target, and twenty-four kilometres nearer to the Turkish border. 'Looks good,' Galloway said. 'Any thoughts?' he asked the other three.

Noonan looked up with a start. He'd been thinking that this particular jaunt was a far cry from boarding a ship in mid-Channel. This time it looked like they were going to be out on a very long and very rickety limb. With no sign of a safety net.

It was Finn who asked the question, though. 'Do we have any idea what sort of opposition we can expect?'

'Not yet,' Galloway admitted.

'There will be KGB,' Raisa volunteered. 'They have new name, but I forget. They are same KGB as always.'

'And the Iraqis may have their own security people involved,' McClure added. 'From the Mukhabarat, probably. The same bastards who tortured our prisoners during the Gulf War.'

Hearing this, Noonan decided that his previous thoughts had been unduly optimistic. This was beginning to sound like one of those adventure-book missions in which most of the medals were awarded posthumously.

* * *

The club was on one of the small streets between the Strand and the Embankment, and Manny Salewicz arrived for lunch not expecting much in the way of culinary joy. 'What the English can cook, they cook well,' as one of his fellow US Embassy colleagues had remarked, adding that they could only cook two dishes – roast beef and roast lamb.

Both, Salewicz was pleased to see, were on the menu. He chose the latter – there was no point in risking Mad Cow Disease – and asked Hanson to what he owed the pleasure of the invitation.

Hanson smiled, for he had grown rather fond of the CIA man over the last few months. 'Let's eat first,' he said, and for the next half-hour they did just that, filling in the spaces between mouthfuls with topics as diverse as the O. J. Simpson trial, the latest *Prime Suspect* and the rumoured government plan to sell off the Houses of Parliament. It was a full hour before Hanson brought them back to business, as they relaxed over a glass of excellent port in a secluded corner of the members' lounge.

'We've received some rather interesting intelligence,' the MI6 chief began. 'It seems that Saddam has decided to become a cuckoo and lay his nuclear eggs in someone else's nest.'

'Whose, for Chrissake?'

'Azerbaijan's.'

Salewicz looked stunned.

'It's a Muslim country, but not a fundamentalist one. It was part of the Soviet Union, so it has the necessary technological base, but it's in a region which no one's very interested in these days – there are too many problems and the only thing they have which anyone else wants is offshore oil. And they're frightened enough of the Armenians to accept Saddam as a nuclear partner.'

The American seemed less than convinced. 'What's the intelligence source?' he wanted to know.

Hanson told him about Raisa Karayeva, omitting only her name, and then widened the picture to include Constantine's theories and other circumstantial evidence that had been gathered over the past couple of weeks.

'Where is the woman now?' Salewicz asked when Hanson had finished.

'In a safe house. We're going to check out her story on the ground,' he went on. 'That's why I asked you to lunch – consultation between allies, I think it's called.'

'Uh-huh. And exactly how are you planning to check it out?'

Hanson sipped at the rose-red nectar. 'We're sending some people in. Special forces people.'

Salewicz nearly choked on his port. 'How? From where?'

'By plane from Cyprus.'

The American studied a mental map. 'Across Turkey. The Turks'll go apeshit if they find out.' He reached for his glass and another thought struck him. 'You can put 'em in with a Hercules, but you can't pull 'em out the same way. How are you planning to get these guys back?'

Hanson told him.

'And I suppose the Turks won't notice this flight from their own airfield?' Salewicz asked sarcastically.

'It's a NATO airfield,' Hanson corrected him. 'And I'm sure we can come up with a story which will satisfy them. The helicopter can be on a humanitarian mission – one of our gallant nurses lost in Nagorno-Karabakh –

something like that. We'll think of . . . What?' he asked, seeing the smile spreading on the American's face.

'And exactly which airfield are you planning to use?' he asked.

'Dogubayazit. It's the only one close enough.'

'And it just happens to be the one the US Air Force uses for patrolling the Iraqi no-fly zone. If the Turks find out they will be hanging our guts out on a line. They take this Pan-Turkic crap really seriously, you know? The Azeris are their long-lost brothers, like the Uzbeks and God knows who else . . .'

'I can't believe anyone in Ankara will want Saddam to build up a nuclear arsenal, in Azerbaijan or anywhere else.'

Salewicz shook his head. 'They wouldn't give a damn. And they have a lot more in common with Iraq than people realize – not only the Muslim angle but a mutual interest in killing off the Kurds. And of course Turkey and Azerbaijan have the same relationship to the Armenians. I wouldn't put it past the Turks to demand a share of these nukes, and use them to threaten the Greeks. These are not people who understand power in the real world – they still think it comes out of the barrel of a gun.'

'Doesn't it?'

Salewicz grinned at him. 'You know, talking to you, I always get the feeling I know exactly how the British both won and lost their empire.'

Hanson smiled back. 'So you'll let us use your strip of Turkish tarmac?'

'Hey, this is a Special Relationship, right?'

10

The countryside beneath her was a patchwork of muted greens and browns, so unlike any part of the land she called home. There was a softness, a moistness, almost a sensuousness about the English landscape. It was like a puppy, she thought, friendly and comforting.

The first time she had stepped forward on to the edge of the C-130's open ramp she had been terrified, and knowing that the young men all around were feeling much the same had been only marginally helpful. They were hiding their first-jump fears in near-hysterical humour, but her grasp of the language still wasn't good enough to let her share in the jokes, and she had found it hard to remember ever feeling more alone. But Finn had squeezed her hand at just the right moment, and after the first petrifying moments – plummeting towards the earth, trying to stabilize her body posture, hoping that her parachute wasn't going to be the first to fail at No. 1 Parachute Training School for years – she had pulled the rip-cord, heard and felt the chute billow open above her, and started to float.

And it had felt more wonderful than she could ever have imagined. In that moment she had understood how incredible it must have felt to fly in the days before air-pressurized cabins and Perspex cockpits.

Here and now, halfway through her fifth jump in three

days, it still felt like magic. The spiralling line of men below, the others above, all floating down towards the runway-bisected green expanse of Brize Norton airfield. Off to the right, in the clear, late-afternoon air, she could see the sunlight washing the spires of distant Oxford.

The ground, meanwhile, was leaping to meet her. The main danger in parachuting, she had decided after her very first jump, was in getting so wrapped up in the wonder of flight that the business of landing properly got relegated to an afterthought.

She concentrated, hitting the grass with legs bending and body rolling, as the instructors had taught them on the practice harness. A perfect landing, she told herself – she was getting good at this. It seemed a shame that when it came to the real thing they would be landing on water.

She got up and started gathering in the chute. Twenty metres away Finn was landing, his roll somewhat less graceful than hers. He grinned at her from the ground.

As they walked back across the grass towards the base buildings she remembered seeing Oxford in the distance, and asked him if there was any chance of a visit. She felt like a child asking for a treat, but that was the way she was being treated; everything was supplied – food, a bed, a programme of events for each day.

'Don't see why not,' Finn said. 'If we're going to go, we'd better do it this evening. Tomorrow we've got the night drop, and then we're finished.'

'Then we are ready?' she asked, surprised.

'Not quite. We'll be practising HAHO drops over the Mediterranean once we get to Cyprus.'

'Into the sea,' she murmured.

Finn looked at her. 'You've enjoyed this, haven't you?'

'Yes,' she agreed, smiling. There was one obvious advantage to being treated like a child – you got to play.

He smiled back. Against his expectations, Finn had come to like her over the last few days. She had guts, and she also had a sense of humour. If he ever got kidnapped by the government and locked up on a North Sea oil rig he hoped that there would be someone like her to come and rescue him. 'I'll try and wangle us some private transport,' he told her.

'Wangle?' she echoed, but he was already gone.

An hour later they were driving through the twilit Oxfordshire countryside in a covered jeep, the last of the day's sunlight flickering through the lines of bare trees. 'So what do you think of England?' he asked her.

'It is beautiful,' she said. And it was, but it was the beauty of shadows, not of light. 'I do not meet many people, and they are not ordinary, yes? You are not ordinary.'

'I suppose I'm better-looking and cleverer than most,' Finn said, grinning. 'Are you ordinary in Azerbaijan?'

'No, I do not think I am. It is a traditional country, yes? Most people live outside the city. They are poor and religious and have the narrow minds. Baku is different, but still the tradition is very important. Only a few women have jobs – you go in the streets and there is only men. And of course I am half Armenian,' she added, almost as an afterthought.

'Have you ever lived in Armenia?'

'No, but I often go to visit my mother's family in the old Soviet days, before the trouble in Nagorno-Karabakh. It is good in the mountains, but I like the sea too much. And in Armenia now I will be half Azeri,' she added.

Finn glanced across but there was no self-pity in her face. He supposed that now ethnic cleansing was all the fashion there had to be millions of people like her, people who had once had a foot in both camps, and who now had nowhere at all to put so much as a toe. 'This is Oxford,' he announced, pulling out to pass a stationary town bus.

While the other two members of the team were honing their jumping, McClure and Noonan were applying their detective skills to the twin rig in the Caspian. It didn't take long to discover that it had been constructed *in situ* by the South Koreans, but diplomatically reinforced enquiries of the firm in question failed to produce the original plans. It was no surprise that the Soviet buyers had included a non-disclosure clause in the original contract – in Cold War terms the rigs would have been a significant military target – but the South Koreans' refusal to consider the clause as redundant as the original purchasers was rather more irritating.

But there was a silver lining to this particular cloud. The rigs in the Caspian, as the South Korean firm's PR admitted to the British military attaché in Seoul, were very similar to another pair which the company had erected in the North Sea. Tempests Alpha and Bravo, the oil company had named them.

When the attaché pressed him on the differences between these rigs and the pair in the Caspian the South Korean smiled coyly and said that he presumed the Soviets had given theirs Russian names.

Armed with this information, McClure and Noonan

flew to Aberdeen and took a chopper out to Tempest Alpha, where the rig boss, alerted by Galloway in advance, gave them a free run of the installation. On the day of their arrival this wasn't such a boon as it seemed, for rain was pouring out of a leaden sky, considerably reducing visibility and the rig's photogenicity, and borrowing one of the divers' boats to take a closer look at the underside was out of the question.

The two men spent the day drinking tea in the canteen and watching crap films on the recreation room video. For over a decade undercover SBS men had held the primary responsibility for security on Britain's North Sea installations, and McClure had already spent several months of his life on a rig similar to this one. Now, sandwiching an umpteenth viewing of *The Dirty Dozen* between scarcely distinguishable porn flicks, he was forcibly reminded of what a miserable experience it had been.

By the next morning the weather had cleared and the two men were able to examine both rigs, inside and out, top and bottom, hindered only by the banter of the workforce. 'They must be from interior decorating,' one man observed, as they checked out the residential quarters. 'In that case we'd like tartan carpets and apricot-white walls and gold-lamé curtains,' his friend remarked, helpfully adding that the style was known as 'Scottish brothel'. 'It usually has a crossed thistle and condom motif,' the first man explained.

Back in Poole the next day they found Galloway had the American satellite photographs waiting for them, and once the North Sea photos had been developed the three men eagerly compared the two twin rigs.

Of course the American pictures could only offer an aerial view, but even so the identical nature of the two basic structures was clear enough. The differences were mostly cosmetic: Aliyev B had lost both its drilling tower and crane derrick, Aliyev A its flare stack. The former actually looked deserted.

'There's our OP,' McClure murmured.

'I'll get the illustrators to run up a model,' Galloway said, referring to the branch of the Royal Marines which provided the corps with the maps, plans and models needed for the fulfilment of its operational duties. 'Now, what's next?' he asked. 'How are you doing with the shopping list?'

McClure pulled a notebook out of his shirt pocket. 'There doesn't seem much point in going in equipped to fight the Azeri army,' he said. 'If nothing goes badly wrong it'll all be down to stealth, and if we do trigger an alarm then it'll all be down to speed. So, the usual light weapons – silenced MP5s, silenced Brownings, a little C4, a few stun grenades for that certain moment . . .' He smiled. 'But I'd like to take a couple of M16/M203 combos, just in case the party gets rough and we need to slow down the pursuit. And an Accuracy International for taking out any guards that we can't get close enough to. We can stack most of this stuff on the pallet with the Geminis.'

'You want to take two Geminis?' Galloway asked.

'Two of the 3.8s with the new silencers. They're so quiet that two sound hardly any louder than one. And it'll give us more flexibility.'

'And a backup,' Noonan added.

Galloway nodded. 'OK,' he agreed, gathering up the photographs. 'I'll get these across to the illustrators.'

Outside the sun was shining, offering a fair reflection of his optimism. McClure was proving as thorough as Galloway had expected, and a job which he had originally thought offered no better than a fifty-fifty chance of success was now looking decidedly doable.

The completed model was the first thing that Raisa and Finn saw on their return from Brize Norton two mornings later. She looked buoyant, Noonan thought, and infinitely more at ease than she had at the first team meeting a week before. 'You two look like you've been having fun,' he said.

McClure just nodded a greeting and moved straight to business. 'Is this what it looks like?' he asked her.

'I only see from long way,' she said, 'but yes, I think so.'

'That's a relief,' Noonan said. 'I don't think the illustrators fancy another all-nighter.'

'It is very good,' she added, as if she thought aesthetic approval was being asked for.

'The one thing we don't know for sure,' McClure said, 'is where things are inside. We assume the professor and his wife will have a room somewhere in the residential section here' – he pointed it out – 'but there are four floors of rooms in the original design, and they could have converted other areas. The scientists could be sleeping in their labs for all we know.'

Raisa examined the cutaway side of the model. 'Where are the way outs from the living quarters?' she asked.

'Here and here,' Noonan said, pointing them out.

'Then the scientists will be here, on bottom level, far away from the way outs. And security people, they have the rooms near the way outs. That is the way, the old

Soviet way, in the military places,' she added. She could remember Tamarlan telling her about it, the usual wry smile on his face, as they sat in his car looking out over the Caspian.

That afternoon, as McClure and Finn scoured the operational plan for potential problems, Noonan took Raisa across to the indoor firing range. When the team had first discussed weaponry she had left them to it, assuming that she wouldn't be carrying any. But the others, and particularly McClure, had persuaded her that she should at least carry a handgun. If they were caught the Brits would stand a chance of a diplomatically arranged return home, but she would in all likelihood have to face a treason trial. She owed it to herself, they told her, not to surrender her life so cheaply.

Which probably made sense, she thought, as Noonan handed her the 9mm Browning High Power and showed her how to load the thirteen-round magazine. It was not as heavy as she'd expected, and neither was the recoil hard to cope with. She stood as Noonan told her – legs braced and apart, both hands holding the gun at eye level with outstretched arms – and emptied the magazine in the direction of the target some twenty-five metres distant.

The two of them walked down to see how she'd done, and Noonan let out a whistle of appreciation. All thirteen bullets had hit the card, and several of them had torn a jagged hole in the innermost circle.

'Incredible,' Noonan said. 'I've never seen anyone do better. You didn't work for a circus in your spare time, did you?'

She laughed. First the parachuting, now this. She was

discovering things about herself that seemed to belong to somebody else.

The next day, a Friday, those concerned gathered in the Poole briefing room for the last time. The model of the Aliyev rigs again took centre stage, with the four-person team arranged in a rough semicircle on one side and Colhoun and Galloway on the other, separated by an easel with a large-scale map of the Caucasus area.

Galloway ran through the entire operation from the starting gate in Cyprus to the finishing post in eastern Turkey, more as an exercise in clarification than because there were any major decisions still to be taken. Few questions were asked, and all of these were concerned with matters of detail.

Colhoun then picked out a few points which he thought needed emphasizing. 'One,' he said, counting off a finger, 'it is important that this mission remains our little secret, both before and after the event, and particularly from the Turks . . .'

'Our gallant NATO partners,' Finn murmured.

'Whatever they are, they won't like us invading their airspace or using their airfield to conduct a clandestine mission against a country which they consider a virtual ally. I don't expect we'd think much of it if the situation was reversed. So keep the lid on it, both in Cyprus – where there are plenty of Turkish ears to the ground – and in Turkey itself. No celebrations until you get back to Poole, right?'

They all nodded their acquiescence.

'Two,' Colhoun continued. 'This may sound obvious, but getting out with a minimal amount of information will be a lot more use than getting caught with a perfectly framed photo of Saddam himself lighting the blue touch-paper. Shadmanov is the prime target – get him and everything else will be a bonus. He'll be able to tell us everything we need to know. Any photos you can get of the rigs and the work in progress will be useful if it comes to further action in the future, but if we have Shadmanov's testimony I doubt if any will be necessary – the politicos should be able to pressurize the Azeris into closing the place down and kicking the Iraqis out.'

He checked the notes he'd made. 'Point three. It may all go as smoothly as Derek made it sound, but if so it'll be the first deep-penetration recce in history which didn't throw up a single surprise. You've got a good plan, but don't get trapped by it. Times and places can be changed. If you feel the need to stay a second day, you'll be in radio contact with Derek at Dog-whatever – I can never remember the name.'

'Dogubayazit, boss,' Finn said fluently.

'Thank you. And the same goes for the pick-up point – you can always change it. These burst-facility radios give us the flexibility, but you have to remember to make use of it.' He looked round at the assembled faces – McClure blank, Finn smiling, Noonan and the woman serious and attentive. 'OK, I know I've probably been telling you stuff you tell yourselves in your sleep – it just gives me the illusion of being involved. Any questions?'

There were none, or at least none that anyone felt they could ask. There were too many variables for anyone to feel certain of success, at least in the manner they were envisaging, and they all knew it. Only time could answer the questions they really wanted to ask.

'Right,' Colhoun said, shuffling the papers on his knees and coming up with a particular sheet. 'Last item. Now with any luck there'll be no need for any of you to come within ten kilometres of the coast, but just in case . . . Apologies to you, Raisa, but these ignorant lads had probably never heard of Azerbaijan before the beginning of last week.'

'It's pronounced Azerbaijan, boss,' Finn said mischievously, putting the accent on the last syllable.

'With the exception of Mr Know-it-all, of course,' Colhoun went on. 'So I phoned the Foreign Office for a regional state of play. Tourists, you will be glad to know, are strongly recommended not to travel anywhere in the Caucasus. There's one intermittent civil war going on in Georgia, and another in the Chechen region just across the mountains' – he got up and pointed it out on the map – 'which the Russians are still trying to stamp out. The war between Azerbaijan and Armenia has died down considerably over the last few months, but I'm told it could flare up again at any time. The Armenians are still occupying most of Azerbaijan's Nagorno-Karabakh region, so it's not over. Most of the fighting is small-arms stuff, but there are some tanks and planes involved, most of them operated by Russians who hire themselves out to the highest bidder. It's nasty stuff – the same sort of ethnic cleansing that's going on in Bosnia. The numbers involved are a lost smaller, and there doesn't seem to be the same predilection for atrocities, but it's hard to be sure, as our media people seem to have lost interest in this war a couple of years ago.

'Moving south, Iran is a mellower place than it was ten years ago, but tourists are not advised to go there either, and the FO doesn't think the current regime would welcome a British military team with open arms – except of course as potential hostages. On the eastern side of the Caspian there's Turkmenistan and Kazakhstan, both of which, like Azerbaijan, are states with large Muslim populations run by ex-communists. Your chances of getting out of either with the Shadmanovs and Raisa here are not good.

'Lastly, there's Russia, and the Foreign Office doesn't seem to have much of a clue as to how the authorities there might react. Yeltsin's regime seems friendly to the one in Baku, but the FO finds it hard to believe that he would condone an Azeri nuclear programme. One thing they are certain of: the Russians will not be happy to find NATO soldiers paddling in their backyard, however good our reasons might be. And their reaction might not be very rational. For everyone's sake the FO would prefer that they didn't find out.'

'The moral of this story seems to be that we keep our feet wet,' Finn observed.

'It's safe at sea,' Noonan agreed.

'Exactly,' Colhoun agreed. 'Raisa, have you got anything to add? Any British assumptions to argue against?'

She thought for a moment. It had been strange hearing her country, and those around it, discussed – dismissed, really – so dispassionately, but she had no argument with any of the judgements Colhoun had made. 'No,' she replied.

'Well, that's about it then,' Colhoun concluded. 'I'll come and wave you all goodbye tomorrow.' He got up to leave, noticing McClure's stony face as he did so. As far as Colhoun could recall, the team leader hadn't uttered a single word during the meeting, which suggested either enormous confidence in team and plan or, less acceptably, a grim impatience to be gone.

*　　*　　*

That evening Raisa spoke to David Constantine on the phone. 'I don't know if I can talk to you about this,' she began, 'but maybe you tell me who is best for talking?'

'About what?' he asked.

'About after,' she told him. 'When we come back. I have no money, no work. It is . . .'

'Scary, I should think,' he suggested.

'Scary, yes. I cannot go home, and there is nothing for me here.'

'I understand,' he said, wondering why no one had had the decency or the sense to reassure the woman. They had probably all assumed it was someone else's job. 'I will be happy to look into it for you, if you like. There's no reason why you shouldn't be reimbursed – paid – for your time . . .'

'I do not want money for this . . .'

'Everyone else is getting paid,' Constantine said, 'and you are right – you cannot live on nothing. But I will also do what I can about finding you work of some sort. Maybe not in your field at first, but we'll see. I don't think you should worry about it now,' he added. 'We'll get something worked out.'

She thanked him, and promised to call him the moment she returned. After hanging up she opened the window of her small room and smelt the salty tang of the English sea on the breeze. It was all one planet, as she and colleagues were fond of reminding the dinosaurs in the economic ministries.

McClure had phoned Annie late that afternoon to ask her out for the evening. They could drive out into the country, he said, and find a pub that served a decent meal. It had not been a very prosperous week for her, but she agreed anyway – his mood sounded too good to waste.

Having obtained her acquiescence he walked down Poole's High Street to the local W H Smith's and, after a considerable time spent searching, finally found what he had come for. He handed over a fiver, took his purchase into the first pub he came to, and found a secluded table to read through the instructions and fill out the form. After finishing his pint he walked down the street to the police station, where he persuaded the desk sergeant and a colleague to witness his signature.

When the idea had first come to him during Colhoun's political speech, he had dismissed it as tempting fate. But the more he'd thought about it the more the opposite seemed the case, and now, walking back to his room at the base, he felt good about what he had done. He'd never tell her, but if the worst came to the worst he wanted her to know that he had appreciated her. Liked her. Loved her even, whatever that meant.

Noonan and Julie drove into Bournemouth, where a film she wanted to see was showing at the big multiplex. He was used to the kind of films that showed in the bigger rooms, and it felt strange sharing one with not much more than twenty people. It was a foreign film too, starring some hippie-looking Frenchman. Much to his surprise, Noonan found himself getting involved in the story.

Afterwards they managed a quick pint and drove back to Poole.

'I've got something to tell you,' he said, pulling the car up outside her parents' house.

She turned to face him, her face thrown into beautiful relief by the street light. 'What?'

'I'll be gone for a couple of weeks, starting tomorrow. Out of the country.'

'Where are you going?' she asked, apparently more interested than upset.

He hesitated. 'I probably shouldn't be telling you, but . . .' He shrugged. 'Cyprus.'

'I'd like to go there. What are you going for?'

'That I definitely can't tell you.'

She examined his face. 'You're nervous, aren't you?'

'No . . . yeah, I guess I am. It's sort of like playing your first game for the school football team – you really look forward to it but you're scared stiff at the same time.'

'Is it going to be dangerous?' she asked, and now he thought he could hear concern in her voice.

'No, I don't expect so,' he lied.

She took his hand in hers. 'I've got some news too,' she said, and grinned.

'Oh, what?'

'Mum and Dad have gone away for the weekend.'

He hoped she meant what he thought she did. 'That's nice.'

'Do you want to come in?'

Ten minutes later they were removing the last items of each other's clothing, and standing naked in each other's arms beside her bed. He couldn't remember his body ever feeling more excited.

'You know what I said about playing the first time . . .'

She took him gently in her hand. 'Don't worry,' she said. 'You'll get more than one game to show what you can do.'

*　　*　　*

On the other side of Poole Finn was lying on his bed reading a book about turn-of-the-century spies and soldier-adventurers in western and central Asia. It was all fascinating stuff, not to mention grist for any quiz addict's mill, but he was having trouble concentrating. That evening he had taken Marie Colhoun out for a drink, and if he was any judge of eighteen-year-old girls – and he had rather specialized in that area – she had been flashing him green lights all evening.

He liked her – she had a lovely body, she was clever, she was funny. But she was also the boss's daughter, and he wasn't sure he liked her enough to risk enraging Colhoun. The Scot might be a wonderfully liberal father, happy to let his daughter go her own way. Then again, he might take violent objection to one of his own men fucking her in the back seat of a borrowed car in a seaside car park. Some parents were like that with their teenage daughters – Finn had heard them say so.

So he had done the noble thing, and probably left her thinking that he was impotent, diseased or gay. Or all three.

He did like her though. Maybe when he came back . . .

He sighed and went back to the book. At least they wouldn't have to walk all the way to the Caspian, like some of the poor fuckers he was reading about.

The following morning Colhoun and Galloway had time for a few words on the airfield tarmac. The SBS boss had woken up worrying in the middle of the night – something he hadn't done for years. He was hoping it wasn't a premonition. 'How's it looking to you?' he asked Galloway. 'Any doubts?'

'There are always doubts. But it looks good. They've

turned themselves into a good team. The woman has exceeded all my expectations, and probably a few of her own. McClure's his usual efficient self. Noonan's nervous, but it's his first big show. I'd be worried if he wasn't. Finn's just Finn. I like the chemistry.'

'Finn's been going out with my older daughter.' Colhoun grunted. 'Doesn't know I know though.'

Galloway laughed. 'Are you going to tell him?'

'Maybe.' Colhoun sighed. 'There's something about this one that worries me. Nothing specific – the plan looks as fail-proof as a plan can be in these sort of circumstances. It's just a feeling.'

'Sink or swim,' Galloway murmured, as the fully laden team emerged from the building behind them.

It was not an auspicious comment. According to the report Colhoun had read the previous week the Caspian was not as salty as other seas. Which made it easier to sink and harder to swim.

11

Cyprus was hot and bright. They arrived at the Akrotiri base early in the afternoon, and were escorted to rooms which offered views of the blue Mediterranean and what looked like the perfect beach.

Not that there would be much time for sunbathing in the week that followed. From the first morning Galloway kept them on their toes, with a training programme aimed at both increasing their overall physical fitness and honing the technical skills which would be needed on the team's thirty-six-hour trip into enemy territory. Early mornings were devoted to running and swimming, the rest of the daylight hours to take-offs in the Hercules and splashdowns in the sea. The HAHO novices, Raisa and Finn, were introduced to the oxygen equipment and thermal suits, and given instruction in the techniques needed for guiding the GQ360 chutes during the long descent. In the meantime the more experienced McClure and Noonan worked to improve their landing of the remote-controlled parachutes which would be carrying the heavy equipment.

Climbing aboard the C-130 for the third time on one particular day Noonan suddenly had a picture of himself clambering up the slide in the park near his childhood home in Liverpool. Up you went, down you came, and up you went again.

For all the demands that the days made on their minds and bodies, none of the team waited eagerly for the hours of darkness. Galloway had decreed from the start that they should stay on-base for the duration, which rather limited the possibilities for entertainment, and the fact that they were unable to divulge the reasons for their presence hardly endeared them to the normal squaddies. Restricted to their own or one another's company, each of the four found him or herself with rather more time to think than they would otherwise have chosen. Even Finn, normally stoical almost to a fault, found himself prone to anxieties about their upcoming jaunt. In particular, he found himself worrying about how McClure would react to the jettisoning of Galloway's restraining influence.

For his part, McClure was reminded again of life on the rigs. He and Noonan watched films in the rec room, read badly researched military thrillers and worked out in the gym. Unknown to each other, both spent most of an evening searching for something to say on postcards to their respective better halves, with equally unsatisfying results.

Given this general state of mind, it was with some relief that they heard, on the eighth day of their stay on the island, Galloway's announcement of their imminent departure. 'You'll be leaving tomorrow at 19.45 hours,' he told them. 'Which should put you at the jump point around three and a quarter hours later – midnight local time. You should be in the water an hour after that. Which will give you about four and a half hours of darkness to reach the rig and set up your OP. The Sea King will pick you up from Narghin Island at 03.00 the following night.' He looked round at the four faces, each with its different mix of emotions. 'So let's go into

Limassol and get a decent meal this evening, and then you can start building up a decent backlog of sleep. You're going to be needing it.'

Tamarlan Shadmanov rubbed his eyes and strained to catch more of the conversation which was taking place several tables away in the otherwise empty canteen. It was a little after dawn, and he had been up all night trying to solve one of those problems which, despite himself, he still found almost unbearably interesting, and he was in no hurry to return to the claustrophobic quarters he shared with his wife.

The Azeris at the other table – three ambitious young physicists whom he had known and avoided at the university – were talking about an escape. One of the Iraqi scientists had apparently grabbed one of the supply boats at gunpoint soon after dark the previous evening, and sped off in the direction of Iran, some four hundred kilometres to the south, presumably with defection in mind. The physicists were unanimous in doubting that the speedboat carried enough fuel to cover even half that distance.

Shadmanov tended to agree with them, but it was still comforting to know that he was not the only person on the platform who would have preferred to be somewhere else.

At that moment Azad Vezirov came in through the heavy doors. He was looking tired, Shadmanov thought.

'Has someone really escaped?' he asked the head of security as he walked past.

'One of the Iraqis has tried,' Vezirov said without stopping.

Shadmanov took his coffee outside, where the sun,

having climbed clear of the horizon, was now taking the chill out of the air. He leaned against the railing of the walkway, staring out across the open water, listening to the wavelets lapping against the giant legs of the rig. For the first time in several days he thought about Raisa, who had invested so much energy in saving this sea. He wondered again if she had contacted Akhundov and got his message, and if so, whether she had decoded it. Now that several weeks had gone by he rather hoped she hadn't.

At the time it had seemed a clever thing to do, but now . . . After all, the only thing she could have done with the knowledge was to get herself into trouble. And for an undeserving cause at that – he had hardly given her a moment's thought since the first few days here, and when he did their affair felt like something which had happened long ago.

He felt old here, he realized. He felt as if his past had come back to haunt him with all the unresolved guilts and fears.

And he missed hiking more than he missed her. Here he could see for nearly fifty kilometres in each direction, but he couldn't move more than two hundred metres in a straight line.

He thought about the young Iraqi, and raised his mug of coffee in a token toast of his escape attempt. He was asleep three hours later when the man was brought back, but he saw him in the canteen that evening, eating dinner with the two Iraqi security guards in close attendance, defeat in his eyes.

That same morning Sir Christopher Hanson and Manny Salewicz met for a stroll through St James's Park in the spring sunshine. 'No problems?' Hanson asked the American, more casually than he felt.

'None. Everything's arranged. The colonel in charge at Dogubayazit – his name's Klesko, by the way – he's been told that a British Sea King will be arriving later today, and that he's to give them anything they want and ask no questions. As you can imagine, he's not particularly thrilled by these orders, but he'll obey them. There's a Turkish liaison officer attached to the base, but he apparently spends most of his time in the town brothel, so there's not much chance he'll notice anything. If by some miracle he does, then they'll snow him under with stuff about NATO inter-force familiarization exercises, or some such corporate newspeak crap – you know what I mean. Third Worlders just eat up that stuff – makes them think they've cracked a code.'

Hanson smiled in spite of himself.

'Everything OK from your end?' the American asked, running a hand across the headful of stubble which he probably thought of as hair.

'I think so,' Hanson admitted, with a reluctance born of thirty years in the job.

'So forty-eight hours from now we should know whether Uncle Saddam really is making bombs in someone else's backyard.'

'And how long before they're operational,' Hanson added.

'And then the crapola will really hit the fan. I don't envy whoever it is gets the job of trying to sell the Russians on a NATO bombing raid in the Caspian.'

They'll probably offer to do it for us,' the MI6 chief said cynically.

'Yeah, but they'll want paying for the privilege,' Salewicz agreed.

Hanson left it until early evening before notifying the PM that action was imminent, for experience had taught him that it was wiser not to allow politicians too much time for second thoughts. 'I thought you'd like to know,' he said informally. 'The SBS team will be on its way in an hour or so.'

The PM's sigh was audible over the phone. 'I'd completely forgotten it was today,' he admitted. 'Well, I wish them luck. Will they be in constant contact with the outside world?'

'I think so, Prime Minister.'

'Then please let me know if anything significant happens. Day or night.'

'Certainly . . .'

'I take it the embassy in Ankara has been alerted?'

'Yes, they're on stand-by.'

'With buckets of water to douse the flames, I suppose,' the PM said drily. 'I wouldn't want to be in the ambassador's shoes if the Turks get wind of this.'

'Well, at least these days they won't send him back in pieces as an expression of their displeasure,' Hanson said.

'I sincerely hope not,' the PM said with feeling, and hung up.

He'd probably seen his latest poll ratings that morning, Hanson thought sourly as he put on his coat. He was halfway through the door when he remembered Constantine. Returning to his desk he punched out the scientist's number, and listened to the phone ringing in the Cambridgeshire cottage.

'Constantine,' a voice said.

'Hanson. Thought you'd like to know, our boys – and girl – will be airborne in a couple of hours.'

'Thanks,' Constantine said. 'How long's the flight?' he asked, more for something to say than because he really wanted to know.

'About three and a half hours, I think.'

'Are their chances good?'

'I hope we wouldn't be sending them if they weren't. Suicide squads are not very English, somehow.'

Constantine laughed, but there wasn't much good humour in the sound. 'Thanks for calling,' he told Hanson, and hung up with an abruptness which both he and his cat found surprising. 'Sorry,' he told the cat, and walked across to the window, from which he could see the lights of the nearest village.

The team sat waiting in the airbase office while Galloway ran through everything one more time. It was hardly necessary, and he could tell that they were not really listening, but that didn't matter, for in moments like this he preferred the sound of his own voice to silence. His past experience suggested that most groups of men in such situations retreated into semi-hysterical humour, but this team was different. Partly it had to be the presence of a woman – and a foreign one at that – but Galloway suspected it had more to do with the personality of Sergeant McClure. The man was either humourless, unaffected by the tension, or both.

Galloway finished up with the weather report. 'It couldn't be much better,' he told them. 'The overnight low will be around ten to twelve degrees, thin cloud at around three thousand metres, not much in the way of wind at any level, and the sea should be calm.'

'That is good,' Raisa said, seeing it in her mind's eye.

'Any last questions?' Galloway asked.

There were none. He led them outside, where they piled into the two waiting jeeps and started off across the wide expanse of empty tarmac. It was a cool evening for Cyprus, with a light breeze blowing and a clear sky overhead. The crescent moon hung in the western sky, lighting the distant Mediterranean. It would be below the horizon in a couple of hours.

Ahead of them the camouflaged Hercules was warming up its engines beneath the yellow floodlights. They clambered out of the jeeps, half heard the good-luck wishes of the two squaddie drivers, and climbed up into the belly of the monster. After the training runs of the previous week the interior was familiar, but not completely so. This was an MC130, the special forces variant with electronic jamming gear, secure communications and precision navigation systems. It had been designed for the insertion of deep-penetration missions and its maintenance crew had obviously taken such an exalted purpose to heart, for the plane was spotless.

The seating was just as cramped though, and no one was in a hurry to strap themselves in. While Galloway and McClure checked the equipment on the two pallets the other three shuffled from foot to foot, listening to the roar of the four engines outside.

The RAF crew of four each came back to say hello. They seemed friendly enough, and not at all nervous about their forthcoming intrusion into Turkish,

Armenian and Azeri airspace. But that was hardly surprising, Finn thought – pilots were known to be the craziest people alive.

Once the ten-minute warning had been given, the four members of the team went through the checking procedures they had been taught, giving a thorough once-over to the main and reserve parachutes, and all the various straps, ties and releases which they would be using. Satisfied, they strapped themselves into the webbed seats and waited. Within a few minutes the plane was in motion, taxiing across the airfield. The Alison turboprop engines hit a higher note and the giant plane accelerated down the runway, creaking and rumbling with discontent, before allowing itself to be lifted into the sky. It was like a fat woman getting out of a chair, Noonan thought – you knew she could do it, but it took so much fucking effort.

For the first few minutes, as the plane gained height, no one tried to compete with the roar of the engines. Finn was the first to speak, wondering out loud why the RAF couldn't lay on a film for long flights.

'I suppose you'd like ice-creams, too,' one of the crew said from the cabin door.

'Popcorn would do.'

Noonan and Raisa laughed, and even McClure managed a thin smile.

This was more like it, Galloway thought. The funereal atmosphere had started him wondering how many of the four would be coming back. He took a trip round the faces, trying to gauge what was going on in the minds behind them. Who needed encouragement? Who needed lightening up? Who needed calming down?

All three men seemed self-absorbed, but Galloway

could detect no signs of incipient panic, or, what would be worse, massive overconfidence. They had been trained for moments like this, and indeed they would have stood little chance of qualifying for membership of the SBS if they hadn't demonstrated such capacities in initial training. Sometimes the jump from the training ground to the real thing exposed an unsuspected flaw in a man's make-up, but not often. All three of these men had made this jump at least once without faltering, and Galloway saw no reason to believe that they would do so now.

As for the woman, she seemed remarkably calm and collected for someone who had never done anything remotely comparable before, but then she had been that way ever since she joined the team. If it was all a façade, then it was a damn good one.

Raisa momentarily felt his eyes on her and smiled back. She was feeling a host of conflicting emotions, some positive, some negative, some neither one nor the other. She had never really been a team player, and, crazy as it seemed, she felt as close to these three men as any group of people she had ever known. It felt good to be part of a team, really good – like an ideal halfway house between solitude and the intimacy of one-to-one relationships. It felt like a new world, a new life, almost as if she was being reborn.

But where was this new life taking her? Where else but back home, back towards the old life, her beloved sea and her married lover. She really didn't know how she'd feel about Tamarlan when the moment came – all that seemed so long ago. But maybe she was kidding herself, maybe the old life was the real one, and this playing at soldiers was just a momentary madness.

She supposed she would find out soon enough, and in

MARINE I: SBS

the meantime there were more important things to worry about, like jumping out of a plane at ten thousand metres and rescuing Tamarlan from the KGB. The plane didn't actually worry her – she was rather looking forward to it – but she did feel anxious about the imminent confrontation with him and his wife. It seemed so utterly unpredictable.

As far as she knew, they were under orders to take Tamarlan with them only if he agreed to go, but such a policy seemed scarcely credible, and she suspected that McClure probably had secret instructions to bring the scientist out whether or not he was willing. If this was indeed the case, she really didn't know what to think. If Tamarlan proved unwilling to leave on his wife's account, then she knew she would find it hard to be sympathetic, considering what else was at stake. But if he had a better reason, one that had not yet occurred to her, then . . .

She was looking forward to the descent, but the real problems would start around sea level.

Sitting a metre or so to her left, Noonan was thinking about the telephone conversation he had had with Julie earlier that evening. It had been OK, but she had seemed so far away, or at least that was the way it had felt to him. According to her, it had been him who had sounded like his mind was somewhere else.

He thought about the night they'd made love, as he often had over the past eight days. It had been so incredible, so much better than anything he'd ever experienced before, and the thought that it might never happen again was almost more than he could bear. If she met someone else . . . The mere thought sent his stomach into free fall.

136

He'd be back in a few days. Provided he made it.

This one was real, he thought. The cling-wrapped grenade-launchers and MP5s on the pallet were real. At the time he had thought the business in the Channel had been the real thing – it had been for that poor Russian bastard – but even before they'd found out it was all a set-up it had been hard to see that op as anything out of the ordinary. They'd only been sixty kilometres from Poole, for fuck's sake. It had felt like a tougher-than-usual training exercise.

Parachuting into a sea surrounded by hostile countries was something else again. There'd be real opposition, a good chance of a real baptism of fire. All those guys in the pubs back home could take their next night of passion pretty much for granted – all they had to do was look left and right before they crossed the road and not get their dicks caught in their zip. Whereas he'd only get another chance to feel Julie's lovely body up against his if he was quick and lucky enough when it came to the crunch.

Funny thing was, he'd never appreciated before just how safe other people's lives were.

'You get used to it,' Finn said softly. He was sitting facing Noonan, a slight smile on his face, looking as though he did this sort of thing twice a week just to keep himself in shape.

'I'll let you know,' Noonan said ruefully.

'You won't need to,' Finn told him, and shut his eyes again. Like fuck you got used to it, he told himself. But maybe saying so would make Noonan feel better. The anxiety in the boy's eyes had been getting to him.

He always found himself asking the same dumb question at times like this: what the fuck was he doing here? It had occurred to him in the helicopter as they headed for the Haitian island the previous summer, and again as he climbed aboard the pirated freighter less than a month before. He was no nearer an answer on this occasion than he had been on those.

There had been three other men on the Haitian and the South China Sea missions: Callum Marker, Rob Cafell and Ian Dubery. Rob and Ian were both in love with the sea, and either of them could have found any number of sea-related jobs which didn't involve such frequent dicing with death. Marker was both clever and competent, and, false modesty aside, Finn thought he could say the same for himself. There was any number of things either of them could have done with their lives, so why this?

He could say the same of Noonan, he thought, though McClure was something else again. Out of the corner of his eye, Finn could see the team leader conscientiously cleaning his Browning High Power, his face an absolute mask. No, it was hard to imagine McClure as anything but a soldier.

But the rest of them . . . they had chosen. He himself could have gone to university, or gone into business – only a couple of months ago he had spent most of a weekend sorting out his cousin's recording studio accounts for him. Or he could have been an adventure holidays tour guide, with interesting information coming out of his ears. Or a gigolo specializing in young heiresses.

He could have gone for anything. So why was he sitting in the belly of this rumbling metal bucket with wings, about to risk getting his balls shot off by diverse foreigners, and all for the greater glory of a Queen and Country which he found about as convincing as

Chelsea's back four? He had no more idea this time than last. The only difference was a growing suspicion that he never would.

To Finn's left, McClure was finding that the rumble of the Hercules provided an almost musical accompaniment to his state of mind. Years ago, as a teenager, he had seen the Vietnam film *Apocalypse Now*, and been really taken by the US Air Cav's use of chopper-borne loudspeakers to blast out stirring music during their airborne attacks. He had found out later that the piece in question was called *The Ride of the Valkyries*, but he supposed it didn't matter much which music was used – anything that provided an adrenalin rush would do.

Not that the SBS was ever likely to need any such accompaniment – their missions, almost without exception, relied on stealth for their success.

This one would be no exception. If there was to be any contact with the enemy it would have to be both silent and invisible, at least up until the moment they had the scientist safely in the bag.

McClure looked round briefly at the other members of his team – the woman, the cocky Londoner, the kid. In a couple of hours they would all be heading into the unknown, where, no matter how many contingencies you planned for, every moment was beautifully unpredictable. It was like stepping out on to a high wire on a windy day, and only the best made it across.

He was one of the best, and a big part of the reason why was a willingness to risk his own life. He had nothing to lose – it was as simple as that.

As always, the thought seemed to prise him open, to offer a fleeting glimpse of unbearable loss. One more heartbeat and it was gone, leaving him staring across the fuselage at Raisa.

He carried on cleaning the Browning.

The minutes went by, and the hours. They were told when they had entered Turkish airspace, then told when they were passing over Mount Ararat and crossing into Armenian skies. Another half-hour and they were nearly ten thousand metres above the disputed Nagorno-Karabakh enclave and heading out over Azerbaijan proper. A few minutes later the officer who was doubling as the dispatcher emerged from the crew cabin and gave them the fifteen-minute warning.

The four team members unstrapped themselves and reached for the dry suits which they would be wearing over their combat fatigues until they reached the rig. Each of them fought their way into the tight rubber garment, pinching their ears as they pushed their heads through the skin-tight neck seal, and then set about hoisting themselves into the parachute harnesses. This done, they cracked the shells of the chemical lights on the back of one another's helmets, put on the Passive Night Goggles, and offered themselves to each other for a thorough check.

'It's time to hook up,' the dispatcher shouted, attaching the plastic hose from his own mask to one of the two oxygen consoles in the centre of the plane. Galloway and the team followed suit, and at a word from the dispatcher the pilot began the process of depressurization. Ears began popping and the air grew steadily colder.

'Switch,' the dispatcher ordered, and they all shifted their hose connectors from the central console to the bottles attached to their belts, each of which contained thirty minutes' worth of oxygen. An additional rumble served notice that the tailgate doors were being opened, but within seconds this symphonic variation had been lost in the overall roar of the Hercules's slipstream. Stars appeared in the widening jaws.

As the ramp settled into place McClure and Noonan pulled the two pallets into position, and then did a final check on the remote units they would be using to manoeuvre the Controlled Air Delivery chutes. Each pallet bore a deflated Gemini and rocket-launcher; one carried two MP5s, the other an MP5 and the sniper rifle. It would all have fitted easily enough on one pallet, but, as with the boats, Galloway had decided that a backup was advisable.

'Two minutes,' the dispatcher yelled over the roar of the engines and slipstream, holding up two fingers in confirmation.

The four of them waited beneath the glowing red lamp, right hands gripping the parachute static line, left hands resting on top of the reserve chutes strapped to their chests. There was a forest of stars visible through the opening, tailing down into the dark vagueness of clouds far below. Galloway was patting each of them on the back, grinning encouragement through his oxygen mask.

The light turned green. The dispatcher and his assistant heaved the first pallet forward across the rattling rollers and out into space. The second swiftly followed, and then the four team members, with what seemed hardly a step between them, were throwing themselves out into the thin air. The slipstream grabbed them, threw them forward, and then, as if deciding it no longer wanted them, allowed them to fall.

Each mentally counted second seemed like an eternity as they struggled to stabilize their plummeting bodies, face down with backs arched, legs and arms extended. Each second count reached ten, each hand reached for the rip-cord, and each chute billowed open, jerking its human cargo upright. Below them the CAD chutes had halted the plunge of the two pallets, and as McClure and Noonan took control of both their own and the equipment's downward trajectory, the less experienced Finn and Raisa concentrated on using their control toggles to keep in line of glide behind the others. Above them the fiercely glittering stars only emphasized how cold it was, while the world beneath their feet seemed composed of dark-grey smoke. It reminded Finn of a black hole as envisaged by the makers of *Star Trek*. Against this emptiness the chutes below seemed like pale-grey flowers, the green pinpoints of chemical light on the helmets like sheltering fireflies.

As the minutes went by this view seemed not to change one iota, and if it hadn't been for the perceptible warming of the air around them the foursome could have been forgiven for believing that they were in orbit around the earth rather than falling towards it.

At the rear of the line, Raisa found that even the daunting prospect of the next thirty-six hours couldn't drain the pleasure from the experience. According to the plan, they would be in the air for around fifty-seven minutes, gliding something like thirty kilometres before splashdown, and there wasn't a lot she had to do in the meantime but keep in line and enjoy the view. There wasn't much to see yet, but the feeling . . . well, it had to be something like the weightlessness astronauts enjoyed, a kind of physical freedom which had no earthbound parallels. From the first jump at Brize Norton she had loved it, and she was damned if this was going to be her last such experience.

For McClure and Noonan there was less time for such thoughts . . . controlling both their own and the pallets' descent was a rather more demanding business. And as they fell towards the thin layer of cloud McClure felt his anxiety building. The one thing which could abort the mission before it started – and see the four of them swiftly marched off to jail or worse – was the presence of unfriendly eyes in their drop zone. The Caspian was not a crowded sea where shipping was concerned, and they had chosen a DZ removed from all the known lanes, but there was no way of knowing where or when any of the various navies might choose to exercise or what sudden whim might motivate the master of a single fishing boat.

An increase in the dampness of the air and a slight fading of upward visibility told McClure that they had entered the highest layer of cloud. The chutes began to sway more as the water vapour grew denser, and for about five minutes the team found themselves gliding silently down through the wet mist, devoid of all reference points save the position of their own bodies.

And then suddenly McClure was out in the open, about three thousand metres above a dark and apparently empty sea. He could see faint and scattered lights far away to the west, and others, closer, to the north, but there were none in the wide expanse of water towards which they were falling. So far so good. He glanced up quickly to check that the others were still holding their positions. They were.

The final fifteen minutes of their descent seemed to

pass quickly. McClure's altimeter was showing two hundred metres when the pallet under his control hit the surface. He released his bergen to hang beneath his feet on the bungee cord and pulled on both toggles to break his forward speed. At a hundred metres above the water he jettisoned the reserve chute and positioned his hands above the cape-well releases. A second before hitting the water he pressed down, the shoulder-straps fell away and the slight breeze carried the billowing chute to one side.

McClure broke back to the surface, treading water as he pulled on the fins which had been hanging from his waist, and then popped open his life-jacket. Fifty metres away the woman was splashing down with an ease and elegance which matched his own. Between them he could see the other two's helmet lights bobbing in the gentle Caspian swell.

They had arrived.

12

Ten minutes after splashdown the parachutes had been weighted and sunk, the Geminis inflated, loaded and motorized. McClure was with Noonan in one, Finn and Raisa in the other.

McClure checked his watch, which had already been adjusted for local time. They were five minutes ahead of schedule, which just about cancelled out their being half a kilometre further south than intended. The Aliyev rigs were fifteen kilometres to the north. First light was still more than four hours away.

'Let's go,' he said softly, and the two muffled 40hp outboard motors came to life with an apologetic cough.

They headed north across the barely rolling sea at a steady 15kph, eyes peeled for other shipping, but for several kilometres the horizon remained empty. Then a bright light loomed above it in the north-east, causing McClure to slow and turn a questioning glance at Raisa. She nodded. It was the night ferry from Baku to Krasnovodsk, which they had been expecting to see in the distance.

Seconds later the ferry had again disappeared below the horizon, and the two Geminis resumed their previous speed. A scattering of faint lights were now visible in the north, and as the minutes went by a thin black line formed around them between sea and sky. This was the man-made peninsula of oil rigs and pilings which arced out into the Caspian from Baku, off the end of which lay the Aliyev twin rig.

Another minute and this too was visible, initially as a faint source of illumination and then, as the distance between them dropped, as an angular shadow flecked with pinpricks of white and yellow light.

They were about one and a half kilometres away when McClure cut the engine on the leading Gemini and signalled Finn to do the same in the boat behind. As the two craft bobbed in the swell, he spent several minutes examining the twin rig through the nightscope.

The larger of the two connected structures, Aliyev A, was certainly occupied – the lighted windows left no doubt of that. The exterior walkways were well lit, but more, McClure guessed, for the convenience of those aboard than as a security measure. He could see no sign of sentries, which suggested either a total reliance on hidden cameras or an assumption that the rig's location was security enough. He hoped it was the latter.

To the east of the illuminated A rig, surrounded on three sides by the open sea, B rig seemed little more than the shadow of its twin. The bright light which adorned the top of the truncated drill tower was clearly intended as a warning to shipping and aircraft, not as a source of illumination, and the bulk of B rig was cloaked in impenetrable darkness. The SBS team could hardly have hoped for better.

They could make the approach as planned, McClure decided, taking a semicircular course which would bring them in on the blind side of the smaller rig. He gave Finn the appropriate hand signal, received a wave of acknowledgement, accepted a paddle from Noonan and settled down to work.

The next half-hour was less nerve-racking than they'd expected. The Stygian depth of this particular night would have made the two small boats almost impossible to see in any case, and the apparent lack of watchers on either rig merely added weight to the team's belief in its own invisibility. Only Finn, with a cynicism borne of recent experience in such matters, found it slightly worrying that so much luck seemed to be coming their way at the beginning of the operation. He liked it better when fate owed him a break.

They reached the base of B rig without mishap, and edged the two Geminis in among the intricate web of girders which supported the platforms above. The girders themselves, as McClure and Noonan had discovered on Tempest Bravo, offered a slippery but straightforward way up to the lowest deck, and Noonan had made several such practice ascents during their time on the North Sea rig. He started upwards now, sacrificing speed for sureness of hold on the barnacle and algae-covered struts. Falling to his death at this stage would be fucking inconvenient.

Beneath him, the others were tying their supply and equipment bags to girders before carrying them up. Having emptied the Geminis they disconnected the outboard motors and stowed them in waterproof bags, before clambering out on to the structure themselves and deflating the boats. These, together with their bagged motors, were then attached to a flotation bladder, which was in turn inflated with carbon dioxide to the extent required to keep the whole package submerged a metre or so beneath the water's surface.

This accomplished, they had only a few seconds to sling the supplies and equipment across their shoulders before the end of the lightweight caving ladder slapped Finn in the cheek. At a nod from McClure he used his own weight to pull it taut, and then started climbing. Raisa followed, with the PC bringing up the rear. Each emerged through a small trapdoor on to the metal floor of the rig's lowest deck.

There they removed the silenced MP5s from the waterproof bag. B rig might seem deserted, but there was no point in taking chances.

The favoured spot for an observation post, picked out by McClure during a thorough exploration of Tempest Bravo, was a derrick control cabin, four floors above. They started up through the labyrinth, climbing steel ladders which showed no trace of ever having been used, and, having reached the right floor, worked their way round to the side which faced A rig across fifty metres of water. Having studied the plans, each member of the team felt familiar with the basic layout, but for McClure and Noonan, who had visited its North Sea counterpart, Aliyev B was something of a shock. It had obviously never been used for its original purpose, and after Tempest Bravo's clutter of pipes, hoists, winches, barrels and drilling equipment it seemed so empty and bare. It felt like a half-built block of flats, with floors and internal supports but no walls. Movement during the hours of daylight would be a lot riskier than they had expected.

The derrick control cabin was beyond empty and bare – it was non-existent. But Lady Luck was still smiling on them, for close to the place where the cabin should have been, several large piles of metal lattice flooring had been lashed together with steel hawsers and left to rust. The space between two of these piles offered concealment from all angles but above, and this omission was made right by the floor of the deck above. Even better, gaps in the stacked sections of flooring provided a selection of views of the towering A rig. It was hard to imagine a more suitable place.

'Home sweet home,' Finn muttered.

McClure was pulling the MIL/UST-1 satellite communications unit out of its pack. 'Get yourselves out of the rubber suits,' he told the others. 'I'll let Galloway know we've arrived,' he said softly, and walked off in search of an open sky at which to aim the satcom's antennas.

It was still only 11.30 in Poole when McClure's brief message reached Colhoun's office. He sat there for a few moments, staring at the few words on the piece of paper, wondering at how little could mean so much. His team were 'in position', hidden on a converted oil rig in the middle of a sea which few Britons had ever laid eyes on. And millions of lives might depend on how successfully these four people spent their next couple of days.

It wasn't right, Colhoun thought. Things like war and peace shouldn't hang by such slender threads.

He supposed he should go home. Nothing was likely to happen in the next eight hours, and Galloway was quite capable of looking after the store by himself. But he felt reluctant nevertheless, for although it was utterly daft, having ordered his men into such a situation he was aware of something inside him which revolted against the idea of sleep.

*   *   *

Nearly five thousand kilometres away, McClure and Finn left the other two in occupation of the OP and began a systematic search of B rig. They didn't expect to find anyone, and they weren't disappointed, though the discovery of several used condoms on the platform above the empty drilling shaft suggested there were occasional visitors. Gazing down from the unprotected rim into the depths of the gaping shaft, Finn decided that these days sex was dangerous enough in bed.

'They're months old,' McClure decided, after examining the condoms with the air of a palaeontologist sifting through recently excavated fossils.

'We could try carbon-dating them,' Finn suggested.

McClure grinned mirthlessly. 'Fucking outdoors is something people do in summer,' he said.

Finn had to admit the man had a point.

They moved down through the decks, finding no other traces of recent human occupation, and eventually reached the eastern end of the covered bridge which connected the two rigs. Its counterpart on the Tempest twin had boasted a narrow walkway enclosed in wire mesh above oil- and gas-carrying pipes, but this bridge was no more than a long and empty metal box suspended twenty metres above the water. Crossing it unobserved in daylight would be nothing more than a lottery, but at night the lack of any bridge lighting would be a definite plus. What ambient light there was came from A rig's catwalk to the left, with the consequence that the northern side of the walkway was shadowed by its own roof.

'Sweep complete,' McClure said softly into the miniature microphone which was pinned to his shirt collar. 'We're alone, for the moment anyway.'

The view of the bridge from the OP was partial at best, and anyone emerging from the distant doors on A rig could get across over to B without their knowledge. So, McClure wondered, was it worth keeping a permanent watch down here on the bottom deck? He asked Finn what he thought.

The younger man thought about it for a minute or so. 'No,' he said at last. 'The other three would get some warning, which might help, might not. It might just draw attention to us all. And the man down here wouldn't have a prayer – there's no cover, and no way he could get back up to the OP without being seen from the other side. I think we should assume that people only come over here once in a blue moon, and just play the odds.'

'Agreed,' McClure murmured. He had reached the same conclusion himself, and it was nice to hear he wasn't just whistling in the dark. 'I think this would be a good time to take a quick look over the other side,' he added. 'The less surprises we have to deal with tomorrow night the better.'

'I was afraid you were going to suggest that,' Finn muttered.

McClure smiled and passed on their intentions to Noonan, who sounded less than ecstatic himself.

A few seconds later the two men were walking briskly across the bridge, their eyes fixed on the double doors straight ahead. No one came through them, and no shouts of alarm rang out from the catwalks above. They stepped across the small open area at the foot of the external catwalk steps and flattened themselves against the doors. Through the small round windows they could see a dark corridor stretching into the distance, but the doors themselves were locked and bolted, and there was no sign of a key, either inside or out.

This was both good news and bad news. Good because it meant that the bridge across to B rig could only be approached by means of those external catwalks which were visible from their OP, bad because it meant they would have to use those same catwalks to gain entry to A rig's interior.

'Is there anyone out above us?' McClure asked Noonan.

'No.'

'If anyone appears, let us know.'

'Roger.'

McClure and Finn walked up the two flights of steps to the next level, where an otherwise identical pair of doors obligingly swung open in response to the PC's push. There was no key here either, and the corridor in front of them was well lit. Colour scheme apart, it could have been the one on which their rooms had been situated aboard Tempest Alpha.

'Two men on the fifth level, coming down,' Noonan's voice whispered excitedly in their earpieces.

'Acknowledged,' McClure murmured, and gestured to Finn to precede him down the steps. At the bottom they flattened themselves against the doors once more, listened to the footsteps above, and waited for Noonan to give them the all-clear.

'They're back inside,' he reported almost instantly.

McClure and Finn recrossed the bridge and climbed back up through four of B rig's five levels to the OP. It was now almost four in the morning, and time for half the team to get some rest.

'Raisa, Finn – gonk time,' McClure announced. 'We'll wake you at ten.'

The Londoner managed a quick leer, but otherwise needed no second bidding, and seconds after curling himself up in the Gore-tex sleeping bag he was dead to the world.

Raisa found it harder. 'Gonk time,' she murmured sarcastically to herself. This was an apt occasion, she thought, for using one of those Marine phrases which made no sense at all. 'Fat chance!' As she lay on the hard metal floor, listening to the sounds of the Caspian lapping at the supports of the two rigs, the whole business seemed far too fantastic for something as mundane as sleep.

Lingering over his coffee in the A rig canteen Tamarlan Shadmanov wondered what, if anything, he should be doing about the young Iraqi scientist. Salam Muhammad's refusal to work was undoubtedly slowing down essential work on the project, a fact which pleased and dismayed Shadmanov in almost equal measure. He had no wish to see the work completed for Saddam's sake, or for the sake of the idiots who ruled in Baku, but he had every desire to see it finished for his own. He didn't want to spend the rest of his life on a converted oil rig, spending his days working on weapons of mass destruction for a lunatic, his nights confined in a cell-like room with a woman for whom his feelings were at best residual.

Twenty-five years ago, as he knew only too well, such a selfish attitude would have filled him with guilt. But time and experience had changed him. For one thing, he was no longer so arrogant as to consider himself irreplaceable; for another, he had come to realize that events of world-shattering importance usually only mattered to politicians and journalists. Not always, but often enough for Shadmanov to give his own interests the benefit of the doubt. After all, if everyone concentrated on making the most of their lives, they might have less inclination to ruin other people's.

But ... he told himself, and left humankind's most powerful syllable hanging there in his brain as he took another gulp of coffee.

'Good morning, Professor,' Vezirov said, looming above him. The security chief placed his tray on the table and stared at his large cooked breakfast with an expectant smile.

'Good morning,' Shadmanov said coldly.

'I hear you're being held up by Salam's intransigence,' Vezirov said, making a neat diametrical incision in the yoke of the first fried egg.

Shadmanov shrugged. 'A little,' he agreed. He didn't want to get the poor kid shot.

'Well, don't worry about it. He's getting a visit from his own people today. I expect they'll point out the error of his ways, one way or another.'

Shadmanov looked up at Vezirov, wondering if the man could really be as big a shit as he made out.

Finn and Raisa were shaken awake at ten in the morning by a bleary-eyed Noonan. The clouds from the night before had appreciably thickened and the wind was fresher; the Caspian seemed almost lead-coloured underneath the heavy overcast. It was warmer though – somewhere in the high teens, Finn reckoned.

McClure was still at his post, staring through the

veiled binoculars. 'We've only clocked two men in uniform so far, and they had the look of internal security – more worried about their own people than outsiders. We've seen a lot of people in white lab coats – men and women.' He smiled at Raisa, who had suggested they bring along such coats for possible use as a disguise. 'But we haven't seen anyone who looks like our man. And there's been no arrivals or departures, either by sea or air. OK? Wake us at four – or earlier if you need to.' He passed Finn his log of sightings and times and crawled away towards his sleeping bag.

Finn looked at the neat entries, the almost childlike numerals. 'Sleep well,' he murmured. 'Now, what about breakfast?' he asked Raisa.

They ate the last of the sandwiches from the Akrotiri canteen, a couple of apples and a packet of mixed nuts. 'I suppose everyone has caviar for breakfast round here,' Finn said. 'This is where it comes from, right?'

'Yes, but I've never had it for breakfast.'

'You're probably a Weetabix fiend.'

'I like your Weetabix.'

'You're not alone. Rumour has it the Queen crumbles a couple for herself each morning.'

Raisa grinned. 'What I'd really like is a cup of tea.'

'I know what you mean, but I'm afraid it's cold drinks for the duration. With any luck the chopper crew will bring a Thermos with them tonight.'

They settled down to watch. In the grey light of day the rig across the water seemed even more massive than it had by night. It was like a combined oil refinery, office building and block of flats on stilts, Finn thought. He had known the dimensions from the model back in Poole, but even so . . . It was fucking *huge*.

Advanced guesswork had placed the main work areas on the far side of A rig, and eight-plus hours of observation had offered no contrary indications. Occasionally there was movement visible through one of the windows in the wall facing them, but the rooms in question didn't seem to be in permanent use for any sort of work. The external catwalks were occasionally used as a short cut between floors – the SBS team assumed the Aliyev A, like Tempest Alpha, also had lifts and internal stairs – but were more commonly employed as the setting for a fresh-air break, with or without cigarette.

A few of those who came out to lean against the rails were dressed in blue overalls – cleaners, probably – but the vast majority wore the white lab coats beloved of technicians and scientists the world over. Both groups came in both genders, though males seemed to preponderate among the lab coats. In racial terms, Finn was pleased to find a spectrum which ranged from blond Slavs to dark-moustachioed Turks. As long as no one expected any of the SBS men to understand Russian or Azeri they wouldn't stick out like sore thumbs.

It was a couple of hours before they saw anyone in uniform, and then it was four men in a group, all wearing what Raisa recognized as the post-independence outfit of the Azeri KGB. They emerged from the doors on the third level and climbed up to the open roof, each carrying a small suitcase. Their heads had no sooner disappeared from view than the reason for their presence filled the air – a Mil Mi-8 'Hip' was approaching from the west. The helicopter loomed briefly above A rig before setting down on the elevated helipad, some two hundred metres away on the far side of the structure. About a dozen passengers climbed out, all carrying personal bags.

Several were women, and at least two of the men were of Slavic appearance.

These arrivals had all disappeared from view by the time the four KGB men reappeared. The latter helped the crew unload some boxes and then clambered aboard. Minutes later the helicopter was airborne again, the drone of its passage fading into the west.

Another hour had passed – it was now almost two in the afternoon – when Raisa suddenly tugged at Finn's arm and handed him the binoculars. 'Third-level doors,' she said.

A woman in a red skirt and blue sweater was leaning against the railing and smoking a cigarette, her medium-length blonde hair twisting in the breeze. A man was with her, also smoking; the two of them were laughing at something, and there was more than a suggestion of intimacy in the way they stood together.

'That's Farida Shadmanova,' Raisa whispered.

'With her husband?'

'No, that's not Tamarlan.' She felt angry with the woman for deceiving her husband so openly, and angry with herself for having such a ridiculous reaction.

'The plot sickens,' Finn murmured beside her.

13

As Madonna crooned *Bedtime Stories* in his ear, Uday al-Dulaini stared stony-faced out of the helicopter window. The light was already fading, and the sea some hundred metres below seemed to be covered in oil. Maybe it was – the way the Azeris talked you could be forgiven for thinking that they had discovered the stuff.

Their flight had been six hours late arriving in Baku, thanks in large part to a long delay in Kiev. As the crow flew it was about eight hundred kilometres from Baghdad to Baku, but the roundabout route dictated by Iraqi's pariah status had now consumed twenty hours of his and Barzan's time, eating deep into Uday's already depleted resources of tolerance. On more than one occasion during the journey he had found himself questioning the wisdom of Saddam's continued defiance of the Americans and their cronies. The Iraqi leader had guts all right, but then so had a bullock. And maybe it was time for the regime to start cutting its losses, get the oil revenue flowing back in and start teaching its internal enemies a few overdue lessons in obedience.

Uday could now see the Aliyev rig up ahead, its windows flashing gold in the late-afternoon sun. Maybe this project would shift the balance of power back towards Iraq, but there was always the danger that Saddam's bluff would be called, and the country would end up an irradiated desert. If that were to happen, Uday planned to be a distant spectator. Like many of his Mukhabarat colleagues he already had money stashed away in Switzerland for what the English – who had never known a real water shortage in their lives – liked to call a rainy day.

His thoughts turned to Salam Muhammad. The man might be a brilliant nuclear scientist, but his refusal to work showed a remarkable lack of intelligence. Uday was looking forward to the look on his face when he saw the family memento which they had brought to show him.

The helicopter was hovering just above the landing pad now, and he could see the rig's security chief waiting to one side, holding his cap to his head against the wind generated by the rotor blades. 'What's his name?' he asked Barzan.

'Vezirov,' was the answer.

'Why don't the Azeris get rid of their Russian names?' Uday wondered out loud.

Barzan just shrugged.

The Russian pilot brought them down gently, the co-pilot swung the doors open and the two Iraqis jumped nimbly down on to the tarmac. Vezirov waited for them outside the radius of the still whirring blades, a smile of greeting on his face, mixed emotions in his heart. He was glad someone else had been given the job of sorting out the recalcitrant scientist, but not overwhelmed with joy at the prospect of sharing either his authority or his rig with these two men. On the occasion of their last visit the senior of the two had probably raped an Azeri technician – she had claimed as much, while he had been apparently unable to grasp the concept – and only a judicious mix of threats, appeals to national interest and financial compensation had prevented her colleagues from taking some sort of collective action. For that reason this visit had been designed as a day-trip, but the lateness of the Iraqis' arrival presumably implied a change of plan.

Vezirov asked as much.

Uday smiled at the Azeri, knowing exactly what was on his mind. 'We don't want any repetition of Salam's behaviour, so I will be talking to all our people, reminding them of their duties.' He smiled again. 'And of the consequences of any failure to discharge them. So yes, we shall have to stay overnight.'

'In that case I will show you to the rooms we have set aside,' Vezirov said. 'They are not luxurious, but . . .' He shrugged.

'I remember,' Uday said.

They took the lift down through three floors, emerging into a cream-coloured corridor. The two rooms were small but clean, adequately rather than lavishly furnished, with a single square window looking south across the Caspian.

Uday left his briefcase on the bed and turned to Vezirov. 'The earlier I see Salam the longer the others will have to consider his punishment,' he said.

'You can use my office,' Vezirov offered.

'No, I will see our people in their own rooms. I want them to remember this visit.' Uday smiled. 'And then perhaps I will not have to make this journey again.'

Vezirov nodded. 'I will take you to Salam Muhammad.' He had to admit, at least to himself, that he was curious to see how the Mukhabarat man intended convincing the young scientist of the error of his ways.

Five minutes later he found out. As Salam looked up defiantly from the bed on which he was sitting, Uday asked him if he would recognize his sister's wedding ring.

The scientist looked up, fear and suspicion in his eyes. 'My sister has nothing to do with this,' he said, but his tone lacked conviction.

'Every Iraqi citizen has a duty to assist the state,' Uday contradicted him. He nodded at Barzan, who removed the small box from his pocket, and handed it to the scientist.

The wedding ring was inside, still on the finger. Salam stared at it in disbelief, his mouth hanging open.

'There are no more rings,' Uday said, 'but you will receive another finger for each day you refuse to work.'

A silence lasting several seconds was eventually broken by Salam. 'I will work,' he whispered.

In the OP on B rig McClure had spent the hour since the helicopter's arrival hoping in vain for its departure. Its presence overnight on the helipad posed one more problem in an operation already overflowing with them. The gradual clearing of the sky that afternoon, though half-expected, had also been thoroughly unwelcome. Now they would have to deal with lunar light, albeit only the faint glow of a crescent moon, for the first few hours of darkness.

The helicopter had brought more than problems, though. It had also delivered two men, at least one of whom was an Iraqi. McClure had recognized the face from the MI6 gallery of senior Mukhabarat operatives which they had studied in Poole, and had had the quickness of thought to capture it on film while the two arrivals were being given the red-carpet treatment on the helipad. If by some miracle the SBS operation failed to turn up anything else, that one photo should go some way towards substantiating Constantine's theory; far enough at least to set some alarm bells ringing through the various NATO defence ministries.

But McClure intended to go home with much more than that.

The prime objective was Shadmanov, with or without his agreement, and with or without his wife. If they failed to find the Azeri scientist, then they were to gather what photographic evidence they could of the rig's work areas before leaving for the rendezvous with the Sea King on Narghin Island. Whatever happened, they would have to move fast and think on their feet, hopeful of escaping detection but ready to deal with any unwelcome interference.

As he watched the last of the daylight drain from the western sky, McClure couldn't help thinking that it had all the makings of an interesting night.

He looked round at the others. Finn was busy keeping watch, now exchanging the nightscope for the binoculars, but the other two were simply sitting with their backs against a pile of flooring sections, the tension obvious in their faces. McClure decided it might be a good time for a team meeting.

'OK,' he said softly, 'let's talk about this party we've been invited to. Finn, you'd better join the rest of us.'

'And miss the excitement of watching someone take a fag break?' He gently laid the nightscope down and crawled across to complete the small circle.

'Right,' McClure began. 'Since the plan of action was worked out before we left England, the first thing we should ask ourselves is what we've learnt since we got here, and what changes, if any, we ought to make.' He looked at each of the faces inviting participation.

'There are less security guards than we expected,' Finn offered, 'and about half of them look like Russians. If someone would lend us a uniform we could probably get away with impersonating one.'

'Raisa was right about the lab coats,' Noonan said. 'And we don't even need to borrow them.'

'None of which . . .' McClure began.

'One other thing,' Noonan said doggedly. 'That bunch who arrived on the chopper this morning. They might be just a returning shift, but they could be new recruits. They could be new faces to the people already here.'

'Good point,' McClure agreed, impressed by the younger man's acumen. 'Anything else?'

'The chopper itself,' Finn said bluntly. 'If the balloon goes up they could use it to track us, which will be trouble. Against that, sending someone all the way to the helipad to disable the fucking thing seems like an invitation to disaster. That would double the chances of someone being seen and mean splitting us into three groups rather than two, which seems like pushing it.'

McClure worked his way through Finn's argument, and decided he agreed. The helipad was just too far away – both in metres and their knowledge of the ground – for the precise coordination and timing an operation like this required. He didn't like it one little bit, but when all was said and done the risks involved in taking action against the wretched chopper seemed greater than those involved in ignoring its existence. 'Agreed,' he said reluctantly, turning to Noonan for a show of male unanimity.

'Yeah,' the third man said. He wasn't sure he did

agree, but he certainly didn't feel strongly enough either way to start an argument with his two more experienced comrades.

'The other new item is the moon,' McClure said. 'We knew it was a possibility, but this morning it looked like we might get away with another blackout.'

'It's kind of lovely,' Finn said with a smile.

'Yeah. So lovely, I think we might give ourselves another hour to watch it set.'

Finn looked up sharply. 'The Sea King can't leave any later and still make it back before dawn.'

'I know.'

'So we'll have to cut our own time margin to almost zero,' Finn persisted.

'I think it's worth the risk. We'll still have time to turn the Sea King round if we come up empty. And we built plenty of margin into the original plan. I reckon we'll still be twiddling our thumbs on Narghin for at least half an hour before they arrive.'

'You could be right,' Finn admitted. 'And you're the boss,' he added with a grin.

'There is one other thing we learn,' Raisa said unexpectedly.

They all looked at her.

'Farida Shadmanova has a lover,' she said simply. 'If she is with Tamarlan she may not wish to come, and if she is not, then he may not be willing to leave her. We have ten minutes to argue with them, right? Maybe we need more.'

'Maybe,' McClure murmured. This was the part, the only part, of the operation which filled him with foreboding, because it seemed utterly impossible to predict how the parties concerned would react. The team's orders were to bring Shadmanov out, voluntarily if possible, by force if necessary. If he said yes and his wife said no, then she was to be rendered incapable, one way or another, of raising the alarm. How Shadmanov would react to his wife being left bound and gagged was anybody's guess, but then again, given the nature of their relationship, there was always the possibility that even if she wanted to go he would insist on her being left behind. Raisa's presence would provide yet another emotional twist to an already overburdened situation, but was necessary both for gaining the scientist's confidence and for handling any linguistic crises encountered *en route* to the living quarters. It had occurred to the SBS man more than once that an assumption of non-cooperation on the part of both husband and wife would have considerably simplified the whole mission. 'But ten minutes is all we'll have,' he added. 'And it'll have to be enough.'

He looked at his watch. It was ten to six. 'Get on the radio,' he told Noonan, 'and tell Galloway we're going into action an hour later than planned. If he wants to know why, tell him.'

Tamarlan Shadmanov found it hard to take his eyes from the table on the other side of the canteen at which Azad Vezirov was sitting with the two Iraqi security men. The story of the gift they had brought for Salam Muhammad had already reached every waking ear on the rig, and, as far as the Iraqi contingent was concerned, had no doubt created an instant upsurge in loyalty to their master in distant Baghdad. Shadmanov couldn't help wondering what sort of people encouraged loyalty in a late-twentieth-century nuclear weapons facility by mutilation of the workers' relatives. The two Iraqis looked like normal people. They didn't have horns or fangs or yellow eyes.

One of the uniformed Azeri security men was walking towards the Shadmanovs' table. To Tamarlan's surprise he stopped and gave Farida a slight bow. There was a half smile playing about his lips, and they seemed to curl with faint contempt as he acknowledged Shadmanov's presence with a curt 'Professor'.

So this was his wife's latest, the scientist thought, ignoring the man. He idly wondered whether they had yet consummated the affair and decided that they had probably not. Farida, as he knew from personal experience, derived a great deal more pleasure from expectation than reality – she loved seduction but she didn't much like sex.

It was none of his business, really. He turned his attention back to the far table, and spent the next minute watching Vezirov's face. The KGB man obviously neither liked nor felt comfortable with his Iraqi counterparts, but he was just as clearly fascinated by them. He would be repelled by the Third World savagery, the scientist thought, but despite himself he would also be attracted by the directness and panache of its expression.

Shadmanov suddenly felt sickened by the whole business. He turned to his wife, who was blowing smoke towards the ceiling. 'I'm going to our room,' he told her. 'Are you coming?'

'Not yet. You're only going to pick up a book and read, aren't you? I'll watch TV in the rec room for a while.' She forced a smile. 'I might even find someone who actually wants to talk to me.'

'I'll see you later then,' he said equably.

*　　*　　*

On the tarmac at Dogubayazit Major Galloway stood beside the bright-yellow Sea King HAR Mk3, hugging himself tightly as the RAF crew went through their final checks. On a clear spring night at almost two thousand metres above sea level it was bitterly cold, and the beauty of the world around him offered only partial compensation for the SBS man's fears of incipient frostbite. Here, six hundred and fifty kilometres to the west of the Aliyev rig, the crescent moon was yet to dip below the horizon, and the snow-covered peaks of Mount Ararat were shining with pale-white fire.

Looking round, Galloway could see no sign of other life on the NATO base. The Americans were minding their own business – while keeping warm – inside the dimly lit base buildings, and the local Turkish military were apparently all away on leave that night. More than a few palms had been crossed with dollars, and the official rumour – that a stupid British journalist with very influential friends had managed to get himself marooned in the Armenian enclave of Nagorno-Karabakh – had been more or less taken for the truth, even before the unarmed RAF Rescue helicopter had arrived to provide further confirmation. The British might be acting illegally, but there was no conflict with the national interests of Turkey, and every opportunity for a few Turkish officers to profit from turning a blind eye to what was, after all, an obviously humanitarian endeavour.

Fortunately, no one had seemed to notice the external fuel tanks which the Sea King was now carrying, and which were needed only because the long return journey to the Caspian was beyond the helicopter's normal operational range.

It was 22.28 Turkish time, and the crew of four had finished their checks. The captain gave Galloway the thumbs up, and the SBS man retreated a few paces as the rotor blades hit a higher note and sharpened the cold wind on his cheeks. Part of him wished he was going along, but there was no good reason why he should – the Sea King crew could find Narghin better than he could, and once there would either pick up the waiting party immediately, or wait the agreed ten minutes before leaving without them. There would be no hanging around on Azeri soil.

The helicopter lifted off, hovered for an instant above the tarmac, and then moved away on a course that would take it just to the south of the lesser Ararat. The crescent moon was no longer visible in the sky, but its light was still shining in the distant snowfields, and despite the cold Galloway stood for a minute or more watching the silhouette of the Sea King dwindle into a speck against the beautiful backdrop.

It was twenty to eleven when he got back to the warmth of the radio room, and interrupted the Americans' card game to send confirmation that the team's transport was on the way. The Yanks good-naturedly invited him to join their game but he declined, knowing that his mind would be elsewhere. In another fifteen minutes McClure and the others would be leaving their OP on the smaller rig and going off in search of the Azeri scientist. And half an hour after that he would receive one of three messages: 'Gold' would mean that they and Shadmanov were on their way to Narghin; 'Silver' that they were heading for the island without him; 'Bronze' that something had gone badly wrong and they wouldn't be able to make the rendezvous.

In the last case Galloway would have to recall the Sea King and try again on the following night, always assuming the SBS team could reach the island by then. Not surprisingly, 'Bronze' wasn't the signal he wanted to hear.

The four-person team on B rig had spent a busy couple of hours. Soon after ten the moon had gone down behind A rig, throwing the sea beneath its twin into deep shadow, and providing Noonan and Finn with the cover they needed to reinflate and reload the two Geminis. At 23.40 hours they had received word from Galloway that the Sea King was *en route*, and now, with the last few seconds of the day ticking away, they sat in the dark waiting for McClure to give the green light.

'Let's go,' he decided, jumping the gun by ten seconds.

'Good luck,' Noonan said. He was staying behind in the OP, partly to warn them of accidental encounters on the steps opposite, partly because a group of four seemed a little on the conspicuous side. And there was always the chance that the threesome would be captured, leaving Noonan to escape alone with the evidence they had already accumulated.

According to the plan, they had ten minutes to reach Shadmanov's room, ten to persuade him and his wife to accompany them, and ten more to retrace their steps. If by some mischance the man was not home at ten past midnight, they would use the ten minutes allotted for persuasion to return by way of the research labs, or at least by way of that area which they believed housed the research labs. If they drew a blank but had not been spotted, McClure had the option of turning the

Sea King round, camping out on B rig for another day and going through the whole thing again the following night.

The prospect of hauling all their gear back up to the fourth level was hardly an appealing one, Finn thought, as the three of them made their way down through the deserted rig to the bridge level. The walkway itself was deep in shadow, and the water lapping at the rig supports covered the slight noise of their footfalls on the metal grating. Once across, in the shadow of the unused doorway, they unrolled and put on their white lab coats.

'All clear,' Noonan's voice sounded in their earpieces.

McClure led the way up the steps and in through the doors on the second level. There was no one in the corridor, but once inside they could hear a loudish thumping noise somewhere up ahead. They walked on past several empty rooms – this part of the facility, which was used for tool and material storage on Tempest Alpha, was no doubt surplus to current requirements on Aliyev A.

The next set of doors, which on the North Sea rig led out on to a catwalk above one of the refinery halls, here opened to reveal a huge chamber, empty save for some eight or ten men in the throes of an indoor game of football. White paint had been used to create goals on opposing walls and pitch markings on the concrete floor. The thumping noise they had heard was the ball bouncing off the metal walls.

Intent on their game, the players didn't look up as the threesome passed above them.

Another pair of doors brought them to a junction of corridors. Following his mental map of Tempest Alpha,

McClure turned left, just as a door some twenty metres in front of them swung open. A man emerged, took one look at them without breaking stride, and walked away up the corridor. So far, at least, their rough disguise was working.

The man soon turned right and they followed him, up a short flight of steps, across a short bridge between buildings, and in through yet more double doors. The air was suddenly warmer here – they had reached a section of the rig in regular use. Voices could be heard now, and the next flight of steps brought them up to the highest level of the accommodation area.

McClure took a deep breath, turned the final corner, and found himself looking in through the open doorway of a large recreation room. There were about twenty people inside, all with their heads turned towards the large TV on the far side of the room.

McClure gave Raisa a questioning look, and she did a quick survey of the heads in front of her. None of them belonged to Shadmanov, whom she knew had always hated TV. 'No,' she said.

One woman had left her chair, apparently sated for the night. Raisa glanced at McClure, who gave her a slight nod, and once the woman was out in the corridor asked her in Azeri if she knew where Tamarlan Shadmanov's room was. 'We're old friends from Baku,' Raisa explained.

The woman looked at them blankly. 'No,' she decided. 'There's a list in the office next door,' she added, looking at Finn.

She was a bit on the old side, the SBS man thought. Still quite sexy though.

'Thanks,' Raisa told her.

The office was open, the list on the wall. The Shadmanovs were in 311, two levels below.

They were still on a roll, Finn thought, as the three of them descended the stairs. The lift had been open and waiting, but McClure had decided that using it would be tempting fate. As far as he knew no special forces mission had ever ended up stuck in one, and he didn't want to be remembered as the leader of the first.

According to his watch two minutes remained of the first ten.

Once his three comrades had disappeared inside the towering bulk of A rig, Noonan had been left with little to do but watch, wait and listen to McClure's sporadic updates on the other three's progress. About seven minutes had passed when the couple emerged from the double doors on the fourth level and started down the catwalk stairs. He didn't pay them too much mind at first, fully expecting them to re-enter the interior, as ninety-five per cent of their colleagues had done, on the third level. When they continued on down towards the second he made ready to warn the team of the impending encounter, but still wasn't feeling any great cause for concern. It was only when they reached the first level that he realized, with a lump in his throat, just where they were headed.

McClure and Noonan's discovery of the used condoms flashed through his mind, and suddenly he could see guilt in the way the two of them seemed to keep glancing over their shoulders, as if they were expecting to be followed. Crossing the bridge, they even made sure to keep in the shadows, just as the SBS team had done.

What if they came up? What could he do?

Then again, if they stayed on the first level they were bound to see or hear the team *en route* to the Geminis below.

A growing sense of panic seemed to grip Noonan's heart as he realized that the mission might depend on his killing these two people in cold blood. He fought it back and, with a supreme effort, managed to keep his voice steady as he reported the problem to McClure: 'Two intruders have just crossed the bridge on to B rig. Looks like they're in search of somewhere private to fuck.'

The group on A rig were on the stairs between the second and third levels. Hearing Noonan's news McClure stopped the party of three in its tracks. 'Courting couple just crossed the bridge,' he told Finn and Raisa. 'Where are they now?' he asked Noonan.

'Somewhere below.'

'Find them and report back,' McClure told him. He turned to the others: 'OK, let's go.'

He led them down to the third level, and up the corridor to the room in question, inwardly praying that Shadmanov would be at home. There was no noise coming from inside, and Raisa had the sudden premonition that they would interrupt Tamarlan and his wife making love.

McClure rapped softly on the door.

There was a noise like a chair being moved, and an irritated male voice asked, 'Who is it?'

Raisa nodded yes to McClure's unstated question. It was him.

The door swung open. Shadmanov's mouth dropped open when he saw Raisa, and seemed to bounce shut at the sight of those accompanying her. As rehearsed, she pushed forward, forcing him back and allowing the two SBS men to get in and close the door behind them.

'What . . . ?' Shadmanov exclaimed, his eyes moving swiftly to and fro between visitors. The open book face down on the small sofa and the half-empty glass of spirits on the adjacent table suggested he had been reading with a nightcap. The room seemed full of female clothes, but there was no sign of Farida.

Raisa took the bull by the horns – another ludicrous English expression she had learnt from Finn. 'Tamarlan,' she said in Azeri, 'these are English soldiers. They have come to rescue you and take you back to England.'

He looked at her as if she was speaking gibberish. 'But what are you . . . how did you get here?'

'We flew from Turkey last night. We were dropped by parachute into the sea and spent the day hidden on the other rig.'

'You were dropped by parachute?' He couldn't believe it, and yet he could see it in her face. It had only been a few weeks, and there was a different person behind the eyes.

'I got your message – the end of the rainbow.' She smiled, hoping to put him more at ease. 'We don't have a lot of time,' she added.

'But I can't . . .'

'Where is your wife?' she asked.

He shrugged, and gave her a glimpse of the rueful smile she remembered. 'With her latest boyfriend, I expect.' He looked at her hopelessly. I can't just leave, not . . .' He shook his head.

'You don't want to do this work?'

'No, of course not.'

'Then what holds you here?'

'Nothing, I suppose.' He tried to get a clearer grasp of what was happening, but it seemed impossible. How could he be expected to abandon the country of his birth and his wife of thirty years at five minutes' notice.

'What's happening?' McClure asked Raisa. She lifted a hand to ask for patience, and turned back to Shadmanov. 'We cannot wait long,' she said calmly. She didn't want to threaten him, knowing from long experience that threats only forced him back into his shell. But unless he grasped what was happening in the next couple of minutes they would have to knock him out, which would suit no one. He wouldn't enjoy the experience, and they would have to bluff their way back to B rig with an unconscious body in tow.

'I can't,' Shadmanov said. He didn't know why, but he just couldn't leave Farida there.

Raisa played her only trump. 'Your friend Arif is dead,' she told him. 'He was murdered by the KGB for trying to find out what happened to you. I think you owe him something.'

He seemed to age in front of her eyes, but before he could say anything footsteps suddenly became audible in the corridor outside.

The door swung open to reveal his wife. 'What a picture,' she began with a malicious smile. 'I . . .' The door clicked shut, and her voice died away as she became aware of the two armed SBS men.

Farida was wearing a man's shirt, jeans and two-inch heels. She didn't look like a woman in her late forties, Raisa thought as she told Shadmanov, 'Explain the situation to her. She can come too. This is not about us,' she added, seeing the surprised look on his face.

Shadmanov told his wife what was happening. She listened more calmly than he had, her eyes flicking across Raisa's face and those of the two British soldiers as surprise and disbelief gave way to calculation. The West, she thought – these people are offering us emigration to the West. The very fact of their presence here was proof enough of her husband's importance to them. They could look forward to a good life in England or America.

And by the same token, it seemed unlikely that such men would be sent so far to take no for an answer. Her husband was going whether he wanted to or not. If he refused they would take him by force, and then they would have to leave her behind, immobilized at best, dead at worst.

'How are we going to get to England?' she asked Raisa.

'There are boats waiting to take us to an island nearby. We will be picked up by a helicopter from there in' – she looked at her watch – 'just over two hours. We will reach Turkey before daybreak.'

'We shall come with you,' Farida said.

'Good,' Raisa said. 'They are coming,' she told McClure and Finn. 'How long have we got? They need to change.'

McClure exhaled noisily. 'Two minutes at most.'

'You have a minute to get some warm clothes on,' Raisa told the two Azeris. 'You'll need flat shoes,' she added to Farida.

'Can we bring anything?'

'No.'

A minute later they were as suitably attired as time would allow. As Shadmanov pulled on a lab coat over his jacket, his wife found time to empty her jewellery box into one of her pockets.

'We're on our way,' McClure told Noonan.

14

Some fifteen minutes earlier Noonan had started down through B rig's four levels, ears straining for sounds of the intruders. He heard nothing until he reached the second floor, and then it was a giggle from further below. They were in the worst possible place, between the SBS and their transport home.

He sought for a better fix on their position, waiting until he heard a slight human noise above the lapping sea and then moving towards it, careful not to make any noise of his own. Finally he could see them through the metal grating floor, standing arm in arm against the railing at the farthest point from the bridge, the open sea behind them.

Actually, only the man was standing. Her legs were off the ground, her body arched backwards across the top railing, riding the rhythmic thrusts he was making inside her.

It might well be an adulterous fuck, Finn thought, but somehow the two lovers, their shadowy figures rocking to and fro above the black waters, seemed the picture of innocence. Watching the two of them filled Noonan with a longing for Julie, and he felt absurdly reluctant to interrupt, let alone end their lives.

As this thought passed through his brain the woman's back suddenly arched in spasm, and a low groan shook the man's frame. For a few seconds they seemed almost to leave the ground, and then she was limply clinging on to him, and he was muttering something, hopefully an endearment, in whatever language it was they spoke.

There was no way he could shoot them, none at all, but they showed no sign of leaving voluntarily. He looked at his watch, discovered that he had less than ten minutes, then laughed to himself at the obvious solution. Their presence below suggested their love was illicit, so what better incentive to move could he offer than the fear of discovery? He had been trying to keep quiet when noise was all that was required.

Noonan retreated to the ladder which led up to the third level, climbed a couple of rungs and then let himself down with a slight bang. Then he walked heavily across the metal floor, talking to an imaginary partner in a language that he invented on the spot. With any luck the Azeris would assume it was Iraqi, or, if they were Iraqis, Azeri. Or something.

After twenty or so seconds he stopped talking, and heard whispers below. They were not by the rail any more, but they seemed to be moving towards the bridge. A few seconds later he could see them, crossing the bridge with anxious glances over their shoulders.

Noonan climbed back up towards the OP, a huge sense of relief flooding his being. He was on the last ladder when McClure came through the earpiece to tell him they were starting back. 'It's all clear,' he replied. 'The love-birds have left.'

They reached the door without meeting anyone, crossed over the narrow bridge between buildings and started down the corridor on which they had seen the man emerging from a room. This time it was empty.

But once through the next double doors they could hear the game of football still underway, despite the lateness of the hour. 'Maybe it's Azerbaijan's World Cup Squad,' Finn murmured to himself.

The group emerged on to the walkway above the refinery hall just as two uniformed men came through the opposite doors some forty metres away. 'Start talking to me in Azeri,' McClure murmured to Raisa, and she obliged, launching into a monologue about the first thing which came to mind – the cat she had owned as a child.

The distance between the two parties narrowed to about twenty metres when one of the security men remembered why he was being paid. 'You can't go out this way,' he shouted.

'He says we can't go out this way,' Raisa translated.

McClure's mind whirled, taking in all the relevant data: the lack of an alternative route which didn't involve a long and dangerous detour back through the accommodation block, the security men's holstered side-arms, the Browning he was holding in the lab coat pocket, the potential witnesses playing football beneath their feet.

What he didn't expect was input from Farida, who was now angrily arguing with the two security men. 'We always go this way,' she was claiming, 'and what difference does it make to anyone? We only want some fresh air!'

McClure didn't understand a word she was saying, but he could see the effect – the man who had spoken was now beginning to shrug his acquiescence.

His partner, though, seemed increasingly interested in their faces, and as he murmured something to the other man his hand was fiddling with the fastening on the leather holster.

There was no more time to argue, no bluff left to call. 'Take them out,' McClure snapped, sliding his Browning free of the pocket, bracing his legs and taking two-handed aim. The silenced gun coughed twice and the security man slumped to his knees. A split-second later Finn opened fire, hurling the other man backwards with three shots to the chest.

For a moment the only sound in the vast hall was the fading bounce of a ball on concrete.

On the makeshift pitch below the players had stopped, their faces turned upwards, some with a questioning look, others with the horror of knowledge. Behind the two SBS men the Shadmanovs seemed struck dumb by surprise, and Raisa's eyes, always large, now seemed intent on colonizing the rest of her face.

Cursing under his breath, McClure urged them all forward. 'The balloon's gone up,' he told Noonan tersely. 'Get down to the water.'

Their brisk walk had turned into a jog. Even more speed might have been advisable, but McClure had no idea how fit the Shadmanovs were, and he didn't think it was worth risking a coronary or a fall for a few extra seconds.

They reached the last doors. He leaned out, half expecting to hear running feet on the catwalks above, but there was only silence, and no one in sight. Any minute now, he thought, as they started across the bridge, and right on cue an alarm bell started ringing somewhere on the rig behind them. Almost instantly a klaxon joined in, as if eager not to miss a rare opportunity to show its worth.

Having readied the caving ladder Noonan was waiting by the rail, half convinced that he could still smell the vanished couple's passion in the air. The two Geminis were only just visible in the water twenty metres below.

'You first,' McClure told him. 'Then you,' he told Finn.

Bell and klaxon continued with their harmonizing, but there was still no indication that the intruders' whereabouts had been pinpointed by human agency.

The Shadmanovs, still pale from the shock of the catwalk encounter, were not eyeing the ladder with much enthusiasm. 'Can they manage it?' McClure asked Raisa. If not, they would have to be dropped into the sea and then recovered.

Perhaps they realized as much, or perhaps being asked simply stung their pride. Tamarlan went first, going down with a nimbleness which surprised McClure until he remembered that the man was an inveterate hiker. His wife needed help getting across the rail, but once on the ladder itself managed to descend at a surprisingly good pace. Even so, McClure was pleased the two of them wouldn't be required to do much more than keep a seat warm for the rest of the trip.

Raisa went down rather faster, using the natural agility which she had honed through hours of practice in the Akrotiri gym, and joined Farida and Finn in one Gemini. McClure took one last look at the empty bridge and followed, joining Noonan and the scientist in the other.

There was still no sign of pursuit, no sound of rotors warming on the helipad. The sky, though moonless, was much too clear for comfort, with the Milky Way stretching like a pale fluorescent band across the sky. The klaxon and bell would drown out the sound of the outboard motors, but was it possible they could get away without being seen?

'Straight out,' McClure decided. 'Keeping B rig between us and them.'

The two silenced outboards purred into action, and Noonan curved the first Gemini away from its mooring at the base of the rig and out into open water. Finn followed with the second, some twenty metres adrift. They were about half a kilometre away when first the klaxon and the bell cut out in quick succession. At the same moment the top of A rig came into view above B, the sound of whirring rotors reached across the water, and the Mi-8 lifted off the distant helipad.

Four hundred kilometres to the west the RAF Sea King had crossed the official border between the warring states of Armenia and Azerbaijan, and was now contour-hopping at an average height of two hundred metres above the disputed enclave of Nagorno-Karabakh.

'It looks quiet,' Eddi Barton's co-pilot, Geoff Johnston, observed, staring down at the dark hills and valleys flashing by beneath them.

'Quiet as a fucking grave,' Barton agreed.

The co-pilot grunted, and reached for the almost empty bag of authentic Turkish Delight which was on the floor between his feet. 'There hasn't been any fighting for a few months, has there?'

'Not that anyone bothered to report. And stop hogging the Turkish Delight.'

'Dead right,' the navigator agreed, abandoning his

seat for a moment to grab the bag out of the co-pilot's hand.

'They've probably just run out of ammo,' Barton said cynically. 'Or volunteers. There's . . .'

He was cut short by Kevin Heywood, who had just spotted activity on the MEL search radar screen, and exclaimed, 'Jesus, they're missiles!'

Barton swung the Sea King violently down and to the right as Johnston half shouted into his mike, 'Home base. We are under fire. Attempting . . .'

It was almost the last thing he ever said. One of the two shoulder-launched SAM-7s lanced into the Sea King's tail section, spinning it out of control and down towards the dark ground.

'Oh shit,' the co-pilot murmured, and then there was silence.

In the lead Gemini McClure was watching the Azeri helicopter draw a second, wider, search circle around the rig. They were almost two kilometres away now, and it was probably time to start drawing the wide circle needed to get them on course for Narghin Island, but the SBS man hesitated. Another kilometre might make all the difference.

It did. The Mi-8 pilot might have seen them or simply made a lucky guess, but whatever the reason he abruptly swung out of his circling pattern and on to a pursuit course.

'Cut the engine,' McClure rapped out, and as Noonan obliged he reached for the M16 with its mounted M203 grenade-launcher, his head full of mental arithmetic. The helicopter was about a kilometre away now, and closing at the rate of about fifty metres per second. Which meant that in about ten seconds it would be inside the M203's maximum effective range of three hundred and fifty metres.

McClure breech-loaded the grenade and raised the combined weapon to his shoulder, counting on the dark sea behind him not to offer the pilot a warning silhouette. In the other Gemini Finn had also loaded up, which doubled their chances of a hit. For what seemed an eternity – but was about six seconds – they sat waiting and watching as the dark shape of the Mi-8 grew larger against the starry sky, trying to judge the range.

Three-fifty, three-twenty-five, three hundred. 'Keep coming,' McClure murmured. Two-seventy-five, two-fifty. It was slowing down, beginning to turn away, offering the chance of a broadside. 'Now,' McClure snapped, and the two Hilton HG40 grenades left the launcher at seventy-five metres per second.

One second, two seconds, three seconds, four . . .

One of the two grenades exploded just behind the helicopter's cockpit, only to be outdone a split second later by the detonation of the adjacent fuel tank. As the fireball reached for the stars the disembowelled remains fell to the sea, leaving only scattered puddles of burning oil to briefly flare, splutter and go out.

'Let's go!' McClure shouted at Noonan. 'Narghin,' he added, indicating with his arm that it was now time to correct their course. The younger man revved the engine and they were on the move again, drawing a wide circle towards the south and east. The rig was now no more than a distant silhouette; both sea and sky seemed empty of pursuit.

McClure did more mental arithmetic. The nearest naval base was just outside Baku, some thirty kilometres distant, the nearest airbase farther still, on the peninsula behind the city. Even if they could get a helicopter in the air within fifteen minutes – which would be pushing it – they would still be ten minutes' flying time away, and in twenty-five minutes they would be well over halfway to Narghin. And nothing he had seen on the Aliyev rig led McClure to believe that those in charge of security would be able to act quickly and efficiently in a crisis. It was beginning to look as if they were home and dry.

In the radio room at Dogubayazit airbase Galloway sat for several seconds with both hands cupping his mouth and nose, trying to digest the news of the Sea King's destruction.

'What's up?' one of the card-playing Americans asked.

'The helicopter's been shot down,' he told them.

'Jesus Christ! Who the fuck by?'

Galloway shook his head. 'God only knows. I can't believe a plane . . . but our best information was that there were no SAMs on the ground. There hasn't been a helicopter shot down over the enclave since 1989.'

The Americans looked at him sympathetically, cards in hands. There was nothing they could do or say, and they knew it. All of them were thinking about the four Brits, with whom they'd been sharing a joke not three hours before.

Galloway rapped himself on the forehead with the knuckles of his left hand, as if he was trying to wake himself up. What was he going to tell the team in the Caspian? That they would have to hang on until another Sea King could be sent? What else could he tell them?

They were supposed to report in on arrival at Narghin, but the sooner they knew their transport had been delayed the more options they would have. He reached for the MIL/UST-1 unit, hoping that McClure would be in position to receive.

He was. 'Where are you?' was Galloway's first question.

'About fifteen Ks from Narghin,' was the answer.

'We have a problem,' Galloway went on, mentally adding 'Houston' to the sentence. It had been something of an understatement the first time round, but at least the Apollo had got back safely. 'Your ride home has been shot down, so you won't be collected tonight.'

'Can you repeat that?' McClure asked.

Galloway did so, adding that the attack had taken place over Nagorno-Karabakh.

'Jesus Christ,' was McClure's comment.

'What's your current situation?' Galloway asked. 'Is anyone aware that you're out there?'

'Yeah,' McClure said, 'we had to take out a helicopter ourselves.'

Galloway's heart sank.

'We're in the clear for the moment,' McClure went on, 'but I reckon in an hour or so they'll be all over the place.'

'Narghin should be as good a place to lie low as anywhere. I'll talk to you again in an hour.'

'OK, boss,' McClure said, a slight smile playing on his lips.

Noonan had worked in close proximity to the man for about three months now, and had a bad feeling about that smile. 'Trouble, boss?' he shouted above the purr of the outboard.

McClure's smile broadened. 'Yeah,' he said, nodding his head meaningfully in Shadmanov's direction, 'but let's keep it to ourselves till we reach Narghin, OK?'

Noonan acquiesced, his mind racing through possibilities. It had to be the Sea King, but he didn't see how . . . Unless . . .

A shiver of fear seemed to race up his spine, and his mouth was suddenly dry.

A few metres away in the Gemini's prow, McClure was wondering how the scientist and his wife were going to like the news that their rescue had sprung a large and dangerous leak.

Galloway's next satellite transmission was to Poole. Colhoun, summoned by the duty officer, listened in angry disbelief as his subordinate recounted the disaster which had befallen the Sea King and its crew, and the consequent marooning of the hunted SBS team for at least another twenty-four hours.

They agreed to talk again in an hour, once the team had reached Narghin. By then either or both of them might have something more constructive to suggest than simply hiding out and holding on, though neither was optimistic.

A twenty-four-hour wait would be bad enough in itself, Colhoun thought as he took the short walk back to his office, but things could easily take another turn for the worse. A lot depended on who had shot the Sea King down, and how eager they were to publicize their success. If the Turkish authorities got wind of how and where the Sea King had met its fate then there was every likelihood that they would forbid the use of the Dogubayazit base for a second attempt. And there were no other bases which could be used, so any hope of a military retrieval would disappear, leaving only the diplomatic option of bargaining the team's way out through one of the adjoining countries. That might be possible, always assuming the team wasn't first apprehended by the Azeri authorities, but Colhoun doubted whether any such deal could be extended to cover the Shadmanovs and Raisa.

And he wouldn't abandon her without a fight, Colhoun realized, pouring himself a generous glass of malt. She might have come to them for help, but she had been more than willing to put herself at risk in return, and he had come to both like and respect the woman.

The malt was the first good news he'd had that evening, smooth as a Tory's tongue and with rather more in the way of integrity. The second sip was sliding gently down his throat when it occurred to Colhoun that the point of the exercise was to talk to Shadmanov, and that if things took another turn for the worse the man might not be available for conversation on an indefinite basis.

David Constantine was watching TV when the phone rang – an American police drama which he couldn't quite find the energy to turn off. He thought about not answering, but as usual his sense of curiosity kicked in somewhere around the sixth ring. There was always the chance – admittedly a remote one – that one of his children had remembered him.

'Constantine? This is Neil Colhoun from Poole. I thought I'd skip the usual channels and ask you to come down here right away . . .'

'Has something gone wrong?' Constantine asked anxiously.

'Yes is the simple answer. They've got Shadmanov but the extraction helicopter has been shot down over Armenia. And since there's a better than even chance that the team will be caught before we can send another one in we need to ask Shadmanov what he knows by radio. And it seems to me you'd be the best person to put the questions.'

'Of course,' Constantine agreed, 'so what . . . ?'

'Just get ready,' Colhoun told him. 'I'll get a helicopter from Lakenheath to pick you up and bring you down. There must be somewhere they could land nearby?'

'The village green, I suppose,' Constantine said, a pleasant sense of expectation warring with his concern for Raisa. She really deserved better than this . . .

'Right, well, I'll get them to ring you for precise directions and timing.'

'Fine,' Constantine said, making a mental note to ask that the pilot not land in the cricket square. He didn't want to spend the next year apologizing to everyone else in the village.

RAF Lakenheath phoned ten minutes later, and an hour after that a Lynx was noisily setting down on the edge of the village green. So much for an anonymous retirement, Constantine thought as he ducked beneath the whirring rotors and climbed aboard. It seemed that half the village had tumbled out of the pub to watch the excitement.

It was almost a quarter to two when Noonan manoeuvred the leading Gemini alongside what remained of the landing dock. Narghin was slightly less than a kilometre in width, and about half as much again in length. According to Raisa's second-hand information, the island was little more than a bare, rocky outcrop, with a few stunted trees, patches of dry grass and the sprawling ruins of its former *raison d'être*. Almost fifty years had passed since its last use as a prison, but it was still restricted territory.

Some of the ruins were visible as they came in to dock, a line of irregular black silhouettes stretching into the distance. Just above them, the Pole Star hung in a depressingly clear sky.

Once they had pulled the two Geminis up on to the dock McClure told the rest of the team about the disaster which had befallen the Sea King.

'Are they all dead?' Finn asked.

'I don't know. Probably.'

'So what can we do now?' Raisa asked. She felt curiously detached, as if she had just been presented with an interesting problem.

'We hope they can send in another helicopter tomorrow night,' McClure said. 'In the meantime we need somewhere to hide during the day. While Paul gets the Geminis deflated and all the equipment ready for transport Finn will find us the perfect spot. Raisa, you'll have to look after our guests. Explain to them what's happened, and try to keep them calm. I'm going to talk to Galloway again.'

He picked up the satcom unit and walked on to the island proper. The ruined façades of two-storey buildings lined three sides of a large open space paved with cobblestones, and McClure set up the antenna in its centre, imagining the shackled prisoners who had paraded there in years long gone by.

Galloway had no fresh news. They still didn't know who had shot down the Sea King, or whether whoever it was would be seeking publicity for their kill. 'But as far as I'm concerned,' Galloway told McClure, 'we'll be trying again tomorrow night. How do you reckon your chances of remaining undiscovered for twenty-four hours?'

'Hard to say. The place looks full of potential hidey-holes, but I guess it depends on how thorough a search the locals can put together. We never did get those Azeri force estimates from the MoD.'

'No,' Galloway agreed. Now that the unspeakable had happened, the paucity of the information they had managed to gather about the area was rapidly becoming critical. The team knew what Raisa knew, and in those areas of which she was ignorant – which included just about everything to do with the police or military – they were all swimming in the dark. Still, it could have been a lot worse: they could have been there without her.

But the team's safety was not Galloway's only concern. Now that capture was a real possibility he needed to ask McClure what they had discovered during their last hours on the rig.

'We found Shadmanov,' McClure said, but even as the words left his lips he realized that, as far as he knew, Raisa hadn't actually asked the scientist what work he had been doing there. He had just assumed from Shadmanov's presence, and from his willingness to leave, that their suspicions had been validated.

Galloway had obviously assumed the same thing. 'Constantine is being flown down from Cambridge to Poole,' he said. 'When he gets there we'll hook him up with Shadmanov and Raisa, OK?

'Yeah.' After breaking the connection McClure walked back to the landing dock and called Raisa over to tell her as much, noting as he did so the depressed look on

Shadmanov's face, and the mixture of anger and fear on his wife's. 'They're not happy, I suppose?' he muttered.

'Will you be happy if you are them?' she asked tartly.

'No, I guess not,' McClure said, but couldn't help grinning as he did so. A voice inside his head was urging him to enjoy every last moment of this, because such a challenge would probably never present itself again. The sea in front of him might be empty, but it wouldn't be for long.

He turned his eyes inland just as Finn materialized out of the shadows and walked across the cobbled square towards them. 'I think I've found somewhere,' he said, and explained what.

'Let's have a look,' McClure said.

Ten minutes later they were all standing inside the ruins of a Russian Orthodox chapel. The interior had long since been gutted by either fire or some other natural disaster, but towers still stood at either end. The taller of the two was topped with a cluster of onion domes, one of which bore the additional weight of a stork's nest; the shorter, which had been stripped of any such previous adornment, offered a wide space beneath its broken ceiling. The spiral staircase which had once connected this space to the ground had long ago rotted away, leaving no simple means of access.

'Send the monkey up with a ladder?' Finn asked, grinning at Noonan.

'It looks good,' McClure admitted, 'but let's hold on a minute. We've still got almost four hours of darkness. Are we sure Narghin is our best bet for the day? How many other islands are there?'

The question was directed mostly at Raisa. 'There

are more than thirty within a fifty-kilometre radius of Baku,' she said, sounding like a tour guide. 'Most are bigger than Narghin. Not many people know of this place,' she added.

'The Azeri army must know about it,' Finn said.

'Maybe, but I am not sure. Look around,' she said. 'It is a long time since men come here.'

'What about the mainland?' McClure asked.

'It is possible. For fifty kilometres south of Baku there is a road and a railway and a pipeline by the shore, and behind them are farms and then hills. But it is open country – there are not many trees.'

'And then we'd either have to ask the RAF to pick us up from the mainland – which won't make us their flavour of the month – or make our way back here tomorrow night, which'll mean two long trips across an open sea,' Finn said.

McClure grunted. 'Yeah. We'll stay. Maybe we'll get lucky and the Azeris won't find out about the Sea King. If they think we're already gone they won't be trying so hard to find us.' He looked up at their home for the next twenty-four hours. Once they were up there it was going to feel like a trap, but then that would be true of any secure hiding-place, and they could hardly spend the coming day sunning themselves on the beach.

15

In the hours that followed the raising of the alarm on Aliyev A Azad Vezirov was a man under siege, distracted from his efforts to organize an effective search party by the need to fend off a barrage of critical questions from his superiors on the mainland and the scarcely veiled scorn of his Iraqi guests.

'We were told this place was escape-proof,' Uday growled when news of Shadmanov's departure reached him. 'First Salam, now this man . . .'

'This man did not escape – he was abducted,' Vezirov interjected, somehow managing to keep his voice calm.

'By whom?'

'We don't know yet. They were white Caucasians, but beyond that . . .' Vezirov had to admit that he wanted to know. Whoever these people were they had been good. The two security men on the second level had both been killed by more than one bullet to the heart, and the helicopter had been taken out at a range of three hundred metres, in the dark, most probably by a simple grenade-launcher. And then the intruders had simply vanished, presumably in the direction of home, wherever that might be.

They were either Americans or Armenians, Vezirov thought. Either the enemies of Iraq or the enemies of Azerbaijan.

Uday was certain that Iraq's number one enemy was responsible, but now that the intruders had made a clean escape from the rig he was beginning to fear that any chance of catching them had probably passed. As dawn approached both men were getting down to what they saw as the real business of the day, which was to protect themselves from the wrath of their political masters in Baku and Baghdad.

This effort proved premature. Soon after seven Vezirov's phone rang with the news that a British helicopter had been shot down soon after one in the morning by Azeri irregulars near the small town of Fizuli, and it didn't take the two men long to guess what its mission had been.

'They will have to wait at least a day for another rescue attempt,' Uday mused out loud. 'Where is this place the helicopter was shot down?'

The Azeri showed him on the wall map.

'So it must have flown from a Turkish airbase,' Uday said. 'And even if the British had permission – which I doubt – the Turkish government will not want anyone to know that they've been involved in military action against Azerbaijan, not after all the Pan-Turkic propaganda they've been putting out recently.' He smiled at Vezirov.

'So?' the Azeri asked.

'So an angry protest from your government – with perhaps the threat of taking the matter to the Security Council – should dissuade the Turks from sanctioning a second rescue attempt.'

Vezirov found himself reluctantly admiring the Iraqi's political acumen. 'There's one problem you're overlooking,' he said. 'These people have Shadmanov and they will be in radio contact with their own country. The secret is out.'

Uday was undismayed. 'They may know what we're doing here, but there's a world of difference between knowing something and proving it. If there wasn't, there would have been no need for them to send these men. And to get international approval for interference in the sovereign affairs of Azerbaijan they will need real live witnesses, not just the taped recollections of a few dead soldiers. Soldiers, moreover, whose mere presence on your territory constitutes a flagrant violation of international law.' The Iraqi flashed his shark's smile. 'Deep in their hearts everyone will know what is really happening, but as long as we can provide a reasonable doubt they'll find it much more convenient to look the other way. If we can wipe out the English soldiers and bring back the scientist then the project will be unaffected.'

He turned to the map. 'And now that we know they're still here, let's start looking for them.'

Two hours later, with the sun lighting the façade of the Presidential Palace in Baku, Gyudar Aliyev shielded his eyes against the glare and gazed out to sea. Vezirov had made the call Uday had suggested, his superior had come straight to the President, and the latter was now agonizing about the options open to himself and his small country.

From the beginning he had felt ambivalent about the project underway on the rig which bore his name, but there had seemed to be several good reasons for pushing ahead with it – the payments from Baghdad, the present threat from Armenia and possible future threats from

Russia and Iran – and few for calling a halt. The Azeri bomb wasn't going to cost a kopek, and no one need know of its existence unless and until the threat of use was required.

There was nothing illegal about the project. Azerbaijan had not signed any non-proliferation treaties in its own right, and there was nothing to stop its government developing its own nuclear weapons if it so wished. There might be legal problems involved in sending such weapons to Iraq, but that was a problem for the future. For the moment those Iraqi citizens who were working on the project were simply selling their skills abroad, like all those ex-Soviet footballers who now earned their living in western Europe.

Such arguments aside, it would no doubt still be preferable if they could present the project in a non-military light. The Western oil companies were probably capable of turning a blind eye to anything, but there was no point in subjecting them to unnecessary embarrassment. No, Aliyev decided, it would be better to seize the high ground now, before the Western powers started to bleat. He took one last look at the shining sea, and walked across to the phone on his desk. 'Get the Turkish Ambassador in here,' he told his secretary. 'And then arrange a press conference.'

It was time the world found out about the terrorist attack on the Caspian Institute for Peaceful Nuclear Research.

After eating an uninspiring breakfast shortly after dawn, the party on Narghin had been left with nothing to do but wait, watch and listen for the widening search to reach their island. During the early hours of daylight they heard several planes and helicopters in the distance, but it was gone ten o'clock before an Mi-8 flew low across the island and hovered briefly about fifty metres above the ruined prison complex before continuing on its previous course, presumably none the wiser. The five people in the chapel eyrie breathed a collective sigh of relief.

Tamarlan Shadmanov had talked to Constantine on the radio for almost two hours, spelling out exactly what was happening on Aliyev A, which scientists were working there and what each was working on, and how far advanced their work was, both separately and as a whole. At the end of the conversation he had felt utterly exhausted, and knew it was not just the talk which had tired him, or the events of that night. He felt as if he was suddenly carrying the weight of his whole life on his back, the burden of all the lies he had told himself to justify the work he had done. He had never felt comfortable with it, but he had allowed himself to be seduced by the intellectual challenges, and, yes, by his wife's need for the status and material privileges which went with it. And now that the Englishmen's escape plan had gone so badly wrong, he couldn't escape the feeling that in some crude way justice was being done. The fact that both his wife and his mistress seemed likely to share in whatever fate had in store for him offered an almost comical twist to an otherwise tragic theme.

Lying next to him, also unable to sleep, Farida had no notion that their situation had a funny side. They might still get to England, she thought, and that would be wonderful. If they didn't, then she and her husband had to be damn sure they didn't get caught in the crossfire, either metaphorically or literally. Provided that they were taken alive, there should be no great difficulty in convincing the authorities that the Englishmen had abducted them from the research station at gunpoint. After all, they had killed the two security guards with no compunction whatsoever. Who wouldn't have been afraid to resist them?

A couple of metres away, Finn was watching the distant landing-stage through a small gap in the masonry. The problem with this job, he thought, was the lack of laughs. Rob Cafell might have been an occasional pain in the neck during their stowaway voyage on the pirated freighter but the two of them had shared a giggle or two. McClure was more together than Finn had feared he would be – in fact he was damned good at his job – but a dead sheep would have displayed more sense of humour. And since it was fucking obvious that the downing of the Sea King had left them all up the Caspian without much in the way of paddles they were going to be sorely in need of a few good laughs just to get by.

Close by, Noonan was sitting with his back to the wall, eyes closed but not asleep. An awful lot had happened in the previous twelve hours, and he was finding it hard to still the thoughts and feelings which were churning in his mind. There was a large knot of fear in there somewhere, but he had expected that, and knew, without knowing quite how he knew, that it was under control. What had surprised him was the insistent buzz of exhilaration which went with the fear. It seemed to heighten everything, from the awareness of his own breathing to the colours of the sunlit weeds which had taken root in the crumbling stonework of the chapel walls. It was like a drug really, one that both fascinated and repelled him. Looking across at McClure, who was cleaning his MP5 for at least the third time that morning, Noonan had the sudden feeling that he had discovered what made the other man tick.

McClure might have recognized Noonan's feelings, but these days he became aware of the drug only when it was withdrawn. Here, at the heart of the action, he felt focused, collected, calm. A little worried, perhaps, but with good reason: Galloway's promise of a second flight had been too personal – 'as far as I'm concerned' were the words he had used – as if he knew that the chances of his being overruled were better than even. And if there was no rescue flight then they really did have a challenge on their hands. When Raisa woke up – McClure smiled inwardly at the realization that she was the only one of the team calm enough to sleep – the two of them would have to go through the options again. Maybe on the second run-through they wouldn't all seem so impossible.

Sir Thomas Clovelly and Dean J. Barclay, the British and US Ambassadors in Ankara, both had bored expressions on their faces as they waited in the anteroom for the required audience with the Turkish Prime Minister. Behind the masks, however, Clovelly was anxious and Barclay angry – not least with his British colleague. As far as the American was concerned, Turkey was too important to NATO for the British to fuck with. He would show solidarity with Clovelly because his State Department superiors had instructed him to do so, but not with any pleasure.

The door opened and a minion invited them in. Kemal Demiru was seated behind his huge desk, dressed as usual in a dark-blue suit, white shirt and maroon tie.

He greeted his visitors courteously enough, but his eyes were not friendly.

'I have just had a report from my people in Dogubayazit,' he began, once the two ambassadors had seated themselves. 'The base authorities there were of the belief that your helicopter' – he looked straight at Clovelly – 'was involved in a rescue mission. Some nonsense about a journalist with connections to your royal family who needed to be rescued from Nagorno-Karabakh.' His lips curled with anger. 'Now I wonder where that story came from.'

'I have no idea, Prime Minister,' Clovelly lied.

Demiru expressed his contempt by eyeballing the ceiling. 'I am aware that Dogubayazit is a NATO base,' he said, 'but it is on Turkish soil, and you have used it to launch a military raid against a state which we consider an ally and a friend, without the diplomatic courtesy of a request, without the slightest trace of respect for Turkish sovereignty.'

'We of course apologize for any perceived lack of respect,' Barclay said. 'But our decision to pursue this matter in secret was taken with the intention of sparing the Turkish government unnecessary embarrassment.'

'It wasn't simply that you knew we would refuse permission?' Demiru asked sarcastically.

Clovelly had the grace to smile at that. 'Her Majesty's Government would also like to offer an apology for any misunderstanding,' he said smoothly. 'Having said that, I would like to stress that the action was taken under NATO auspices, and that it is in the interests of the Alliance – and all its members – that it be brought to a speedy and successful conclusion.'

Demiru looked at him. 'You are not suggesting another attempt?

'These men are trapped . . .'

'That is of no interest to me.'

'I can understand your anger,' Barclay tried, 'but we are talking here about Iraq getting hold of a substantial nuclear arsenal. Surely the securing of such intelligence is as crucial to Turkey's interests as it is to ours?'

'Are you not in contact with these men?' Demiru asked.

'Yes, but . . .' Clovelly began, before he realized his mistake.

'Then they will have already passed on what intelligence they have gathered,' Demiru said triumphantly.

'We have no other way of reaching them,' Barclay said.

'You should have thought of that earlier,' Demiru told him. 'There will be no more flights from Turkish territory,' he added. 'Is that clear?'

It was.

The first search party arrived on Narghin soon after one. A motor launch disgorged a platoon of troops, who cautiously edged their way into the prison complex. After ten minutes of fruitless searching they began to relax, moving almost nonchalantly from building to building, without even bothering to maintain silence.

Raisa listened to them chatting to each other in Azeri, mostly about the prison and who had built it. 'It must have been the communists,' one voice said, and she found herself smiling at the *naïveté*. She had seen the eighteen-year-old faces through Finn's binoculars when they landed – they were just children really, and would have been just entering puberty when the Soviet Union disintegrated.

Another half an hour and they were gone, presumably *en route* to the next island.

Raisa sat staring at the stork's nest atop the tarnished onion dome, thinking that not many of Narghin's visitors would have stayed such a short time. The prison had been built by the original Russian invaders of the Caucasus more than a century and a half earlier, as a holding area for Persian prisoners of war. Since then there had been common criminals, political prisoners of the Czars, victims of Stalin. The last inhabitants had been gypsies, moved there during the Nazi push towards the Caucasus in 1942. They had been considered a potential fifth column by some paranoid moron in Moscow.

Raisa wondered how long she and the others would be staying. They might have found a safe hiding-place, but sooner or later they would have to leave its shelter for the dangers of the open sky or the open sea.

In London it was almost ten in the morning. The sun was shining, the early season tourists thick on the ground in Whitehall and Trafalgar Square, as Sir Christopher Hanson's car carried him towards his meeting with the Prime Minister, but the delights of spring were not exactly uppermost in the MI6 chief's mind.

The PM and Martin Clarke were already sipping coffee in the Cabinet Room when he arrived and took a third seat at the head of the huge table.

The PM wasted no time. 'This is a disaster,' he said coldly. 'I have the Russian Ambassador demanding an audience, and about a dozen others lining up behind him. Azerbaijan of course, Turkmenistan, Iran, Kazkiz-something – I can't even remember some of their names – every last one of them brimming over with righteous rage because their precious sovereignty has been infringed. The Turks have already given our ambassador in Ankara a tongue-lashing, and the Americans are furious.'

'But we have got the information we needed,' Hanson quietly reminded him.

'I know.'

'What did they find out?' Clarke asked. Unlike the other two he had not been briefed by Poole.

'The Iraqis are assembling nuclear-armed missiles in the Caspian,' Hanson told him. 'And according to Shadmanov they're not much more than a year away from deployment. Unless we do something within the next twelve months Saddam will have the power to irradiate anyone or anything within Scud range, which includes Israel, Tehran, Kuwait, all the Gulf oilfields.'

'Oh boy.'

'Exactly. I'd say we've given new meaning to the phrase "priceless intelligence".'

The PM looked slightly mollified.

'And the team which collected it needs help,' Hanson went on, hoping to press his advantage. 'For all our sakes,' he added, gilding the lily somewhat. 'Seeing them paraded in chains through the streets of Baku is not likely to increase the government's reputation for competence.'

'I didn't shoot the wretched helicopter down,' the PM complained.

'You sent it,' Hanson said brutally.

The PM looked suitably distraught. 'But what can we do?' he asked hopelessly. 'The Turks refuse point-blank to sanction another air rescue mission, and – you heard me – every nation which borders the Caspian is crying out for blood. They won't be in any hurry to offer sanctuary.'

'Not publicly, at least,' Hanson agreed. 'But none of these ex-Soviet states are in good economic shape. The promise of a development grant might work wonders.'

The PM sighed. 'I doubt it. The leaders would have to care more about their people's development than their own images as defenders of the national honour. And what if a deal leaked? They'd be pilloried, and I'd be answering questions in the House about the payment of ransom to get our men back. No, I don't think so . . .'

'So what . . . ?'

'I don't see what we can do,' Clarke interjected on the PM's behalf.

'You're just going to leave these men hanging?' Hanson asked icily.

'We don't have many other options,' the PM retorted, answering ice with heat. 'The only place we can exercise any real leverage is Azerbaijan itself, and that'll be courtesy of the oil companies . . .' He paused for a second. 'In fact, our best chance might well be for the SBS team to surrender itself to the authorities in Azerbaijan. If they did so, I think there's every chance we could get them back in a reasonably short space of time.'

'You might be right,' Hanson said, 'but what about the Karayeva woman, and the scientist. They're both Azeris. They'll probably face treason charges and a firing squad.'

The PM shrugged. 'I don't know what else to suggest. What else can we do?' he added again, more plaintively this time.

The fact that he was probably right was the only thing that kept Hanson from both losing his temper and offering his resignation. There probably wasn't anything they could do. Back in his own office he put through a call to Poole, expecting Neil Colhoun to like it even less than he did.

He wasn't disappointed. 'The government's washing its hands of them?' the SBS boss asked in cold disbelief.

'They'll do all they can to get the Azeris to send your lads home, and I'd say there's a fair chance they'll succeed. The Azeris really need deep-water drilling technology, and they can only get it from us or the Americans, and since Yank intelligence was in on this from the beginning they'll presumably help put the pressure on. That's the good news. The bad news is that this scenario involves washing our hands of Karayeva and Shadmanov. He'll probably be too useful to shoot; she looks like the necessary scapegoat.'

'Bastards,' Colhoun murmured.

'I have to admit that seems a fair assessment,' Hanson agreed.

'They won't do it, of course,' Colhoun said eventually.

'Won't what?'

'Surrender to the locals. Not if they know they're handing Raisa over to a firing squad.'

'They're on an island in the middle of an inland sea surrounded by hostile countries. What other options do they have?'

An hour or so later, as darkness fell across the Caspian, the same question was exercising the minds of the SBS team on Narghin. Galloway's apologetic transmission was received with barely concealed satisfaction from McClure, but the reaction of the others was rather more ambivalent.

'Another fine mess I've got myself into,' Finn murmured on hearing the news. But look on the bright side, Stuart, he told himself. If you get out of this in one piece you'll probably make sergeant, and be given more chances to die in countries that your mother never even heard of.

Next to him Noonan was feeling the same strange mix of emotions as before, fear and exhilaration dancing together in his stomach.

'We won't tell our passengers just yet,' McClure was saying. 'Not until we've decided what we're going to do.'

'Being given a "free hand" in this situation is fucking rich,' Finn said. 'It's like telling people who are being laid off that you're "letting them go", like you're doing them some sort of favour.'

'Probably,' McClure said drily, 'but at least they haven't tied our hands, and we do have options.' He looked around the other three faces. 'First off, it's been suggested by the politicos that we surrender to the Azeri authorities. They reckon there's a good chance the three of us' – he included Finn and Noonan in his look – 'will probably get sent home without too much delay. Raisa probably won't be so lucky. And as for Shadmanov . . .'

'Fuck that for an idea,' Finn said. 'I'll think about surrendering when someone rams a Kalashnikov barrel up my arse.'

'As long as you're not enjoying it,' Noonan added.

'That would be different,' Finn agreed with a grin.

Raisa stared at the two of them with amazement.

'Right,' McClure went on. 'No surrender. So we have to get home one way or another. We could try heading for one of the other countries around this sea, but it doesn't look promising. For one thing, we don't have enough fuel, and finding any to steal on the open sea could be a bit of a problem. For another – he allowed himself a rare smile – 'we've become quite famous over the last twelve hours, and most of the governments around here have been queuing up to slag us off. Even if we could reach their shores none of them are likely to welcome us with open arms.'

'Great,' Finn murmured.

'But there is one possibility,' McClure said.

'Armenia,' Raisa murmured.

'Yeah. Any enemy of Azerbaijan's is a friend of theirs.'

'Hmm,' Finn said. 'And since we're the lads who discovered the Azeris are building a bomb, they might even make us national heroes. Only problem is, Armenia doesn't have a Caspian coastline.'

'A mere detail,' Noonan muttered.

Finn grinned. 'So how far are we from these new friends?'

McClure shone the torch beam on the crumpled map which lay between them. 'If we take the shortest route to the mainland, landing here' – he tapped the spot with his index finger – 'we'll be about two hundred and seventy-five kilometres, as the crow flies, from Armenia proper, but only about two hundred from Nagorno-Karabakh, which is under Armenian control.' He looked up at the others, pausing to let the idea sink in.

'So how do we do it?' asked Finn. 'I don't suppose there's a train with de luxe sleeping compartments – the *Flying Armenian*, maybe?'

Raisa smiled. 'There *is* a train to Georgia.' She traced the route with a finger. 'And it comes close to Armenian border – maybe thirty kilometres. But since war begins there are many checks on passengers – more than ten between Baku and border. With six people – and three not speak Azeri – I do not think so.'

'How about freight trains?' Noonan asked.

'There are some,' she admitted, 'but I do not know when.'

'And there's no way of finding out,' McClure said. 'Raisa's right. With our faces, and not speaking the lingo, we haven't got a prayer in the open. We'll have to use the roads, and maybe this river' – he picked out the Kura with his finger – 'to get within striking distance, and then hoof it over the mountains. Travelling only by night.'

'Do we have enough fuel for a river journey?' Finn asked. 'Those new outboards may be a damn sight more fuel-efficient than the old ones, but this river seems to bend a hell of a lot. Eighty Ks on the map will probably be more like twice that.'

'We'll have to pick up more on the road, and then maybe steal some extra from boats on the river. We could be into these mountains before dawn – which would be nice – but there's no reason we have to be. We've got food for another forty-eight hours, and as long as we're not spotted we can use all that and a bit more. And we're less likely to be spotted or blocked on the river.'

For several moments they all looked at the map in silence.

It *sounded* feasible, Finn thought. A trip across Azerbaijan with the best saved for last – the crossing of a war zone. Who said there were no adventures in the modern world? 'I can't think of a better idea,' he said.

Noonan nodded his agreement.

Raisa smiled and shook her head. They were all quite crazy.

'One more thing,' McClure said, turning to her. 'Galloway thinks we should give Shadmanov and his wife the option of sticking around before we try and drag them over the mountains. If we leave them here they could always claim they were kidnapped. Which might be a lot safer than coming with us. On the other hand, you can point out that the rig's not likely to be one of the world's safest places over the next few weeks.'

'I'll talk to them,' Raisa agreed. She crawled on all fours to where the scientist and his wife were watching and waiting. The three SBS men watched their faces as Raisa gave them the bad news – anger on Farida's, anxiety mixed with wry amusement on Shadmanov's. Farida started to say something, but her husband seemed to shut her up with no more than a couple of words, and then said something to Raisa.

She nodded and crawled back to the others. 'They come with us,' she said.

'The wife didn't look too keen,' Noonan observed.

'She was told this was a luxury tour, and she doesn't like the downgrading,' Finn said. 'I can't say as I blame her.'

211

16

It was twenty-two minutes past seven when Noonan's feet touched the floor of the gutted chapel. Once the others had followed, the party threaded its way through the silent ruins of the prison and down to the dock. The moonlight was now dimmed and diffused by the clouds Galloway had promised them.

McClure had informed his immediate superior of their plan and, as expected, had not received a particularly enthusiastic response. Still, during the course of the conversation the notion had seemed to grow on Galloway. The fact that he had no alternative to offer had probably helped.

That had been almost two hours ago, and by this time the Old Man in Poole should be pestering the politicians. McClure wanted the Armenians to know they were coming before they got there, just in case someone at the front was short-sighted or trigger-happy enough to take them for Azeris.

While Noonan and Finn reinflated the two Geminis, lowered them into the water and reattached the outboards, McClure and Raisa kept watch. There had been neither sight nor sound of a helicopter for over an hour now, and there was no movement visible on the surface of the sea, all of which boded well. With the lack of ambient light and the Caspian being the size it was, it would take an incredible piece of luck for anyone to spot them making their way to the mainland. The helicopter would have to be almost directly overhead, and well within range of the grenade-launchers.

In any case, McClure thought, the lack of aerial traffic suggested a different type of search. In the Azeris' shoes he would have first reckoned possibilities, and then created an escape-proof outer cordon, before starting on a thorough search of the enclosed area. The big question was whether they would have included the mainland in their calculations. McClure didn't think the enemy would initially expect an attempted escape overland, but they could make the same political deductions as he had. At the very least there would be the Azeri equivalent of an APB out, and probably a few roadblocks. But there was no way they could cover hundreds of kilometres of coastline.

The Geminis were ready. McClure, Raisa and Noonan got into one, Finn and the Shadmanovs into the other. The two motors burst into restrained purrs, sounding only slightly louder than the breeze tugging at the rippling waters and the trees behind the dock.

'Let's go,' McClure told Noonan. Fifteen kilometres to the west the thin line of the mainland coast was just about visible.

As Narghin receded behind them, McClure again quizzed Raisa on the geography of what lay ahead.

'I told you,' she said equably. 'I am on this road only three, maybe four times. There is beach, some hills of sand, the road, the railway, the pipeline. And then there is steppe. For hundred and fifty kilometres, maybe. Dry steppe, except near the rivers and irrigation channels. Then there is farms. Cotton and fruit trees.'

'What about traffic? Will there be much at this time of the evening?'

She shrugged. 'Some. Not a lot.'

The Geminis skimmed forward across the wind-ruffled surface. There were no signs of pursuit, either to the naked eye or McClure's nightscope. A couple of moving lights far away to the east were probably helicopters, but both grew fainter as the minutes passed.

In the opposite direction two pinpricks of light were approaching each other along the narrow strip of black land which divided sea from sky. They crossed and pulled away from each other, one heading north towards Baku, the other south towards the River Kura.

The highway was far from crowded. Five minutes passed before another light appeared, and by this time they were close enough for McClure to pick out the shape of a small car through the nightscope.

At almost exactly eight o'clock the two Geminis made landfall. Both were pulled ashore and deflated, but only one was efficiently buried in the soft sand of the dunes which lay between the shore and the road. Then, as the others crouched in a dip nearby, Raisa walked out into the middle of the road with her trousers rolled up and her hair hanging loose.

The road ran straight as a die, and she could see a long way in each direction. A minute went by, and another. It was a pleasantly warm evening, like so many of those she had shared with Tamarlan. She wondered about herself, wondered why the news that there would be no helicopter rescue had hardly ruffled her, much less thrown her into the panic she might once have expected. This whole business, beginning with Shadmanov's disappearance, and perhaps ending with their meeting again in such strange circumstances, had set her free of something. Inhibition perhaps. Or fear of being herself.

Through a gap in the dunes she could see the black mirror of the Caspian. An inland sea, locked in. They had been locked in together, she thought. She and her precious sea.

A distant light had appeared to the north, which was good. They wanted to go south, and it would be risky taking a hijacked vehicle back the way it had come.

It was another minute before she could make out that it was a lorry, and that was good too. Packing six people, a small armoury and a deflated Gemini into a Lada would be more than uncomfortable – it would be downright memorable.

She walked out into the centre of the road, feeling slightly ridiculous. What would the driver think when he saw her? Would he be wondering how she had got there? Thinking that her legs were too thin? That his favourite cousin was still single, and that here was the perfect chance to indulge himself in the grand Azeri pastime of wife-stealing?

The lorry was only fifty metres away now, and for a moment she thought it wasn't going to stop, but as she hurriedly stepped aside there was the squeal of worn brake shoes and the grinding of an ancient clutch. The five-tonner – one of the Togliattigrad's earlier and cruder models – pulled up about twenty metres past her, and as she walked forward the face of a middle-aged Azeri leaned out of the window. 'What are you doing out here?' he asked disapprovingly.

'I am lost,' she said.

He spat out of the window. 'What will you give . . . ?'

215

he started to ask, then jerked his head round, and she knew that one of the SBS men had opened the other door and shown him the muzzle of a gun. By the time she reached the front of the lorry he had climbed down to the road. His face looked more sullen than scared.

There was a loud rattling noise as the back door slid up, following by Noonan's shout: 'It's almost empty.'

'Get the gear loaded,' McClure told Finn, his Browning still pointing at the driver's stomach, his eyes gazing down the empty road. As Finn and Noonan went for the Gemini, he turned to Raisa. 'Can Shadmanov drive this thing?' he asked.

She asked the scientist if he could, and relayed the 'yes' to McClure.

'Right. You and I will sit up front with him. Tell his wife she'll be in the back with the other two.' He turned his head to check the road in the other direction, found there was still no one coming, and went back to the problem of the driver. If they tied him up and left him in the dunes he might escape, might even be found. In either case he would then be able to give away the lorry's number and type. If they took him with them, then they would have to knock him cold each time they stopped, whether for petrol or a roadblock. And in any case there was no way they could take him in the boat – getting the six of them in one Gemini was going to be a tight enough fit – so the same problem would arise again later. But by then they would know him better, and it would be harder to kill him, or at least harder for the others to accept the need for his death.

There was no doubt in McClure's mind. Alive, the driver was a possible threat to their mission. He abruptly raised the Browning to the man's forehead, saw the light of terror leap from his eyes, and squeezed the trigger.

'What the fuck . . . ?' Finn exclaimed as the corpse collapsed on to the tarmac, but his voice trailed off. He heard Noonan gasp behind him, and saw Raisa's lower lip hanging loose in surprise. It made sense, he thought. If the only thing that concerned you, the *only thing*, was maximizing the odds on their making a successful escape, then it made perfect sense.

So why did it feel so wrong?

This was not a good time to get philosophical. McClure was already dragging the body towards the nearest gap in the dunes, apparently unaware that he had upset the feelings of anyone other than the dead driver.

Finn exhaled noisily and checked the road in both directions. 'Get in the back,' he told Noonan.

'But I want to . . .'

'Yeah, I know. But get in the back.'

Through the wide window of the control tower Uday al-Dulaini watched as the refuelled Mi-8 lifted off and headed back out across the dimly lit tarmac towards the black emptiness of the Caspian. Behind him, Barzan al-Hassan and Azad Vezirov were leaning back in their chairs at either end of the table which held the open map. The Azeri was nursing his third glass of vodka, the Iraqi his second can of Coke.

Uday turned back to the map and looked at his watch. It was twenty past eight. 'Almost twenty hours without a sighting,' he said angrily.

Vezirov shrugged his shoulders. 'They have gone to ground, that's all. When they try to move we shall have them.'

'It's been dark for more than two hours,' Uday snapped. 'Unless they're waiting to be picked up they'll be on the move now.'

'But the Turks have promised there will be no pick-up,' Barzan said.

'That's what they said,' Uday told him. 'Who knows what deal they might have done with the Americans?'

'I believe them,' Vezirov said. 'But it doesn't matter anyway – our defence forces are on full alert. If a second helicopter did enter our airspace it would be shot down even quicker than the first.'

'So we are back at the beginning,' Uday argued. 'If they are not waiting for a rescue then they will be moving.' He leaned over the map again, and tried to put himself in the intruders' shoes. Which way would he head? According to Vezirov's experts the boats they were using had a limited range – they wouldn't be able to reach the Turkmen or Iranian shores to the east and south, much less the Russian or Kazakh coasts to the north.

'Perhaps they intend to stay where they are, give us the chance to tire of the search and convince ourselves that they are long gone. They could stay hidden for days, a week even.' Vezirov looked at his empty glass and reluctantly placed it on the table. 'Tomorrow we will search the islands again,' he decided. 'More thoroughly.'

'You might be right,' Uday conceded, 'but I don't think so. They were only expecting to be here for twenty-four hours – they will have some emergency rations but not that much. And there are at least five of them – six, according to the pilot they shot down. No, I think they are moving. The British, the Americans, whoever they are, they don't have the temperament of the desert. They are only happy when they are active. They are moving. I feel it.'

'If they cannot go north, south or east, they must go west,' Barzan volunteered.

'It seems crazy, but I think they have no other options,' Uday agreed.

'They have plenty of options on land,' Vezirov said, leaning across the map. 'They can head north towards Russia, south towards Iran, west towards Georgia or Armenia. But they won't get far – there are block on all the major roads.'

'What if they don't use the major roads?'

Vezirov smiled. 'In Azerbaijan these are the only roads. If they try to escape overland we shall catch them.'

Uday looked at the Azeri, hoping his confidence wasn't misplaced. He wondered what price Vezirov would pay for failure. Demotion? Retirement? His own punishment was likely to be more severe.

He went back to the map, staring fiercely down at it, as if he was hoping to force a disclosure of the enemy's location by sheer will-power. The map stared back at him, its symbols beginning to blur in his tired vision. Through the connecting door he could hear another pilot reporting in: 'No sighting, repeat, no sighting.'

In London it was shortly after half-past four in the afternoon. Outside it was raining, but in Martin Clarke's room at the Foreign Office he and his research assistant were oblivious to just about everything but the insistent ring of the phone.

Since he had given his secretary strict instructions that their preparation of a written reply was not to be interrupted, Clarke could only assume the caller was someone who mattered. It turned out to be the SBS chief, whom he supposed just about qualified.

'Will this take long?' he asked, looking down at his naked partner. 'I'm very busy.'

'As long as it takes,' Colhoun said, 'unless you'd rather I take it up with the PM in person.'

That was the access which qualified him, Clarke thought. 'Go on, then,' he said.

Colhoun gave him an update on the SBS team's situation.

'Let me get this straight,' Clarke said, caressing his research assistant's nipple with the palm of his hand. 'They have decided to walk through Azerbaijan to Armenia?' He tried to remember any geographical facts about Azerbaijan's interior, and came up empty. Was it a desert, a jungle, mountains?

'I don't expect they'll do the whole distance on foot,' Colhoun said, struggling and failing to keep the sarcasm out of his tone.

A hand was reaching between his legs, but Clarke, suddenly aware of what Colhoun's information implied, pushed it away. 'Are they intending to fight their way across the country?' he asked coldly.

No, they're planning to give a string of benefit concerts, Colhoun thought acerbically. 'I am sure they'll be bending over backwards to avoid the use of force,' he said. 'They don't want to bring attention to themselves. And if they do find it necessary, they won't use any more than the minimum required to ensure their own safety.'

'In other words, they *are* planning to fight their way out. Lieutenant Colonel, I don't think you quite appreciate what is at stake here . . .'

'Minister, I don't think you quite appreciate . . .' Colhoun stopped himself. His men needed this bastard's help, and he wouldn't be doing them any service by letting his own temper get the better of him. 'I understand,' he went on more calmly, 'why Her Majesty's Government have found it necessary to abandon these men, but abandoned they have most definitely been. If we can't extricate them, the least they deserve is the chance to extricate themselves, a chance to get home.'

Clarke was silent for a moment. He could probably get the PM to force either Colhoun's removal or his acquiescence in ordering the men to surrender, but without the SBS chief's goodwill he suspected there was no way of actually influencing the men themselves. And there was certainly no political capital to be gained from publicly disowning national heroes. In which case, damage limitation seemed to be the name of the game. 'What do you actually want?' he asked Colhoun.

'What I want is for our embassy in Armenia – I presume we have one – to start preparing the Armenian government for my men's arrival at the border. Given the nature of their mission I see no reason why they shouldn't expect a parade in their honour through the streets of the capital, whatever that is.'

'Yerevan,' Clarke told him.

'It won't look too good if British soldiers are shot dead because no one thought to tell the Armenians they were coming.'

'I get the point.'

'They could get there before dawn tomorrow,' Colhoun persisted.

'I'll get on it straight away,' Clarke said, somewhat economically with the truth. First, he had some research to do.

In his Poole office Colhoun put the phone down and reached for the more prosaic comfort of a Kit-Kat. He would keep pestering the politicians until it was no longer necessary, but the only people who could help his men to reach the border were the men themselves.

The stolen lorry motored down the Caspian coast road. The view from the front seat was less than inspiring: empty sea to their left, an empty ribbon of tarmac ahead, an empty steppe on their right. They would be on this road for another twenty-five kilometres, before turning inland at the small town of Alyat.

In the back of the lorry, hidden from a cursory examination by the late driver's load, Finn, Noonan and Farida were each wrapped in their private worlds. Noonan was still seething with the anger and confusion brought on by McClure's summary execution of the driver, going round and round the arguments in his head, trying and failing to convince himself that the man's death had been necessary. And yet there was Finn, his face a mask of innocence. How could he be so unconcerned? Had he seen such things so many times that he no longer cared?

In the front seat the other three sat in an unbroken silence. Shadmanov was concentrating on his driving. Raisa was asking herself the same question as Noonan, and finding just as little in the way of clear-cut answers. McClure, meanwhile, had put himself in neutral.

The lorry continued to eat up the kilometres. There was not much traffic on the road, but enough to prevent a single vehicle becoming an object of suspicion. No train passed by on the adjacent tracks, and the few seaside villages which the road skirted seemed dark and devoid of life.

It was just after half-past nine when they entered Alyat. Here there was a semblance of night-life, most noticeably in the vicinity of one well-lit and obviously smoky bar, and a couple of hundred metres farther down the main street they found a garage. It was closed, but the owner and his wife could be seen playing cards with another couple through the open door of their living quarters. He proved more than happy to sell Shadmanov a tankful at twice the normal rate, and on hearing that Raisa's car had run out of petrol a couple of kilometres down the road gallantly sold her a couple of cans at not much more than cost.

Walking back to the lorry, Raisa couldn't resist a last look back at the Azeri foursome gathered round the table, the half-finished bottle of wine shining in the yellow light, their laughter rippling in the silence. She would miss Azerbaijan, she thought with a pang. Not the Caspian, not the bigotry, but the wonderful simplicity of life, the appreciation of basic things, like the smell of pilaff on a warm evening.

They drove out of the town, turning inland at the point where both road and railway bifurcated, and saw the checkpoint a few hundred metres in front of them. No attempt had been made to block the road, and for a very simple reason: the two cars and one lorry were all being used for the purpose of illuminating a makeshift football pitch beside the road. About a dozen men were involved in the game itself, leaving only a couple to man the checkpoint.

McClure clambered over the back of the seat and squeezed himself into the space behind it, rapping out the prearranged warning to Finn and Noonan on the partition wall.

One of the two soldiers waved them down. He was not much more than sixteen, Raisa thought, and the effect of the cradled Kalashnikov was offset by a boyish grin. His partner, who looked even younger, stayed back a few paces.

'Licence, Grandpa,' the older boy told Shadmanov, and then caught sight of her. She smiled at him.

'What's all this about then?' Shadmanov asked, handing down the dead driver's licence.

'Foreign terrorists,' the boy said importantly. He gave the licence a cursory glance and then looked at Raisa again.

'She's my wife's sister,' Shadmanov explained conspiratorially.

'Oh yeah?' the boy said, grinning back at him.

'You want to look in the back for terrorists?' the scientist asked.

'I'd probably find the rest of your harem,' the boy said. 'Go on, on your way.'

Shadmanov ground the lorry back into gear, gave him a salute and set off again.

'There's such a thing as overplaying a scene,' Raisa told Shadmanov sternly, but he could tell she had enjoyed it as much as he had. They looked at each other and burst out laughing, both remembering in that moment what they had once enjoyed in each other's company.

McClure clambered back into his seat, breaking the spell. 'No problems?' he asked her.

'No problems,' she agreed. Maybe this was going to be easier than they expected.

For the next half-hour they drove west along a fairly straight road, across an expanse of rolling steppe studded with plants which looked like stunted cacti. A few kilometres from Kazi Magomed – the only sizeable town in their intended itinerary – they entered an irrigated area, with the neatly dug channels criss-crossing the tidy grids of fruit trees. An occasional light shone in the distance, but there was no one on the roads, and the town itself, when they reached it, seemed even deader than Alyat.

The main street was deserted, and the two visible garages were closed and dark. McClure thought about waking someone but decided against it – they certainly had enough petrol for the lorry, and if there were no more roadblocks then there seemed nothing to stop them driving all the way to the border. Not that he wanted it to be that easy.

After one false turn they found the road which led south towards the nearest bridge across the Kura. Since the pipeline and railway had continued in a westerly direction, there was now nothing to look at but the empty road, the dry steppe and the overcast sky. Half an hour later they reached the small town of Ali Bayramly, a mere kilometre from the bridge, and just beyond the town they sighted a second, more imposing checkpoint.

This time the road had been blocked by a V-shaped arrangement of two cars, and the five men who had been sitting round a roadside fire were now walking forward to meet them, cradling their weapons as they did so. In the lorry's headlights they didn't look to Raisa like regular army.

'Militia,' she whispered to McClure, who was already hidden behind the seat.

Shadmanov pulled the lorry to a halt some ten metres from the cars and leaned out of the window with a grin. 'Looking for foreign terrorists?' he asked.

The leader of the militiamen, a man in his mid-twenties with a short moustache, white teeth and limpid eyes, ignored the question. 'Get down,' he told Shadmanov, 'And you,' he told Raisa.

She hadn't missed the flash of interest in his eyes, and she didn't much like the looks on his companions' faces, but she complied with a smile. Up closer, she could see that the other four 'men' were probably in their late teens. She could also smell the liquor on their breath.

Looking round she could see the sleeping town half a kilometre to the north, but in every other direction the flat steppe stretched away into the darkness. It didn't feel like the safest place in the world.

'Papers!' the leader ordered, crushing his cigarette underfoot.

Shadmanov showed him.

'And yours,' the man demanded of Raisa.

'I left mine at home,' she said calmly.

'She's my wife's sister. I can vouch for her,' Shadmanov told the man.

A slight smile was creasing the leader's mouth. 'You can go,' he replied. 'But we will have to hold the woman until her identity can be verified.' He turned to his men. 'Move the cars,' he told two of them.

'But you can see she is not a foreign terrorist,' Shadmanov insisted.

The leader curled his lip. 'Go,' he told him, one hand on the holstered automatic. The other man, having grabbed Raisa by the upper arm, was pulling her away.

As Shadmanov took a step towards her abductor, the leader rammed the barrel of his automatic into the scientist's stomach, pushing him back with enough violence to make him lose his balance. 'You animal,' Shadmanov said from his position on the ground, and the leader put two bullets into his chest.

Several things happened at once. The two men who had been sent to move the cars stopped in their tracks, one with his hand on the door handle. Raisa tried to break away from the man who was holding her, her eyes fixed on the body of her former lover. And the man who had shot him walked into McClure's field of fire.

McClure had caught the tone of the exchange between Shadmanov and the militia leader, but had understood none of the particulars, and from his position deep inside the cab interior he had been unable to fill them in with his eyes. He had seen the two men walk towards the cars, but the other two were still out of sight, and he couldn't remember if both had been holding weapons. He could rap out the agreed signal on the partition for activating Finn and Noonan, but the noise would give the enemy the gift of a precious second's warning. He was still computing the odds of a successful intervention when the automatic barked twice, Raisa let out her cry of distress, and the leader's head appeared perfectly framed in the open cab window.

McClure sent a double tap through the man's left ear, and then lunged forward across the seat towards the window, the Browning in his hand desperately in search of its second target.

Raisa felt a spray of something hit her face, and

realized it came from the leader's shattered head. At the same moment she felt her booted heel make violent contact with the shin of the man who was holding her. In that instant her brain seemed to be racing in several different directions – wondering at her own instinctive reaction, crying for Shadmanov, wanting to scream for the blood and brains splattered across her face.

McClure's Browning coughed again, she felt the man behind her suck in air like a vacuum cleaner, and suddenly all she could see was the militia leader's automatic lying where he had dropped it. She lunged forward, grabbed the gun and rolled on towards the shelter of the standing lorry, just as McClure landed nimbly on the ground nearby.

At the same moment an engine sprang to life and one of the cars accelerated backwards on squealing tyres. McClure braced his legs, grasped the Browning in both hands with arms extended, and fired. The windscreen exploded, and the car ran backwards another ten metres or so, crushing a cactus-like plant before expiring with its back wheels in a dip and the nose pointing slightly upwards.

The fourth man had vanished into the darkness, and the sound of his progress across the steppe was fading fast.

'Shit!' McClure hissed, looking down at the dead scientist. 'I'll get the others,' he told Raisa, but she wasn't listening. Kneeling down beside Shadmanov, she gently closed his eyes, and stared at the familiar face. There was a touch of a smile on his lips, she thought. He had enjoyed the last twenty-four hours.

A few paces behind Raisa, Farida was staring down at her dead husband, lips pursed, an angry confusion swimming in her eyes. He had only ever wanted her for her body, and she had never been able to forgive him for that. The fact that he had later reneged on their marital bargain – denying her the money and status when he no longer wanted sex – had just been a twisting of the knife. Even in death, she thought, he had contrived to let her down. The West would have no interest in her on her own. She turned away with a sigh.

McClure was checking the bodies of the militiamen. Finn and Noonan, who had heard the initial shots and then spent several very nasty moments waiting for the signal that never came, were now grimly surveying the carnage their leader had wrought in their absence.

'They're all dead,' McClure reported with evident satisfaction. 'See if you can find some way of siphoning the petrol out of the cars,' he told Noonan. 'And get that one off the road.' He turned to Finn. 'One of them got away on foot,' he said, nodding in the direction the man had gone. 'He went that way, but presumably he'll double back towards the town, so we haven't got much time. Any ideas?'

'I don't know. I guess there's no point trying to clear this up. Get the bodies out of sight?'

'I'd rather get moving.'

Finn stroked his chin. 'How far are we from the river?'

'Only a few minutes.'

'Time to take to the boat, then?'

McClure nodded. 'Seems like the best place.'

'We *are* the SBS,' Finn added facetiously.

McClure's answering grin turned into a frown. Noonan had found the necessary piece of tubing and was busy siphoning petrol, Raisa was still bent over Shadmanov. 'Where's the wife?' McClure asked.

'In the back?'

She wasn't. And there was no sign of her on the road until McClure thought to use the nightscope. There she was, already several hundred metres away, walking briskly towards the sleeping town.

McClure walked back up to where Raisa was mopping her face with water from the militiamen's enamel pot. She looked shell-shocked, but this was not the time or place to deal with that. 'She's gone,' he told her. 'How much does she know?'

Raisa took a deep breath. 'She knows we go to Armenia,' she said. Her voice sounded like someone else's.

McClure thought about it as he watched Noonan back the car off the road. They were ready to go. And there seemed nothing to be gained by going back for Farida, only time to be lost. 'Let's go,' he ordered.

Finn took Shadmanov's place at the wheel, which left Noonan alone in the back, tasting the petrol on his tongue and acutely aware that his emotions were having a hard job keeping up with events. His anger at McClure over the shooting of the driver already seemed ancient history.

In the front seat the other three were watching the dry steppe give way to scattered stands of trees and farmland as the river grew nearer. Raisa was still in the middle of telling Finn what had happened back at the roadblock when the tower of a suspension bridge loomed out of the darkness ahead, and at almost the same moment McClure spotted a dirt track leading off to the right through an orchard. 'That way,' he told Finn. 'And cut the engine,' he added, as it became apparent that the track ran downhill.

The lorry rumbled slowly down the rutted road, with Finn's foot on the brake each time his eyes had trouble seeing the way. The only other sound was the swish of overhanging branches being parted.

If there was a farm nearby they didn't see it. The track ended in a copse of acacias beside the wide and silent Kura. A couple of hundred metres downstream a car was crossing the long bridge which stretched gracefully between the low banks.

It seemed like a good place, McClure thought. With any luck, no one would find the lorry before dawn.

Fifteen minutes later Noonan was easing the fully laden Gemini out into the centre of the river. Finn sat beside him in the stern, Raisa and McClure on either side of the bow. Between them, weaponry and spare cans of petrol had been arranged for optimum weight distribution.

By Finn's reckoning there was enough fuel to take them about a hundred kilometres, so they shouldn't have any trouble reaching the middle of nowhere.

17

It was a couple of minutes to eight in Poole, and strains of the *Coronation Street* theme music could be heard seeping out from somewhere on the base. His wife and daughter would have been watching it at home, Colhoun thought. He wondered if Marie had any notion of the mess her latest boyfriend was currently in, and realized there was no way she could. Which, in the unlikely event that she was serious about him, was a damn good thing.

Colhoun was sitting with Galloway and Constantine in the little-used guest lounge, not so much for the use of its comfortable chairs as for its proximity to the base radio room. Galloway had been declared *persona non grata* by the Turkish government earlier that day, and, taking advantage of a lift from the USAF, had managed to reach Poole soon after six. Constantine had insisted on staying on in case Shadmanov remembered something else to tell him, but a stronger, more personal motive, was a desire to share vicariously in Raisa's run for home. He knew it was ridiculous, a fifty-eight-year-old man mooning over a woman who was younger than his own daughters, but there it was. And Shadmanov was about the same age as he was, so she obviously liked older men.

'Incoming transmission,' the duty officer told them

from the doorway, and the three men hurriedly followed him back into the radio room.

The team was heading up the Kura, McClure told them. Shadmanov was dead, killed by militia at a checkpoint. His wife had run off. Another four of the enemy had been killed.

Colhoun winced at the use of the word 'enemy', and could well imagine Clarke's reaction to what he would see, rightly or wrongly, as a killing spree. Maybe McClure was exceeding the needs of the situation, but Colhoun was damned if he was going to tie his men's hands to mollify the same government which had washed its hands of them.

McClure's report ending with a request for better geographical information, since the map they were using would be adequate only for as long as they stayed on the river.

Colhoun told him they would do the best they could, and once the transmission was over got straight on to the chief of the RM Illustrators Branch, who seemed less than hopeful that they would find anything. 'If you can't dig up anything here, get on to the Foreign Office,' Colhoun suggested. 'The embassy in Moscow may be able to fax us something.'

By this time Constantine and Galloway were back in their comfortable chairs, each sipping at their glass of the CO's malt, trying to draw mental pictures of the team's boat as it journeyed up a river neither of them had ever seen. Unable to satisfy himself in this respect, Constantine found himself thinking about Shadmanov. During their conversations earlier that day the scientist had sounded incredibly tired, but it had seemed to Constantine more a weariness of the spirit than a tiredness of the body. And after nearly forty years in the same line of work he had thought he recognized a fellow-sufferer. Working on nuclear weaponry in almost any capacity seemed to have a soul-sapping effect, as if those concerned were obliged to bear the full moral burden of the horror they had dutifully unleashed.

The Azeri Air Force helicopter landed in the centre of Ali Bayramly shortly after one in the morning, giving new life to the wave of local interest which had followed the 'Armenians-are-coming' scare of an hour earlier. Vezirov, Uday and Barzan were escorted across to the old Soviet hall, where the young militia-man and the mystery woman were being held. 'Madame Shadmanova,' Vezirov greeted her. 'Where is your husband?'

'He's dead,' she said.

'How?' Uday asked angrily. The loss of the scientist was bound to add several months to the project, which wouldn't please either Kusai or Saddam.

'These idiots shot him,' she said contemptuously. 'He was probably trying to defend his mistress,' she added, and shook her head with apparent amusement.

Vezirov stared at her in amazement.

'Do you want to see where it happened?' the local man asked him. 'There's a car you can use . . .'

'Yes,' Vezirov said wearily. 'You,' he said, pointing at the militiaman, 'come with us. And you too, Madame.'

In the car he extracted the boy's story. It had seemed like there was just an old man and a younger woman in the lorry's cab – she was dressed like a man but a bit of a looker just the same – but suddenly this other man who'd been hidden just started shooting. He hadn't seen that man's face.

Vezirov turned to Farida for confirmation. 'I don't know what happened,' she said. 'I was a prisoner in the back of the lorry.'

At the scene of the confrontation nothing had been moved. Three bodies were arranged in a neat row by the side of the road, each with fatal bullet wounds. Another dead man, his throat blown away beneath a face planted with shards of glass, sat behind the driving wheel of the car farther from the road.

'What the fuck were you doing here?' Vezirov asked the militiaman.

The boy looked at him with the air of someone who had just been asked a particularly stupid question. 'It's a checkpoint,' he said.

'Right. But what were you checking for?'

The young brow creased in thought. 'Armenians?' he suggested.

Vezirov smiled to himself as he watched Uday walk towards him.

'There's petrol on the ground,' the Iraqi said. 'They've siphoned the tanks.' He reached inside the car for the large-scale map of Azerbaijan and spread it across the Volga's bonnet. 'They don't seem to have many choices,' he said eventually.

'They don't,' Vezirov agreed. He looked at his watch. 'They can't have gone more than fifty kilometres in the time they've had, and if they're heading west they only have two roads to choose from for at least a hundred kilometres. If it's south there's only one. And all three roads will soon be blocked by troops and armour, if they aren't already.'

'Looks like we've got them,' Uday said.

'Looks like it,' Vezirov replied. And all because some local toughs tried to kidnap a woman, he thought.

Uday's mind was already on another tack, scanning down a mental list of missile engineers, trying to decide on a replacement for the corpse laid out on the other side of the road.

The Gemini purred up the centre of the Kura. The river was about half a kilometre wide, but in places the banks were so low that it was hard to make them out, and then it was only the strength of the smooth current which gave the lie to the impression that they were skimming across a vast lake. It was the spring thaw in the mountains, Raisa told them; at any other time of the year the river would be half this size.

In the three hours since they took to the water, they had seen little in the way of human presence. Sixty kilometres had passed without a bridge, and the clusters of buildings on the distant banks were few and far between. The nightscope would reveal squat cottages, a rickety landing-stage and a few moored boats, most of them unpowered, but with an occasional outboard thrown in for good measure. In the event that they needed petrol there seemed likely to be a source to hand.

It was hard to make calculations without a better idea of exactly where they were. The lazy twists and turns of the Kura seemed to bear little relation to the twists and turns on their map, and there was nothing to distinguish the settlements from each other. McClure had the distinct feeling that the next bridge would give them their first real fix, and that was still a couple of hours away. Or at least he hoped it was.

Their other problem was the weather. As predicted, the cloud cover had thinned to almost nothing, leaving large stretches of starry sky. The moon was down at least, but there was still more light than McClure felt comfortable with. Out in the centre of the river they would still be hard to spot by accident, but they were now far from invisible to anyone looking.

Still, all in all, he felt good about the way things were going, the way they had gone. Reviewing the mission to date, he could think of only one major mistake – their over-reliance on air rescue – and that had been made before they left England. It had been a mistake borne of necessity, moreover, since there had been no other available method of extraction. Given that, they had got the professor out and kept him alive long enough to get his intelligence home. The team had suffered no casualties. Yet McClure had few doubts that the difficult bit was still to come. Now that they'd left their tracks in the sand the hunt would begin to close in.

The plan was to leave the river at a small town called Nadzha-something – the name was as long and unpronounceable as the famous Welsh station's – borrow a suitable car or lorry and drive some way into the mountains before daybreak. But it was beginning to look as if they would be lucky to reach the town much before dawn, in which case they wouldn't have time to do much more than find a suitable spot to hide up for the day. And even if they did get there with an hour or so to spare there was no guarantee of finding the transport.

The difficult bit was still to come, all right.

On the other side of the bows, Raisa was brooding about her responsibility for Shadmanov's death. If she hadn't set off to England, told them about the rig, insisted on taking part in this mad adventure, then he would still be working out in the Caspian. Not happily perhaps, feeling a little guilty even, but in a year or so he would have been back in Baku, able to go hiking in the mountains . . .

Not with Arif Akhundov though. What was she telling herself? She hadn't set up the project on the rig, or jumped into bed with Saddam Hussein. She hadn't kidnapped Tamarlan, or killed his friend to stop him talking.

And he wouldn't have blamed her. She knew he wouldn't.

Sitting at the tiller, Finn had let his thoughts drift into anger, which was rare. Mrs Finn had raised a happy-go-lucky lad, who took life pretty much as it came, enjoying the bits worth enjoying and just getting on with the bits that weren't. Politics wasn't something that usually concerned him, but for once, here on a river a very long way from home, he felt distinctly pissed off with the British government. Not because they had left the team in the lurch – he would have understood them not wanting to risk another Sea King crew even if the Turks had agreed to it. No, it was an old decision that was making him angry – the one that had led to Saddam getting away with the Gulf War, when they could have gone in and finished the bastard once and for all. If they had done that then none of this would have been necessary, and he could have been doing something slightly less dangerous, like climbing into a back seat with Colhoun's daughter.

*   *   *

On the other side of the purring motor, Noonan watched the featureless landscape slide past. He was thinking about the dead bodies at the checkpoint, the first he had ever seen properly. Of course there had been the Russian on the boat, but what with the rain and the mist and everything happening so fast it had seemed almost like a scene in a film. Then there was the lorry driver, but McClure had started dragging him away the moment he hit the ground.

He had seen the ones at the checkpoint though, really seen them, particularly the one in the car, whose glass-encrusted face had stared out at him through the shattered windscreen. One minute sitting by the brazier with his mates, the next ... And it was over, just like that. It was so simple, yet so hard to really grasp. This had been that boy's last night on earth, and it might be his too. And this river would keep on rolling, and the stars would keep shining. It would go on without him.

He shivered, and dipped his hand in the water to remind himself he was still alive.

Uday paced to and fro across the dusty space in front of the old local Soviet headquarters, headphones clamped across his black hair, but only half conscious of the sweet nothings which Madonna was whispering in his ear. Vezirov was sitting with the pilot in their helicopter, laughing at something or other. Barzan was nowhere to be seen – probably hiding somewhere with a cigarette. Didn't the idiot know that his breath stank from the stuff?

Vezirov laughed again, further angering Uday, who walked across to the helicopter, tugging the earphones off his head as he went. 'Something's wrong,' the Iraqi snapped. 'We should have had a sighting by now. There must be other roads.'

'There are no other roads,' Vezirov said placidly. 'Either the lorry's broken down or they've gone to ground again. Hoping that we'll get impatient and make a mistake,' he added pointedly.

Uday shook his head. 'I don't . . .' he began, just as a message started coming in on the Mi-8's radio. It wasn't the hoped-for sighting, though – just the discovery of the lorry driver's body on the Caspian shore.

Vezirov was about to break contact when a light suddenly appeared in Uday's eyes. 'What about the boats?' the Iraqi asked.

They hadn't found them.

'Look again,' Vezirov suggested. 'A couple of hundred metres in each direction.'

Uday was already headed for the open door of the Soviet building. He found Farida walking listlessly round the room in which she had been confined. 'Did they have a boat with them?' he asked without preamble.

'Yes,' she said. 'They buried one and took the other with them.'

'Why didn't you tell us this earlier?'

She shrugged. 'You didn't ask.'

Uday slapped her so hard across the face that she lost her footing. Back at the helicopter he told Vezirov that the fugitives had taken one of the boats with them. 'They must be on the river.'

Vezirov sighed. 'Maybe,' he said after a few moments.

'We need to send a helicopter upstream to look for them,' Uday insisted.

Vezirov grimaced. 'To see anything they'll need to fly low, and you know what happened out near the rig.'

Uday shook his head impatiently. 'Then have the pilot transmit continuously . . . no, better still, send two helicopters, with one hanging back behind the other. That way, if the first gets shot down finding them, the second will be able to keep the boat in sight.'

It was a quarter past three, and by McClure's reckoning they had travelled over eighty kilometres. For a while now he had been approaching each new bend hoping to find the bridge looming into view, but so far there had been nothing more to see than another empty stretch of river. In fact, over the last few kilometres the river's course had seemed to grow even more contorted, as if the water was prolonging its journey just for the sake of it. And to make matters worse the last clouds had vanished from the sky. There were still nearly two hours of darkness, but already he was beginning to feel like a sitting duck.

At least the fuel problem had been solved. A few kilometres back, spotting two outboards tied up at a small jetty, they had cut their own, paddled silently across and helped themselves to the contents of the fuel tanks. Unless the river really did disappear up its own arse they would get to where they were going. The problem was when.

McClure was studying the map for the hundredth time when the noise of the approaching helicopter seeped out above the dull purr of the outboard. 'Fuck,' he muttered. They were traversing a long bend in the river, quite a bit closer to the shorter south bank, but there were no sheltering trees on either side, and not a cloud in the sky to dim the ghostly starlight.

He could see the helicopter through the nightscope.

A cone of faint light was shining beneath it, like one of those beams for stealing humans which flying saucers always used in science-fiction films. It seemed to be moving slowly, probably zigzagging slightly to cover as much of the wide river as possible.

'Move in towards the bank,' he told Noonan, working on the assumption that either side offered better odds than the middle of the stream. 'Grenade-launcher,' he told Finn, who bent forward to extract one of the M16s and attachable M203s from the canvas holdall.

It was about three kilometres away, McClure thought, looking back with the naked eye. And then he noticed the second light, moving in the opposite direction from the first, presumably in response to a bend of the river. He picked out the second helicopter with the nightscope, and reckoned it was flying at least half a kilometre behind the first, which put it way beyond rocket-launcher range. The bastards had learnt their lesson.

He quickly explained the situation to the others. 'If neither of them see us,' he summed up, 'that's fine. But if either of them does, then we have to get both of them, or our chances of getting off this river sink to just about zero.' He dug into the holdall for the Accuracy International sniper rifle. 'This is going to take a hell of a shot, he said. 'At least five hundred metres, in the dark. We can stop the boat but there's no way of holding it still. Raisa, you had the best scores in Cyprus.'

She hesitated for only a second before reaching out her hand.

McClure took the other M16 and M203.

The first helicopter was about a kilometre away now, and obviously flying a zigzag course. In less than a minute it would be passing by or over them.

'Cut the motor,' McClure told Noonan. 'And sit still,' he added unnecessarily.

Raisa had attached the ten-round box magazine and was cradling the adjustable rubber butt against her right shoulder. The first helicopter loomed large in the Schmidt and Bender telescopic sight, the starlight reflecting silver on the bulbous windscreen.

'Fire on my command,' McClure rapped out. 'Raisa, just put as many bullets into the cockpit as you can.'

The leading helicopter was about six hundred metres away, trailing its cone of light across the black water . . .

Four hundred . . .

The zigzag was going to take it very close to them . . .

Two hundred . . .

The other helicopter was more like seven hundred metres behind the first, but it was flying even more slowly to compensate for the other's zigzags. Raisa rested her finger on the trigger, glad that she couldn't see any human shapes. With its inhuman sheen the helicopter looked more like a giant insect . . .

The cone of light swept over them.

'Fire,' McClure shouted.

The whoosh of the two grenade-launchers was instantaneous, the crack of the Accuracy International only a split second behind.

There was a blinding flash fifty metres upstream as the first helicopter exploded, showering burning debris down into the river.

Ramming the bolt home, Raisa fired again, and this time the second helicopter seemed to buck slightly in the air before arcing downwards with sudden venom, like a bird swooping for the kill. It hit the ground close to the water's edge, igniting another orange fireball.

'The helicopter industry's gonna love us,' Finn said drily.

'We know where they are,' Uday said triumphantly, his finger jabbing at the point on the map which corresponded with the last reported position of the helicopter search party.

'For the moment,' Vezirov agreed. He was still finding it hard to believe that both helicopters had gone off the air at precisely the same moment.

'The idiots in the second helicopter must have got too close,' Uday said, as if reading the Azeri's mind.

'Maybe,' Vezirov muttered. But he doubted it. There was something about these Englishmen, something almost superhuman. Unless of course they were armed with a hand-held missile launcher. But if they were, then why hadn't they used it before? The experts all agreed that the helicopter in the Caspian had been brought down by nothing more esoteric than a grenade-launcher.

'Have you got men on this bridge?' Uday asked, breaking the reverie.

Vezirov followed the finger on the map. 'They're on their way,' he said. 'This is Azerbaijan,' he added, sensing that the Iraqi's frustration was building towards another angry outburst. 'We haven't got an unlimited supply of troops, and we don't have sufficient means to move the ones we have. Added to which, we've lost three helicopters in a single day.'

Uday restricted himself to an angry sigh. 'Well, at least we should be on our way,' he said.

'Agreed,' Vezirov said. 'The Zardob bridge,' he told the pilot. 'And keep us at least a kilometre north of the river.'

*   *   *

Two more bends of the Kura brought the bridge into view. The sight of the graceful black silhouette was cause for relief in itself, and the sensation was amplified by the evident lack of waiting troops. There wasn't even any lighting on the bridge, just a dim yellow lamp on each of the approaches, and no sign of a settlement nearby.

All of which begged a new series of questions. Now that their presence on the river was known, should they immediately take to the land once more? The local traffic at three-thirty in the morning would be light to the point of non-existent, and they were still almost a hundred kilometres from the presumed safety of Armenian-held territory. On the other hand, Nadzha-something was only about forty minutes upstream. They would arrive quite a while before dawn, and there was likely to be a choice of transport for stealing. The Azeri military would probably be slow to react to their latest losses, and even if they weren't, it seemed unlikely they would have a surfeit of available helicopters in the immediate area.

Spending another forty minutes on the river, McClure decided, would be marginally less risky than setting out across flat, open country with no guarantee of transport. He would stick to the original plan.

A couple of minutes later they passed under the long bridge without sight or sound of the enemy. The Gemini was almost half a kilometre upstream and approaching the next bend when the lights of several lorries appeared behind them, edging out on to the bridge and coming to an eventual halt. Through the nightscope McClure could see men tumbling out of them, and taking up position along the parapet. They were clearly under orders to face east, but McClure had no fear that the

Gemini, which was now hidden in the silhouette of the winding river's higher banks, would be visible to any westward-straying gaze. A few seconds later the bridge was gone from view.

This mission was in danger of mimicking one of those Indiana Jones films, he thought, in which the hero was rarely more than half a step ahead of the pursuit, and a succession of doors clanged shut at his heels. Only this wasn't a movie, and the odds were that sooner or later one of these doors would slam shut in their faces.

Still, McClure thought, as he rigged the satcom radio for transmission, it hadn't happened yet. And glancing round the faces of the other members of his team he found himself thinking that they still had a pretty good chance of making it. He gave Poole a rundown of the latest developments, their current position and immediate plans, and signed off.

The next half-hour passed with agonizing slowness, but their passage was uninterrupted from either river-bank or sky – with any luck their pursuers were still waiting at the bridge downstream. The Kura meandered as aimlessly as ever, but there were more trees visible on the banks, more small landing docks lining the water's edge, and move evidence of agriculture in the wide irriga-tion channels which had been dug away from the river.

At twenty past four a sprinkling of dim lights up ahead gave notice that they were close to their immediate destination, and about four hundred metres from the outskirts of the riverside town McClure gestured for Finn to take them off the Kura and up a convenient channel. They found no effective hiding-place for the Gemini, but at least it was off the river, and the hours of darkness were running out.

They unloaded the bergens, weaponry and cans of spare fuel, pulled the inflatable ashore and left it sitting innocently beneath a tree. Then, after distributing the burden between them, they started off up the riverside track towards the town, which, hopefully, was still sleeping. Just as the track turned into a road a helicopter emerged from the silence, flying down the river at a height which suggested the pilot was more interested in a long life than finding a boatload of foreign soldiers.

The hum of its rotors faded into nothing just as they reached the first houses, one-storey affairs which faced the street with walls broken only by narrow gateways. The street had the look of the Third World about it, but there were power lines to each dwelling, and no smell of sewage in the streets.

From a couple of houses they could hear sounds of movement, and once their passage set off a dog, but the street ahead remained empty. Finn found himself wondering what McClure's reaction would be if some innocent civilian suddenly emerged from one of the gateways and found himself face to face with this strange band of heavily armed foreigners.

A parked car swam into view some fifty metres ahead of them, and as they walked towards it another appeared some thirty metres farther down the road. People were moving in the house beside the first car, but the owners of the second, a new-looking Lada, still seemed dead to the world. The doors were not locked.

'Let's push it out of earshot,' Finn suggested, and McClure nodded. The four of them bundled their hand-held gear on to the back seat and pushed the car some thirty metres. They were now outside a largish building which looked like a school. A crossroads was visible about a hundred metres ahead, and as Finn hot-wired the engine, McClure counted lights going on in different dwellings. The town was waking up.

The car's motor burst into life. 'The tank looks more than half full,' Finn said.

A minute later they were heading in towards the town's centre, eyes peeled for any sign of the road to the west which was on their map. The town was bigger than McClure had expected, and they passed by several medium-sized industrial premises before reaching the older buildings at its heart.

'That way,' Raisa said, pointing over McClure's shoulder to where an old Soviet signpost in Cyrillic script announced the road to Agdam.

They started heading back out of town, passing the police station, where a man in plain clothes had just climbed out of his car. He glanced up as they passed, and raised a hand in greeting before turning away. Presumably he knew the owner of the car.

The town abruptly ended, and the road angled away across the plain, straight as an arrow. The dark line of the distant horizon seemed higher than it had, offering the promise of mountains. There was still no break in the darkness behind them, but the sunrise was only forty minutes away, and the sky would start to lighten in not much more than ten. After that they would have to pay for each extra kilometre with an ever-increasing risk of being sighted or stopped.

Finn was coaxing eighty-five kilometres an hour out of the Lada, and it took only ten minutes for them to reach and speed through the small town of Agdzhabedi, where a couple of sleepy-looking men watched them pass.

It was definitely getting lighter now, and the wall of hills ahead seemed to be slowly climbing out of the horizon. So near and yet so far, Finn thought to himself. The distance was still too great to risk driving on.

'There's another crossroads in a couple of kilometres,' McClure announced. 'We'll dump the car nearby, keep 'em guessing.'

'I was afraid you were going to say something like that,' Finn murmured. He couldn't argue with the decision, though. Another fifteen minutes and they would be sitting ducks.

The road was even climbing slightly, its first deviation from the flat, and their first view of the crossroads came from above, through a welcome curtain of trees.

'Stop the car,' McClure told Finn.

They all looked down at the meeting of ways, which lay in the middle of a shallow valley, surrounded by the buildings of a large farm. There was smoke pouring from a couple of chimneys, and moving figures visible on the road beyond.

'It's one of the old state farms,' Raisa said.

'Time to get out and walk,' McClure decided. To the south of the farm buildings a wide swathe of trees would give them the cover they needed to pass by without being seen.

They pushed the car off into the inadequate cover of the roadside trees and spent a couple of precious minutes draping enough foliage across its roof to fool any airborne eyes, but there wasn't enough time to shield it from searchers on the ground.

There was still half an hour's worth of twilight,

McClure reckoned. More if there was tree cover. They could get another five kilometres closer.

He lifted his eyes away to the west, where the highest slopes of the distant hills were now awash with sunlight, beckoning them forward. The last lap, he thought. The last fucking lap.

18

Vezirov briefly examined the interior of the stolen car, and found what he had expected – nothing. There were no traces of the men who had been inside, no clear proofs of English occupation, like a picture of the Queen or a pile of empty beer cans.

The Azeri security chief smiled to himself. It wasn't as if there was any doubt as to the vehicle's last occupants. The policeman in Nadzhafkulubayl had seen the car leave town on the Agdam road at around the right time, and its owner had reported it stolen a couple of hours later. Two men had seen it race through Agdzhabedi, and one of the workers at the farm below had seen it stop on the road nearby just before dawn. He had not seen anyone get out though, nor any strangers walking across country.

Vezirov crunched back through the undergrowth to his own car, and the familiar sight of Uday al-Dulaini poring over a map. 'At least the scale is getting larger,' the Azeri said cheerfully. They had started the day with a map of Azerbaijan, and now Uday was using Map 10 of the national 1:150,000 series, which covered only the currently occupied autonomous region of Nagorno-Karabakh and the western rim of the Kura lowlands.

The Iraqi had already marked their current position with a neat X. 'These roads,' he said, indicating them with twitches of his index finger, 'they are all sealed off?'

'Yes, but our friends must be on foot. Where could they have got another car? And why would they have wanted one? They ran out of darkness, so they've gone to ground again. Tonight they will try to reach the armistice line. I suppose they might try to steal another car, but I doubt it – they will know that all the roads are blocked. Their only chance is on foot.'

'So what about the paths into the mountains? How many of them are there?'

'Not many. Even less that strangers could find. And first they have to reach the mountains. I'd lay odds they're not more than five kilometres from where we're standing – they wouldn't have risked going on once the sun was up. These are not men who take unnecessary chances.' He smiled. 'They might even be watching us at this very moment.' Vezirov raised a hand. 'But before you ask, there is no way I can block all the routes into Nagorno-Karabakh *and* comb up to a hundred square kilometres of hills.'

Uday looked up at the faint line of mountains some thirty kilometres to the west. 'You are beginning to sound more confident,' he said.

Vezirov shrugged. 'They may be supermen, but they don't know this country. There are a lot of paths up into those mountains but they funnel through only a handful of passes. With another two hours of darkness I think they might have made it, but not now. They've given us a whole day to put the cork back in the bottle.'

Four hundred kilometres to the west, in the Armenian capital of Yerevan, Garnik Mangasaryan listened to the

British consul with a sinking heart. It was Friday, and he had hoped to leave early for the family's first weekend in their new summer cottage, but now it seemed as if he was unlikely to be leaving at all.

'Let me get this straight,' he said in the American-accented English he had polished for three years as a Soviet diplomat at the UN. 'These four men have . . .'

'Three men and one woman,' Brian Dickson corrected him. 'And the woman's half Armenian.'

'What's the other half?'

'Azeri,' Dickson admitted. He had been hoping that the Foreign Ministry official wouldn't ask.

Mangasaryan sighed. 'Not the luckiest combination these days.'

'No.'

'So, this group has verified the existence of a nuclear weapons plant in the Caspian, which you say has been set up as a joint project between Azerbaijan and Iraq, the aim being to provide them both with nuclear missiles?'

'That's the essence of it.'

Mangasaryan let out a sound which was half laugh, half snort. 'The Azeris are crazy enough to use them, you know?'

In Dickson's view it would have been hard to find someone in this corner of the world who wasn't, but that didn't seem an appropriate response. He went into his prearranged spiel, pointing out how important living witnesses would be when it came to gathering support for some sort of action, and stressing how obstructive the Turks had been in the matter of rescuing them. The Armenians had a double opportunity here, Dickson argued: in picking up the international kudos which their old enemy to the west had spurned, they would be paving the way for punitive action against their current enemy to the east.

Mangasaryan had no trouble identifying the self-interest behind Dickson's arguments – no doubt the British Government was wetting itself at the prospect of publicly losing these men – but there was no denying that Armenia would benefit from the international discrediting of Azerbaijan. 'What exactly do you want from us?' he asked.

'Your people in Nagorno-Karabakh . . .'

'They are not part of the Armenian Defence Forces.'

'Of course. But just between the two of us, let's not split hairs. You can get in touch with them, right?'

'Probably. Where and when do you expect . . . ?'

'We don't know yet. What our men need is an accurate idea of where the Azeri border posts are. Once they have that information they'll be able to decide on the best place to cross.' He looked enquiringly at the Armenian.

'That shouldn't be too difficult,' Mangasaryan agreed. 'And once we know where they intend to cross we can start arranging a friendly welcome.'

In Poole Colhoun and Galloway had been trying to fill McClure's shopping list. The Illustrators Branch had been drafting an operational chart of the relevant area, but until that morning the only available source material consisted of two maps which had been privately purchased by a member interested in the Nagorno-Karabakh war. One of the two maps was annotated in Russian Cyrillic script and showed relief, the other was in English and didn't.

Between nine and nine-fifteen this situation took a

marked turn for the better. First, a copy of Map 10 of the Azeri national series – the same map which Uday and Vezirov were using – was faxed from the British Embassy in Moscow; then one of Colhoun's contacts on the other side of the Atlantic came up trumps. Having realized that any attempt to involve the politicians would be a fraught and lengthy business, the SBS boss had simply phoned an old Gulf War colleague. Stephen McGriff had recently taken over as CO of the SEAL Training School at Coronado, in the USA, and he obviously recognized a friend in need, because the latest American satellite photos were arriving on the Poole fax machine within minutes of the Moscow Embassy's contribution.

While the Illustrators visually collated all the new information, the Meteorological Office in London was passing on detailed weather updates from its sister organizations in the former Soviet Union. And as far as Galloway could see it was good news all the way: the afternoon and early evening in western Azerbaijan would see an overcast sky, allowing the team to cross the first stretch of open country in pitch-darkness, while the cleaning of the sky by midnight would illuminate their journey through the more difficult terrain of the mountains.

At around ten Her Majesty's Consul in Yerevan was patched through with Armenian intelligence of the Azeri positions on the border, and the final touches were added to the Illustrators' creation. If the team had been equipped with one of the latest American satcom devices, Colhoun thought sourly, the completed map could have been digitally transmitted to the hillside hide five thousand kilometres away. As it was, one of the team would have to transfer it on to a pre-drawn grid, square by square, over the radio link.

Still, it was better than waiting for the Pony Express, Colhoun thought, ordering tea for himself and Galloway. With the completion of the map their work seemed more or less done. It was going to be a long day.

The SBS team had travelled almost six kilometres through the brightening twilight before McClure called a halt on what seemed a reasonably secluded and adequately forested hillside. Lacking any real entrenching tools, they had taken rather longer to dig even a basic rectangular hide than seemed safe, but no one had come wandering over the hill, and there seemed little reason why anyone should.

McClure had given himself the first watch, and had spent much of the morning staring out through the roof of rearranged foliage at the tree-broken vista of the plain below. As the hours had passed the lack of enemy activity had made him increasingly suspicious. He had seen one helicopter and heard a couple of others, but there had been no line of troops beating their way across the distant grassland or up through the trees. Either the man in charge hadn't seen *The Thirty-Nine Steps* or he had other fish to fry.

And McClure had a pretty shrewd idea which fish these might be. His opposite number had decided to employ all his available resources in blocking the routes to the border. Which was both good news and bad news. Their chances of being discovered during the hours of daylight were lower, but their chances of running into the enemy after dark were that much greater.

At noon he woke Noonan and Finn, then raised Poole

on the satellite link. After receiving the unexpected bonus of a perfect weather forecast, he handed over to Noonan and lay down beside the still-sleeping Raisa to get some rest.

While Finn kept watch, Noonan began the laborious task of transcribing the map on to the grid which McClure had prepared. It took the best part of an hour, but by the end of that time he had a pretty good idea of the country which lay between them and the armistice line in the mountains.

About ten kilometres east of their current position lay the town of Agdam, and from there a road ran due south for about forty kilometres through the foot-hills of the mountains to the much smaller town of Fizuli. From these towns two thirty-kilometre roads ran respectively south-south-west and east-north-east through deep river valleys to Stepanakert, the capital of Nagorno-Karabakh. Both roads were blocked by heavy concentrations of the Azeri army.

There was no other road across the mountains between these two pincer-like highways, but three smaller roads wound up from the Agdam–Fizuli road to villages perched high above the Azri plain, and beyond each of these settlements a path led across the mountains. There were Azeri military positions on all three paths, but only two of them were manned: the strongpoint covering the highest of the passes was deserted. The Armenians said so, and the satellite photos confirmed it. Better still, many of the slopes which this particular path traversed seemed heavily wooded.

'Why would they leave this door open?' Finn murmured.

'The pass is over fifteen hundred metres up,' Noonan observed. 'It'll be fucking cold.'

'Mmm. Maybe they only guard it in summer. What's the distance from here to there?'

Noonan did some calculations. 'Between thirty-five and forty kilometres. And mostly uphill.'

Finn grunted. 'A mere stroll.'

'It's a good job Mrs Shadmanov decided to go walk-about,' Noonan said.

'Yeah. Pity about her husband though. He seemed like a good bloke.'

'Yeah, he did.'

A few feet away Raisa was lying awake, listening to them. Tamarlan had been a good man, she thought. And if the manner of his life had left him with any outstanding moral debts, then the manner of his death had paid them in full.

When the darkness was full the team set off in single file across the landscape of low hills. McClure had found nothing to argue with in Finn and Noonan's plan, and they were aiming for that point on the Agdam–Fizuli road from which their chosen route led up into the mountains. In the interests of speed and mobility they had dispensed with one of the M16-M203 combinations and one of the MP5s, leaving both unloaded in the hide. Noonan and Finn, as lead scout and Tail-end Charlie, were carrying the other MP5s, McClure the remaining rifle and grenade-launcher, Raisa the Accuracy International.

The landscape alternated stretches of obvious farm-land with grassy slopes that seemed, despite the lack of animals, ideal for grazing. There were small vineyards in some of the valleys, fields recently planted for arable crops, stands of acacia trees on the banks of small rivers. Even through the bilious glow of the Passive Night Goggles it seemed a nice area, and Raisa found herself wishing that she had visited it in daylight when she still had the chance.

The walking was certainly easy, with fences, streams and the occasional irrigation channel the only real obstacles. There were farm tracks but no paved roads, and they gave a wide berth to any light which appeared in the distance. The kilometres slipped away behind them, and up ahead the denser shadow of the mountain wall grew ever more distinct.

They reached the vicinity of the Agdam–Fizuli road shortly before nine, and the others waited while McClure conducted a forward recce. Ten minutes later he returned with the news of a T-62 standing guard at the junction with the mountain road. Both routes were effectively blocked to wheeled traffic, but there seemed no comparable impediment to pedestrians. The tank's crew, moreover, were playing cards in a nearby bus shelter.

McClure led the team off at an oblique angle, aiming to cross the road some two hundred metres from the stationary T-62. Five minutes later they were slipping across the tarmac and up through the wooded slope on the other side, before breasting a low ridge and finding themselves just above the river and road which shared the climbing valley. The river lay between them and the vulnerability of the road, but the ruggedness of the terrain soon made it obvious that they had little choice in the matter. They forded the fast-flowing stream and set off up the dark road, ears straining for the sounds of traffic above or below, eyes peeled for any indications that they were walking into an ambush.

The sky above them was beginning to break up, and every now and then a patch of thin cloud would glow with primrose light as it passed across the invisible moon. The tank at the road junction worried McClure. Getting past it had been much too easy, which suggested that the real problems still lay ahead.

For the next hour and a half the road crossed and recrossed the river as it climbed, and soon the members of the team could look back out across the plain on which they had spent the last twenty-four hours. Twice approaching traffic forced them to take cover in the deeper shadows, but neither the driver of the empty bus nor the motorcyclist seemed interested in anything more than the road ahead.

Shortly before eleven the lights of the village which marked the road's end appeared a couple of hundred metres above them, and once that distance had been halved the team struck off across a bare slope with the intention of giving the settlement a wide berth. The terrain soon became difficult, and they took over an hour to circumvent the village, finally reaching the path above it, looking down at the sprinkling of lights below, glowing green through the PNGs.

It was almost midnight.

'Ten minutes' rest,' McClure decreed, and used the time to bring Poole up to date. 'The boss is arranging our Armenian welcoming committee,' he told the others, and lurking there, inside the pride he felt for a job well done, he could also feel the first intimations of panic. Soon it would all be over.

Now the moon was riding high in a rapidly clearing

sky, and there was more than enough light to dispense with the goggles. The four of them forced their weary limbs back into action and set off up the path, climbing alongside a tributary of the river which had accompanied them up the road. At this point it was leaping and falling as the valley steepened and narrowed into a virtual gorge, and after only a few minutes a long wooden bridge came into view, carrying the path across the top of a high waterfall.

It looked like a textbook spot for an ambush, but as far as McClure could see there was only the one way of checking it out. On this side of the stream the valley sides were too steep to climb, and the only way over to the other side was via the bridge itself.

'When we reach the near end of the bridge, run like hell,' McClure said conversationally. He thought he heard Finn grunt with amusement behind him, and he had to admit the words had sounded pretty ridiculous coming out of his mouth, but there was no point in taking chances.

As it happened, the admonition probably saved more than one of their lives.

The moment Noonan set his front foot on the planking several other things seemed to happen at once. Two searchlights sprang simultaneously to life, bathing the wooden structure, the rushing water and the walls of the valley in a dazzling white glow, the SBS team broke into the preordained run and a megaphone-enhanced voice started talking in heavily accented English. 'Eeengleeesh soldiers,' it began, but the rest was drowned in gunfire.

If the Azeri unit commander had expected his quarry to be frozen like so many startled rabbits by the bright lights and the music of his own voice, he was doomed to be disappointed. The team were almost across the twenty-metre bridge before the Azeri soldiers opened fire, and both Noonan and McClure escaped unscathed.

Raisa was not so lucky. A bullet slammed into the left side of her back, exiting just below and to the side of her left breast. She went down as if she'd been tripped, and it wasn't until Finn saw her face that he realized she'd been hit.

'Fuck,' he muttered, just as the ambient light was cut in half by Noonan's destruction of a searchlight. As he covered Raisa with his own body Finn felt a bullet catch him in the fleshier part of the inner thigh, and a split second later the whoosh of McClure's grenade-launcher signalled the onset of a darkness deeper than any that night. The gunfire stopped, then started again, more hesitantly this time.

'Can you move?' he asked Raisa.

'Yes,' she whispered.

Her breath was ragged but he'd heard worse. 'Let's go then,' he said, and the two of them, she on her hands and knees, he pulling himself along on his stomach, started forward across the five or so metres of planks which separated them from solid ground.

They had gone only a metre when more gunfire erupted up ahead, and then the Azeris behind them opened up in earnest once more. Most of the bullets passed above the two of them, but several slammed into the woodwork of the bridge, showering splinters, and one gouged a neat little groove across Finn's back, like a particularly painful whiplash. He cried out involuntarily, then muttered a few choice curses as he resumed his forward progress.

A few moments later and they were both off the

bridge and crawling into what looked like a sheltered niche in the rocky walls of the gorge. Somewhere above them Finn heard the mingling of two familiar sounds – the spitting cough of Noonan's MP5 and the crack of McClure's Browning – and hoped that the enemy on this side of the river would soon be history.

Raisa's breathing seemed better now, but even with the moonlight reasserting its sway it was hard to see how serious her wound was. His own both hurt like hell, and he was probably losing more blood than Tony Hancock could spare, but he didn't think either of their wounds was anywhere close to life-threatening. How he was going to walk another ten kilometres up a mountain was something else again.

There was a slight noise somewhere above him. He brought the MP5 into firing position and waited.

'Finn,' a voice whispered.

'We're down here,' he whispered back.

'How bad is it?'

'Raisa's worse. I'm just not as mobile as I was.'

'We've taken care of everyone on this side,' McClure said matter-of-factly. 'We've got the bridge covered, and we've got a pretty good idea where the rest of them are. Those that are left, that is – I heard someone heading down the path as fast as he could go.'

There was something distinctly crazy about the tone of the man's voice, Finn thought.

'So if you can get yourself and Raisa about twenty metres up the path you should be in the clear.'

'OK.' It was only the length of a cricket pitch, after all. Sticking his head out for a brief glance up the path, he could see where it bent out of sight. 'We've gotta move,' he told Raisa.

She opened her eyes and managed a smile.

A solitary burst of gunfire chipped away pieces of rock above their heads as they started off, but an instant reply in kind from Noonan and McClure deterred a repeat, and the twenty-metre crawl became solely a test of physical endurance. It took almost ten minutes, and utterly exhausted both of them. Once around the bend in the path Finn just lay on his side waiting for the others to come, staring up at the stars scattered across the heavens and wondering which was supposed to be his lucky one.

Suddenly lightning seemed to leap past him, and an explosion engulfed the silence. The bridge, he realised. McClure had blown the bridge.

A few minutes later McClure was examining his comrades' wounds. He had a surprisingly gentle touch, Raisa thought, and for a moment she found herself wondering what it was in his past that had hurt him so irreparably. She was recovering from the shock, she realized. Being shot was not an experience she had ever really expected to have.

He had managed to stanch the bleeding, and was now carefully wrapping the bandage around her, his mind racing through possibilities and options. The enemy now knew where they were, and could concentrate against them. Blowing the bridge had removed the immediate threat of pursuit, but there was no way of knowing for how long. Also, now that their intentions were known, there seemed nothing to stop the enemy from using helicopter-borne troops to leapfrog ahead and block their escape route. But there was obviously no going back, and there was still a chance they could evade any cordon higher up the mountain, for the enemy couldn't cover every square metre of ground. If they could reach the top before dawn . . .

They had less than five hours. Both Finn and Raisa could walk, but both had been weakened by loss of blood, and an uphill trek of ten kilometres or more was hardly what the doctor would have ordered. One of them could be carried on a makeshift stretcher by himself and Noonan, but the team's speed would still be dictated by the one who wasn't, and such an arrangement would deprive it of both forward and rear defence. McClure doubted whether there would be other ambushes higher up the path, but he wasn't prepared to count on it. The two casualties would have to struggle up the mountain under their own steam.

He explained his thinking to Finn and Raisa as he bandaged the other man's leg.

Raisa just nodded, as if it was all self-evident.

Finn stood up, wincing as he put weight on his injured leg. 'Fuck,' he said with feeling. 'If the worst comes to the worst you and Paul can leave us behind. We can dig in, rest up . . .'

'Forget it,' McClure said.

'It's important someone gets through,' Finn insisted.

'Not that important. And we'll only start worrying about it when we have to,' he added, cutting off the conversation.

Twenty metres away Noonan could hear the voices of both his comrades and the Azeris still alive on the other side of the broken bridge. He hadn't looked at the corpses strewn all around him since McClure's departure, but his mind's eye seemed unable to leave them alone. There had been at least six of them, maybe seven or eight, and the two SBS men, emerging above and behind them, had simply mown them down. For some reason it had reminded Noonan of watching his mother pour boiling water on ants. He had been about six years old, and the utter helplessness of the insects had made him want to cry.

It was us or them, his brain told him. They had fired first, and that, as any Western hero knew, made anything OK.

So why did he feel like crying?

He found himself feeling angry at the Azeri commander, who, half an hour earlier, had probably been congratulating himself on setting the perfect ambush.

'Time to go,' McClure whispered out of the dark, and Noonan edged away from the position, crawling backwards through the spread-eagled bodies of the dead.

The valley opened out again, the stream slowed its rush downhill and the trees on the slopes around them began to thicken. McClure led the way up the moonlit path, the two invalids behind him, with Noonan bringing up the rear. It was just a matter of putting one foot in front of the other, Finn told himself, but his body proved increasingly reluctant to cooperate.

McClure called frequent rest-stops, checking the bandages while Noonan scanned the slopes above and below them with the nightscope. There was no sign of pursuit on the ground, but during one such stop, sometime around three o'clock, a helicopter appeared to the north of them, heading up the mountain on a parallel course to their own. McClure identified it as a Kamov Ka-27 Helix-B, one of the newer Soviet helicopters. They were capable of carrying sixteen troops.

The sky was completely clear now, the moon nearly

down behind the mountain, and the air was growing colder with each upward step. The wind seemed to be rising too, particularly as the forest thinned, and bald patches of rock-strewn meadow began alternating with ever-smaller swathes of pine.

By four o'clock McClure reckoned they were only an hour away from the top, but at that point Finn's thigh wound reopened and they had to stop again. McClure sent Noonan back down the path to check on any possible pursuit while he struggled to stem the flow of blood. By this time both Raisa and Finn bore more than a passing resemblance to ghosts, but there was nothing wrong with them that a few pints of blood and the odd day in hospital wouldn't cure. If only he could get them to one.

It was fifteen minutes before he was sure that the bleeding had stopped, and at that point Noonan returned with the unwelcome news that there were troops on the path below. 'They're a long way behind us, but . . .'

'They're moving a lot faster,' McClure completed the thought.

They started off again, their pace even slower, fighting their way up and across what had become an almost barren wilderness of rocky slopes. For a while the path was hard to follow, but as they neared the summit it dug itself deeper and deeper into a rocky cleft, restricting their view of what lay ahead and creating the opposite problem – it was now impossible to get off.

They were several hundred metres up this narrow channel when a faint glow in the sky ahead announced the existence of an artificial light source. McClure was still digesting this information when the sound of another helicopter emerged through the whistle of the wind. The craft – a Kamov Ka-26 'Hoodlum' – loomed into view for a few seconds before disappearing behind the glow which emanated from the horizon ahead. But there was no stilling of the rotors, and a few minutes later the helicopter made another brief appearance, before the sound of its passage faded down the mountain.

Another delivery, McClure thought. But at least the 'Hoodlum' only carried half a dozen passengers.

He looked at the others, two of whom were obviously glad of the unscheduled break. He looked at his watch; it would start to get light in less than half an hour. 'I'm going to do a forward recce,' he told Noonan.

'OK,' Noonan said. 'If you pass a newsagent, I could use a bag of Hula Hoops. Original flavour.'

McClure grinned and started off up the cleft. The glow in the sky grew rapidly bright, indicating that its source was even nearer than he had thought, but there was still no way off the path which didn't involve some serious climbing, and neither of the invalids was up to that sort of exercise.

Rounding a bend in the almost tunnel-like gorge McClure suddenly noticed light on the walls ahead. He cautiously advanced to a position from which he could see around the next bend and found that his worst fears had been realized. He had reached the end of the cleft, which opened out into an almost bowl-like space some thirty metres wide and a hundred metres long. At its far end it narrowed once more, into a gap between the upraised teeth of two ridges. A concrete pillbox had recently been placed on the high ground to the right, as a modern companion piece to the ancient stone tower which perched on the ridge to the left.

The only good news about this arrangement was that

the pillbox had obviously been built by the Azeris. The Muslim moon and stars painted on its side were one giveaway; the fact that it was facing away from McClure was the other. On this side there was only the doorway, and the steps which had been blasted from the rock leading up to it.

The sixteen troops brought up by the Helix-B were much in evidence. Two of them were manning an old-fashioned, but doubtless well-oiled, machine-gun on the open roof of the stone tower, and most of the rest seemed to be lining the walls of the gap, taking what shelter they could from the topography of the rock. There might be more troops in the pillbox itself, but it seemed more likely that it was being used to shelter their commander from the cold wind.

It was not a good defensive position, McClure thought. The searchlights behind the Azeris made them harder to pick out, but they had little in the way of physical protection.

Trouble was, the odds against a successful attack could hardly have been worse. There was only one way forward, and that led into an almost perfect killing field, where, both blinded and illuminated by the lights, they would have to charge across a hundred metres of open ground in the face of concentrated fire from upwards of twenty automatic weapons. It would be a highly efficient way of committing suicide.

McClure crouched in the shadows, searching for the inspiration that would turn reality upside down, turn black into white, failure into success.

None came.

There was no way forward, no way back. In a few minutes the sky would begin to lighten. He and Noonan might still be able to make a run for it across the rocks, but not Finn or Raisa.

There was nothing for it but to surrender.

The word tasted bitter on his tongue.

His eyes examined the Azeri positions one more time, willing a chink in the armour. There had to be some way of profiting from their lack of physical protection.

And then he saw it. For almost a minute he stood there, thinking it through, trying to make it real. He calculated times and distances, ran through an imaginary sequence of events, put himself in the enemy's place. And then, his mind made up, he retreated a few metres down the path, took off his bergen and began rummaging around for what he needed.

Five minutes later he was back with the others, explaining the hopelessness of their situation. 'We'll have to give up,' he told them, and the others could think of no good reason to argue the point.

'But I don't want us lined up like ducks in a shooting gallery,' McClure went on. 'We'll walk up the path, me out front, with you two' – he indicated Finn and Noonan – 'supporting Raisa like she's badly injured. As we walk forward I want the gap between us to widen, right? Because if they just decide to open up I want you lot far enough back to take some of the bastards with you. And just in case they're the worst shots in creation, Paul, you take out the men on the tower to the left. Got that? The tower on the left. Sling your MP5 across your back.'

'Yeah,' Noonan said. He felt almost disoriented by this sudden let-down. Thirty-six hours of adrenalin-pumping flight, and here they were trying to survive a surrender.

'Let's do it,' McClure said.

The four of them walked slowly up the path, stopping in the final, tunnel-like section to arrange themselves in the formation McClure had suggested. Then he strode purposefully out into the open, both hands high above his head, one of them grasping his MP5. As he entered the edge of the searchlit area there was a shout from up ahead, and he involuntarily braced himself against a fusillade of bullets, but no one fired. Squinting against the lights he could see the Azeri troops with their guns raised, and three men emerging from the pillbox, one of whom was the Iraqi he'd seen at the rig.

Without breaking stride McClure ostentatiously tossed his MP5 to one side. Glancing backwards he saw that the others were already ten metres behind him.

The three men were still watching his approach from the top steps. Come down, he pleaded silently, and, as if in response, the man in the Azeri uniform brushed past the Iraqi and began descending. The Iraqi said something to him, which he seemed to brush off with a wave of the hand.

McClure was thirty metres away now, Bobby Charlton range. He took another glance back over his shoulder, found that the others were almost as far behind him, and quickened his pace.

The sky was lightening at last, and through the gap in front of him, way across the invisible valley beyond, he could see the rising sun strike a spark on one towering, snow-capped peak. It was beautiful, he thought, but far beyond his reach.

It didn't matter. There was nothing for him on the other side of the gap. Jobs like this came only once in a lifetime.

The Azeri commander and the Iraqi were now at the foot of the steps. The latter spoke again, causing the former to raise a hand and shout 'stop' in English.

He was fifteen metres away from them. The spread was as good as he could have hoped for – there was only the pair in the stone tower, and if Noonan kept his wits about him . . .

McClure pressed the trigger on the electronic timer and burst into a run.

The Iraqi was quicker than he had expected, and the first bullet hit him somewhere in the chest just as he was reaching full speed, but he kept going, absorbing hits like an American footballer surging and stumbling his way through tackles, before bullets to the head and the heart dropped him dead at Uday's feet.

A split second later the world exploded.

Noonan, Finn and Raisa were knocked backwards by the force of the blast. 'Jesus Christ!' Noonan half yelled, scrambling to his feet a lot easier than the other two. The smoke was already being blown away by the wind, and in the nick of time he understood what McClure had been getting at. As the two reeling figures on the stone tower swam into view he opened up with the MP5, dropping them both with a single burst.

And now there were excited voices on the path behind them, and only death in front.

'Come on,' he shouted, pulling Finn to his feet. 'He's given us a chance.'

Finn and Raisa looked at him as if he was mad, but allowed themselves to be hustled forward through the cleft and on to the downward slope beyond, apparently oblivious to the coating of human remains which lined the walls of their escape route.

Noonan was not so lucky. Here and there he could make out a uniformed arm or leg, but there was no identifiable trace of McClure.

19

Galloway raised himself up one shoulder to finish the story.

'The three of them had only been walking a few minutes when the Armenians showed up. They carried Raisa and Finn down the mountain and drove them to the hospital in Stepanakert. The two of them were kept in for a couple of days, leaving Noonan to cope with the gratitude and congratulations. The way he tells it, the whole town was queuing up to buy him a drink. And then the three of them were taken to Yerevan, where the British consul arranged their flights home via Moscow.'

'Will McClure get a medal?' his wife asked.

'I should think so.'

The two of them lay there in the dark, listening to a late train going by on the Weymouth line. As that sound receded they could hear their neighbour's daughter giggling on the pavement outside. A cat suddenly began to howl.

It all sounded so normal.

'What sort of man was he?' she asked.

Many of those who attended the memorial service in Poole were asking themselves the same question, and Neil Colhoun was no exception. His feelings towards

McClure remained as ambivalent as ever. In the most difficult of circumstances the man had been resourceful, decisive, effective. From a purely military standpoint it was hard to imagine the job being done any better.

And yet . . . There was no excuse that Colhoun could find for the killing of the Azeri driver. Murdering the man had just been more convenient than any of the alternatives.

Was there any way of separating the brilliant soldier from the murderer?

Colhoun sighed. He had been hoping that this service would let him lay the ghost, but life wasn't that simple. Gary McClure wasn't responsible for the frayed edges of Colhoun's moral universe; he had merely been the means by which they were pointed out.

And maybe growing older was about learning to act without that kind of certainty.

Almost a month had passed since the events in Azerbaijan, and though he was still walking with a noticeable limp, in all other respects Finn seemed fully recovered. He was a bit older, and maybe a bit wiser, though he wouldn't have put money on the latter.

As he listened to the usual string of platitudes Finn could see the expression on McClure's face as they all set off on the last lap. There had been a smile in the man's eyes, and it hadn't been ignited by anything as boring as bravado. McClure had been going home. He had wanted to die.

Finn couldn't understand that. Over the past couple of months he had seen more than his share of violent death, and it had only served to make him more aware of how much he enjoyed life.

There was so much to fucking live for.

And so much fucking to live for, come to that.

The night before he had been the only person in the pub to remember the make of Steve McQueen's motorbike in *The Great Escape*. The tie-breaker had won them the quiz, and he'd been rewarded with more than a share of the pot. If life had anything better to offer than the feeling of easing himself into Marie Colhoun's naked embrace then he wanted to know what it was.

Raisa had slept with David Constantine on the team's return, but more as an expression of affection and gratitude than from any real desire. She had found it hard to tell him that there was nothing more on offer, but after a week or so he had said it for her. And if he harboured any ill feelings he hid them well, pulling every string he could find to secure her a research assistant's job in nearby Cambridge.

Her co-workers seemed nice, the work was interesting, the city was more cosmopolitan than Baku. She found the variety of consumer goods truly amazing, the variety of culture even more so. One night she discovered that an old Soviet comedy set in Azerbaijan was showing at one of the art cinemas, and while the rest of the audience laughed at the jokes she cried her way through half a box of tissues. Coming out of the cinema she felt as she had on her first day in England. There was no sea to smell, no purple mountains in the distance, no groups of people sat outside to share their evening. Here the streets were for movement, not life. The people were all inside, watching TV.

She had smiled to herself at that moment, and she did so again now, emerging from the church into the spring sunshine. This was a different world, but she would adapt. If the past couple of months had given her anything, it was freedom from the fear of change.

Soon after his return to England, Paul Noonan had begun having nightmares. By day his experiences in Azerbaijan seemed long ago and almost unreal, but at night they returned to haunt him. It didn't take a genius to work out that his unconscious was making hay with what his conscious mind was trying to repress, but knowing it and changing it were not the same thing, and after a week of wallowing in death he had been worried enough to ask Finn's advice. The Londoner had told him the Marines didn't employ a psychiatric counsellor out of any concern for political correctness.

The counsellor helped, and so did talking to Julie. 'Sometimes when a patient dies,' she told him one evening, 'I have this stupid sense that he or she has let me down, as if there's some cosmic battle going on between life and death and we can't bear to see life lose a single round. I suppose we can't, but it's crazy just the same. Life and death are just two sides of the same coin – you can't have one without the other.'

He smiled at her. 'And how did you get to be so wise?' he asked.

'By watching *Blue Peter*,' she said with a straight face.

He grinned and pulled her towards him. 'There's things you do for me that I've never seen on *Blue Peter*.'

'Now that's what I mean,' she said, pushing her hand between them. 'Do you know that three erections a day can help keep you healthy?'

'I didn't know that.'

'Life is full of wonderful coincidences.'

*　　*　　*

As the weeks stretched into months, and there was still no news of international action against the nuclear weapons facility in the Caspian, Colhoun's curiosity finally got the better of him. As it happened the timing of his call to the Foreign Office was near perfect. Martin Clarke told him that the diplomatic offensive had finally been adjudged a failure, and that he should watch the news for the next few nights.

Three days later the fifth item on the BBC's *Nine o'Clock News* concerned a massive explosion in the Caspian Sea. This had apparently been triggered by a gas leak, but low standards of maintenance on the old Soviet rigs were cited as a contributory factor.

Colhoun wondered whether it had been the Israelis or the Russians who had done the honours.

A week after that Annie Martin received a solicitor's letter in the post. After so long a silence she had half suspected he was dead, but seeing it confirmed in black and white was still something of a shock, as was the news that he had left her over twenty thousand pounds.

That part made her cry. Not for the money and not for his death, but with sadness for a life that had never known love.

She walked across to her living-room and stared up the sunlit street, remembering the night he had almost killed one of her customers.

He had sometimes been good to her, she thought, but there was no way that he had been a good man. Maybe he had never been given the chance to be one. Or maybe that was something people had to seize for themselves.

She was damned if she knew.

TITLES IN SERIES FROM 22 BOOKS

Available now at newsagents and booksellers or use the order form provided

continued overleaf . . .

All at £4.99

All 22 Books are available at your bookshop, or can be ordered from:

22 Books
Mail Order Department
Little, Brown and Company
Brettenham House
Lancaster Place
London WC2E 7EN

Alternatively, you may fax your order to the above address. Fax number: 0171 911 8100.

Payments can be made by cheque or postal order, payable to Little, Brown and Company (UK), or by credit card (Visa/Access). Do not send cash or currency. UK, BFPO and Eire customers, please allow 75p per item for postage and packing, to a maximum of £7.50. Overseas customers, please allow £1 per item.

While every effort is made to keep prices low, it is sometimes necessary to increase cover prices at short notice. 22 Books reserves the right to show new retail prices on covers which may differ from those previously advertised in the books or elsewhere.

NAME ....

ADDRESS ....

....

....

☐ I enclose my remittance for £_____
☐ I wish to pay by Access/Visa

Card number
☐☐☐☐ ☐☐☐☐ ☐☐☐☐ ☐☐☐☐

Card expiry date
☐☐ ☐☐

Please allow 28 days for delivery. Please tick box if you do not wish to receive any additional information ☐